W9-DBQ-215

Savage Grace

Also by Cassie Edwards
in Large Print:

Savage Moon
Savage Obsession
Fire Cloud
Passion's Web

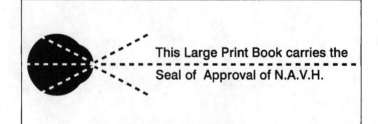

Savage Grace

Cassie Edwards

WHEELER
PUBLISHING

Copyright © 2000 by Cassie Edwards

Published in 2002 by arrangement with Leisure Books, a division of Dorchester Publishing Co., Inc.

Wheeler Large Print Romance Series.

The text of this Large Print edition is unabridged.
Other aspects of the book may vary from the original edition.

Set in 16 pt. Plantin.

Printed in the United States on permanent paper.

Library of Congress Cataloging-in-Publication Data

Edwards, Cassie.
    Savage grace / Cassie Edwards.
      p. cm.
    ISBN 1-58724-333-4 (lg. print : hc : alk. paper)
    1. Cherokee Indians — Fiction. 2. Women pioneers —
Fiction. 3. Large type books. I. Title.
PS3555.D875 S25 2002
    813´.54—dc21   2002028091

With much affection I dedicate Savage Grace *to my dear friend Mary Whitaker of Arkansas.*

ACKNOWLEDGMENTS

I wish to thank Mary Whitaker, a wonderfully talented poet and friend, for allowing me to print her poetry in *Savage Grace*. All of the beautiful poetry that is printed in *Savage Grace* is Mary's.

Naantam — Wolf

Child of the mighty wolf,
Growing so strong and brave,
Omens will guide your heart
Dreams will carry your feet.
While time leads your paths,
And your heritage: your soul,
Climb the mountains to the sky
On wings of courage, you can fly,
Your life-circle will be complete,
When your omens and dreams sleep.
A wild spirit, bravely goes before you,
Child of the mighty *Naantam*.

— Mary Ann Whitaker,
Cherokee, poet, and friend

Chapter One

Here, now, this minute,
Sometimes vague,
Each moment keeps changing
Its course,
Its meaning,
Its distant voice.

Arkansas, 1850

The air was sweet with spring. The sky was as blue as the deepest, clearest ocean. Birds sang with vigorous new life, their nests ready for their hatchlings. Overhead the breeze was gently turning the new leaves and swaying the branches of the huge blackjack oaks.

His thick black hair hanging down past his waist, his bow in his hand, Standing Wolf was making his way beneath these oaks.

Standing Wolf — called *Wah-e-yuh-kat-to-kuh* by his people, the *Anisahonia* or Blue Clan of Cherokee — was hunting wild turkeys on this early morning in May. He was dressed in a

9

short buckskin hunting shirt, coarse homespun breeches with a beaded belt around his waist, and moccasins that made no sound as he walked.

He wore the traditional turkey mask. Groundhog skin had been used for the face, and the ears were those of a wildcat.

When he was a very young brave and his *e-do-da*, Stands One Feather, was alive, Standing Wolf had learned from his father about the turkey masks.

He smiled now as he recalled seeing one for the first time. He had been frightened and had run and hidden behind his mother's skirt, only slowly going back again to his father's side to look more closely at the mask when Stands One Feather gently explained why such a thing was needed for the turkey hunt.

Using kind words that would be easily understood by a child of three, his father had said that turkey hunters wore this sort of mask as they stalked the *gi-na*. Wearing the mask, the hunter would sneak up on several turkeys, because the turkeys were curious and would come close, wondering whether or not the mask was a true wildcat.

Standing Wolf's father had told him that no hunter of turkeys who wore the mask ever arrived home without food for his family's table.

Still walking stealthily beneath the trees, listening for a distant gobble, Standing Wolf was lost in thought. He and his people were full-blooded Cherokee, of the old nation. His father had been the chief of this clan of Cherokee until his untimely death. Unfortunately, Standing Wolf had been too young to step into the chieftainship after him.

It tore at his heart to remember how his parents had died. It had happened many moons ago while they were in a canoe on the White River. A storm had come out of the sky so suddenly, his father had not been able to steer his wife safely to shore. Their lives were claimed quickly when their canoe capsized in the thrashing waves brought on by devastating winds.

Since then Standing Wolf had also lost his beloved wife.

He had married young, at age eighteen. His beautiful, sweet-voiced Sunshine had passed to the other side during her early pregnancy and he had never married again. At 28 he still remained single to honor the wife of his youth. His mourning for her would not end until he found another woman such as she, who would make his heart sing at his very first sight of her.

Thus far no woman had even come close to taking the place of Sunshine. . . .

Making sure that he was not far from the White River, where he had left his canoe beached for his return home, Standing Wolf gazed through the trees at the silvery shine of the river in the sunlight. Although his parents had died in this river, he loved it no less. It was the queen of all rivers. Meandering beneath towering limestone bluffs and along grassy meadows, it began as a mere trickle in a rocky ravine deep in the Arkansas Ozarks.

It slowly gained strength from thousands of natural springs and mountain creeks as it rushed northwest to eventually join the mighty Mississippi.

White River was the home to smallmouth bass, monster catfish, and nine-pound rainbow trout, all of which were staple foods of Standing Wolf's Blue Clan Cherokee.

With two slain turkeys downed earlier with his bow and arrow, and stored safely in a nearby limestone cavern that he had found while hunting, Standing Wolf concentrated once again on hunting. His ears alert for the sounds of turkeys, he had walked onward through the forest, but he had purposely back-tracked and was again in close proximity of his canoe and the cavern where his turkeys were stored. He was almost ready to call it a day, but it had been an enjoyable hunt with the new bow that he had only finished carving the prior evening.

Yes, he was proud of his new bow. The strings, which were fashioned from twisted bear gut, were very strong. For greater flexibility his hickory wood bow had been coated with bear oil, then warmed by a fire to cause the oil to sink in.

His quiver, filled with many arrows, was made of basketry. When not in use, his bow was slipped through buckskin bands on the side of the quiver.

His arrow points were made of turkey-cock spur and barbed so that they could not be easily pulled out if an enemy was downed by one.

Standing Wolf stopped suddenly and stiffened when he heard a twig snapping behind him, and then a rush of footsteps.

Before he could turn around to see who was there, his body lurched with pain and pitched forward as a war club came down hard on the back of his head.

Standing Wolf took another staggering step forward, then fell to the ground, unconscious, his bloodied turkey mask falling off and rolling away from him.

Wet with blood, his long, coarse black hair lay spread out on the ground beneath his head. His eyes were closed, yet his pulse still beat in a steady rhythm at the vein in his neck.

His bow lay next to his outstretched fingers. The arrow had been released the moment the bow hit the ground and had landed out of sight amid thick bushes.

Smiling smugly so that the white scar on his right cheek picked up the shine of the sun, Short Arrow knelt down beside Standing Wolf and gazed at him through wicked, narrowed eyes. He wiped Standing Wolf's blood from his war club onto the thick grass only a few inches from Standing Wolf's face.

Short Arrow chuckled and gave his allies in crime a quick look over his shoulder as they came to stand behind him, staring at the fallen warrior. A mixture of renegades and outlaws, they nodded and grinned back at Short Arrow.

"Finally I will achieve the vengeance I have sought for so long against Standing Wolf," Short Arrow said, gazing triumphantly at Standing Wolf. "He will wish that I had hit him hard enough to kill him."

Handing his war club over his shoulder to one of his cohorts, he untied the buckskin knife sheath at Standing Wolf's left side and with a trembling hand slid the huge, thick-bladed knife from inside it.

"Standing Wolf, this knife which you always wear so proudly will be used against you and will be the cause of your demise," Short Arrow said, slowly running a hand over one side of the knife's blade. "Everyone knows that this knife belongs to you. When you are brought before your people, you will not be able to deny your ownership of this knife. My only regret is that I will not be there when the knife is found in the old chief's body. I would enjoy gloating as you stand accused before your people . . . a people who were once also mine!"

He would never forget that it had been Standing Wolf who had pointed an accusing finger at Short Arrow, causing his banishment from their village. Standing Wolf had caught Short Arrow in many underhanded deeds, but none had been severe enough to cause his banishment, not until Standing Wolf witnessed Short Arrow killing wolves and selling their pelts to whites. To the Blue Clan Cherokee, it was bad luck to kill wolves. It would bring bad luck to their people if the person who took the wolf's life were allowed to stay in the village. And Short Arrow was guilty of having taken many wolves' lives, for he had set a vast number of traps and had placed bait in them that had lured the wolves into the steel jaws of death.

"We should leave now," suggested Black Horse, Short Arrow's best friend, as he placed a gentle hand on Short Arrow's bare shoulder.

Short Arrow glanced up at him but did not agree right away. He looked past his friend and gazed slowly upon the faces of the others he had befriended after his banishment. There were white outlaws and red-skinned renegades. They had come together as one entity and had enjoyed terrorizing the white communities whose towns and plantations were located across the river from the Cherokee village of *Kuhlahi*, "the place of beech trees."

From the beginning it had been agreed that they would join Short Arrow's quest for revenge and would help him once they found Standing Wolf alone.

Laughing sarcastically, Short Arrow shoved

Standing Wolf's knife into his own sheath, which he had purposely left empty so that he could wear the knife until it found its resting place in the heart of Chief Bear Sitting Down.

He gazed at length at Standing Wolf's bow, and then at his quiver of arrows. Smiling, he removed the quiver of arrows and positioned them on his own back. He grabbed up the bow, which bore a warrior's soul in the etchings that the warrior himself had carved into the wood.

"Oh, how you will wish that you had not hunted alone today," Short Arrow said. He hurried to his feet and backed away from Standing Wolf, feasting his eyes on the fallen warrior one last long moment before leaving. "Too bad your friend Good Shield did not hunt with you today. It would have been such a pleasure to have downed him, also, but I would not have left him alive. His living would serve Short Arrow no purpose. Only yours, Standing Wolf. Only yours."

Laughing raucously, he ran into the dense forest with his friends until they came to the horses they had left tethered far enough away so that Standing Wolf would not hear their hoofbeats.

Pleased with what he had achieved today, Short Arrow untied his reins and quickly mounted his horse, while his friends mounted theirs.

Holding Standing Wolf's bow high over his head, Short Arrow rode away, his voice echoing all around him as he shouted out his triumph.

"*Ai-e-ai-ee!*" he shrieked. "It is done! Finally he will pay for what he did to me!"

Black Horse rode up next to him and sidled closer. "The knife," he said. "Are you certain it will be enough to cause your old friend's downfall?"

Short Arrow's smile faded. His eyes narrowed as he glared at Black Horse. "Never was he my friend," he said in a snarl. "And, *ho,* yes, the knife is enough to cause his final demise. The knife was a gift to Standing Wolf. It is a knife known by everyone of my village! A white man gave this knife to Standing Wolf after Standing Wolf saved his life. He found the man's leg caught in one of my traps. Standing Wolf took the man to our village, where our healer cared for his wound until he was well and ready to leave. Before the man left the village, he made a special presentation of the knife to Standing Wolf. It was a knife so fine Standing Wolf wore it everywhere he went . . . a knife known by all and envied by many."

"If it is so valued a knife, will you truly want to part with it?" Black Horse asked, flipping his sleek, raven-black hair back from his face so that it lay long and thick down his bare, muscled back.

"My Chippewa friend, this knife has its place," Short Arrow said, inhaling a heavy sigh. "And that is not in my sheath, friend. Its place is in the old chief's heart!"

"You hate the chief so much that you would take his life in order to get your revenge against Standing Wolf?"

"Standing Wolf and the old chief are one and the same in my plan of vengeance," Short Arrow hissed out. "One pointed an accusing finger that caused my banishment. The other spoke the words that banished me."

"I see," Black Horse said, nodding. "I, too, would feel as you do about how the knife should be used."

Their eyes gleaming, their lips twisted into ugly grins, they began whooping and hollering a war chant. Their horses' hooves thundered over the ground as they rode out into a clearing, leaving behind them the forest where Standing Wolf lay.

Chapter Two

Passion for life.
Passion for clear, blue streams.
Passion for beautiful skies!

Standing Wolf awakened in a daze. He tried to get up, but fell back to the ground, overcome by dizziness. His head throbbed with excruciating pain. He reached a trembling hand to his head and winced when he found a large lump.

He brought his hand down and stared at the blood on his fingers. If he thought hard enough, he could remember hearing a noise and then feeling the pain of a blow.

Someone had ambushed him.

But why?

He was liked and admired by everyone.

He had only one true enemy that he knew of.

Short Arrow!

But many moons had passed since Standing Wolf had caused Short Arrow's banishment from their village. It did not make sense that

Short Arrow would wait so long to seek vengeance.

Suddenly Standing Wolf noticed that his knife was no longer in its sheath. Also he saw that his bow and quiver of arrows were gone!

But were they worth a man's life?

To him the bow and arrows were special. All warriors had their own special bond with their weapons which were made with such loving care.

And then there was his knife. *Ho,* many desired it, but surely not enough to kill over it.

All of this led to the only answer that made sense. He had been downed for vengeance's sake alone.

And there was only one man who would seek such vengeance against Standing Wolf.

Short Arrow.

Suddenly Standing Wolf became aware of the air washing over the land with its cool, evening mist of dew. He knew he must find shelter before darkness fell around him like a shroud.

The cavern that he had found earlier in the morning — that was where he could seek warmer shelter for the night. He began crawling along the ground.

Ho, he . . . must . . . make it to the cavern.

He groaned, his head pounding. The pain was so severe he had to fight hard to stay conscious.

He was relieved when he finally reached the opening to the cavern.

With the last few ounces of his remaining strength, he crawled inside the cave. Still fighting off unconsciousness, he managed to get far enough back from the entrance to be away from the cold night air, for although it was May, the nights near the river could be dangerous to someone weak and injured.

Suddenly he heard a pack of wolves outside the cavern, far in the distance, howling into the evening wind.

"Naantam," Standing Wolf whispered, as though responding to the call of the wild beasts he had been named after. He reached a hand out toward the cave entrance, then it fell to his side as he drifted off into the black void of unconsciousness.

Chapter Three

This interval in every lifetime,
Infinite, as it may always seem,
Will become only an intermission,
Temporarily suspending our dreams.

Enjoying the wonders of spring, wishing that with it came hope again for the future after the terrible ordeal of burying her beloved husband, Shaylee Whiteside sat on the porch of her two-room log cabin. She was rocking and feeding her three-month-old son, Moses.

Every time she thought of her husband not living to see his son, she felt an ache inside her very being. David had not even known that Shaylee was pregnant. That night, the very night that he had been murdered on his way home from buying supplies from a small trading post upriver, she had planned to reveal the wondrous news of her pregnancy.

Tears swam in her eyes as she recalled how she had planned to let him know. During those long days when David had been away from the cabin, Shaylee had been secretly knitting a tiny pair of booties for their baby. She had planned to place them on her husband's plate that night after he came in for supper from his gardening.

But the murdering thieves stole that breathless moment from David when they spilled his life's blood along the roadway to kill him for a few measly dollars and the supplies in his wagon. The thieves stole not only her husband away from her that day, but also her child's father.

Shaylee's home sat some miles from the White River. Her parents, and also David's, lived far away in Boston. When her husband died, she had been left alone to fend for herself and her child, for neither she nor her parents had enough money to pay for her return to Boston.

When she had met David Whiteside in Boston, and agreed to marry him and go with him to a faraway plot of land that he had inherited from a favorite uncle, she had never thought to worry about anything happening to David. She had never imagined that she would have to fend for herself, alone, so far from her parents.

She gazed out at the vast land that her husband and she had owned when he was alive.

Now that land was no longer Shaylee's, nor anything else except for her two-room cabin. She had planted a tiny garden out back which supplied her with vegetables.

Without money, she had been unable to pay her taxes, and the land had been auctioned off. Those who bought the acreage would soon bring cattle and horses onto the land and build a large house down the road from Shaylee's tiny home.

Needing to get back to her daily chores — she had only stopped long enough to feed Moses and enjoy the fresh, clean smell of spring — Shaylee gazed down at her son, who lay contentedly asleep in her arms, his tummy filled with warm milk.

She slid the blanket back farther from his face and ran a finger over the butterfly-shaped birthmark beneath his left ear.

"A butterfly's kiss," she whispered, smiling. The birthmark was identical to his father's, but her son had *her* hair, a shock of red curls, and he also had her blue eyes.

In her mind's eye she saw David standing before her, his gaze sweeping slowly and appreciatively over her. She could remember him so vividly talking about how delicate and slender she was — so tiny that he worried the wind might sweep her away as though she were no heavier than a feather.

Her waist was so slender, he had laughed about how he could almost encircle it with his hands.

As Moses smiled in his sleep, surely dreaming of angels, Shaylee hugged him to her bosom and rocked him for a moment longer, then folded the blanket snugly around him and placed him in a small cradle beside her rocking chair.

Longing to just be with Moses, to enjoy these precious moments awhile longer, she didn't get right up and leave, after all. It *was* such a beautiful day, something to cherish. Soon the weather would be hot and sticky, when one dreamed of times like this, which sometimes seemed so fleeting and unreal.

"Moses, Moses," Shaylee whispered as she gazed down at him. She reached inside the cradle and took one of his tiny hands in hers. "One day, Moses, you will be all grown up. My son, I wonder what your dreams will be. What you will wish to be . . ."

Her thoughts were interrupted by the distant sound of horses' hooves. She looked quickly down the small lane that led from the main country road to her cabin.

Her breath caught in her throat when she saw dust flying and through that dust many men on horseback hurrying her way.

"Who are they?" she whispered, a stab of fear in her heart. She remembered how her husband had died. There was a band of outlaws and renegade Indians who had been ravaging the countryside and she'd always believed they were responsible for David's murder.

Shaylee's knees were weak as she rose from her chair, for she could now see the color of the skin of those who were advancing on her home. There was a mixture of red and white skins.

Her shotgun!

She always kept it just inside the door, leaning against the wall.

Oh, dear God, she thought frantically to herself, she . . . had . . . to get her shotgun.

She had already seen some Indians notching arrows onto their bow strings!

"Lord, please have mercy," she whispered as she turned to go inside for the shotgun.

Her back now to the men, the horses' hooves like claps of thunder erupting inside her brain, Shaylee cast Moses a frantic look over her shoulder, and then caught sight of a fast-approaching Indian.

She screamed when she saw that he had fired an arrow in her direction.

She lurched when she felt the sting of the arrow as it pierced her back.

In the blink of an eye she saw a livid white scar on the Indian's right cheek. She also saw dark, evil eyes in a narrow face. . . .

So tiny and fragile, Shaylee's body made hardly a sound as she crumpled down and lay on her side on the wooden floor of the porch.

Everything was fuzzy now, so fuzzy that she felt no pain where the arrow protruded from her back. Shaylee reached a trembling hand toward her child's cradle.

"Moses . . ." she whispered. "My . . . dear . . . Moses . . ."

Feeling her life drifting away, she dropped her hand onto the porch, and as she lay there, she saw the Indian who'd shot her leap from his horse. He rushed to the porch and took Moses from his cradle.

Unable to do anything, Shaylee was conscious long enough to see her son taken away on horseback in the arms of the Indian.

She was also conscious long enough to see white men go inside her cabin and come out again, cursing when they found no valuables among her belongings.

As Shaylee's eyes locked in a stare into space, torches were thrown onto the roof of her cabin, and soon smoke was swirling as the fire spread on all sides of her.

Shaylee was suddenly aware of a pure white light which seemed to buoy her up. She had never experienced such quiet. And she was aware of a soft weightless feeling.

Serenity seemed to fill her being, yet she fought to hold on to the remembrance of her child.

Not wanting to forget her son or the fact that he needed her, Shaylee fought the euphoria, yet she wished to give in to it and forget all the ugliness she had ever known.

Yes, it would be so easy to think only of this precious sweetness that was engulfing her.

But where was she? she wondered as she gazed in awe around her.

What was all of this beautiful white light?

What were those clouds that she was now passing through?

And why wasn't she feeling any pain? An arrow had struck her.

She reached back and discovered that the arrow was no longer there. It was as though it had dissolved into thin air.

She suddenly heard a voice and realized that she was no longer moving among the beautiful, swirling clouds. Yet she saw no one.

But the voice she had heard was kind. It was gentle. It calmed her fears. For the moment it took away her need to question anything.

She listened to the unseen force which she now believed was God. . . .

"Shaylee Whiteside, some who are taken too soon from earth, and who were good while there, are brought to this halfway place," the voice said. "Because of your goodness, Shaylee Whiteside, you are among those few who may choose whether or not they wish to enter into Heaven, or return to earth for a second chance at life, to finish what they were not able to accomplish."

Not even stunned that she was in the presence of God, Shaylee pondered what the voice had said to her.

She thought of her husband David, and of her grandparents and aunts and uncles who were now a part of Heaven's peaceful bliss.

Yes, it *would* be so wonderful to see them and to be able to wander among the beautiful clouds with them.

But there was one not among them who she loved with all of her heart. Her child!

And he was at this very moment at the mercy of the wild, heartless renegades and outlaws.

"Has my son Moses lived through the abduction?" Shaylee asked softly. "Is he still alive?"

"Yes, Moses is still alive."

"If I choose to resume my life on earth, can I have Moses with me again?"

"That depends on you."

"What do you mean?"

"If you decide to choose earth over Heaven at this moment in time, you will be given a test," the voice said gently, with infinite caring. "You will be sent to earth to help someone in need, to show compassion where you might not want to show it, and if you do, you can at that time either stay on earth or enter the doors of Heaven. If you are not capable of this compassion, then you will no longer have choices."

"Why is the person I am to help so important that he or she is a part of this test?" Shaylee asked.

"This person is a man. He was wrongfully attacked, as you were. He still has much left to do on earth to guide his people," the voice said in its gentle tone.

"What is expected of me? What must I do to prove my compassion toward this man?" Shaylee asked, wishing that she could see to whom she was talking. In her mind's eye she envisioned the pictures she had seen of God in paintings that hung on the walls of churches, and in storybooks she had read as a child.

In his eyes there was always such peace and love. She could almost feel his arms around her now, comforting her as he spoke.

"You are to help the man," the voice said. "He has been injured and will soon be unjustly accused and hunted for a crime he has not committed. You will help him in his time of trouble."

The voice paused, and then said, "Do you still wish to be tested?"

"Yes," Shaylee said, now without hesitation, for Moses had been her main reason for existing before, as he was even now. "How will I know this man?"

"You will know him," was the response.

Again there was a pause, then the voice said, "The Lord goes with you on your journey of the heart. Go now and be careful in your choices."

"Why can't you just make it happen for this man who is in need?" Shaylee asked. "God has the power to do anything he wishes, doesn't he?"

"Yes, he does, but he does not work in that way," the voice said softly. "*That* is why there are *angels*."

Shaylee was taken aback by that, for she suddenly realized she would be returning to earth as an angel.

She had always wondered if there were angels.

Now she knew!

Chapter Four

He wears moonlight, stars,
Spirit and fearless pride.
Dreams to set him free,
His woman by his side.

"There is one more thing," the voice said, interrupting Shaylee's awe of what she now was.

An angel.

She . . . was . . . an angel.

"Yes?" she asked softly.

"When you return to earth as one of God's special angels, you will be able to touch things, even move them, but no one will be able to touch *you*," the voice said. "You have the ability to touch so that you can help the injured man.

"But let me remind you that no one can feel your touch, nor can anyone touch you. You will not feel the warmth of man's flesh, nor will you smell the fragrance of God's creations, those things you once enjoyed with all of your being."

"I shall no longer smell the grass, the river, or the flowers?" Shaylee asked, sad to think that she would not be able to smell the lilacs that grew along the river, or the roses that grew wild in the forest.

"You may, later, but only should you return to earth as a living, breathing being once again," the voice said softly. "Go now, my child. The man who needs you has been alone and unconscious a full night. No one but you must find him where he has gone to seek shelter."

"Where is this shelter?" Shaylee asked. Then her breath caught in her throat when she realized that her time in the clouds was over. She now felt herself being drawn downward until she again saw the bright morning sunshine, the fresh green leaves on the trees, and the sparkling clear waters of the White River.

She found herself standing just outside a limestone cavern that was mostly hidden behind a huge stand of oak trees.

She saw a strange sort of mask lying a few feet from the cavern, and then noticed that blood was on the mask. When she also saw a trail of blood leading inside the cavern she believed that this must be where she was supposed to find the person she'd been sent to help.

She waited a moment to gather up enough courage to go inside the cavern.

Her heart raced inside her chest. Her knees were weak, for she knew the importance of passing this test.

To be able to see her son again depended on

her making the right decisions . . . on her being able to show compassion where it was needed.

It seemed so little a task, for she had never been anything but compassionate.

Yet she recalled that she had been told she might not want to help this person.

"I must find out," she whispered to herself. "And I must do it now."

She picked up the mask and slipped inside the cavern. There was enough light from the sun's rays for her to see two dead turkeys lying at her right. She looked past them and saw a man stretched out on his side on the rocky floor of the cavern, his back to her.

She noticed blood dried on his scalp where he had obviously been injured.

Again she hesitated. There must be a powerful reason why she might not want to help this man. What if she couldn't bring herself to overlook it? What would happen to her Moses?

"Faith," she whispered to herself. "I must have more faith."

Effortlessly, as though her feet didn't even touch the floor of the cavern, Shaylee went over to the man. She stopped and took an unsteady step back from him and dropped the mask when she saw that he was an Indian.

Flashes of those brief, horrible moments when she had seen the red-skinned man grab Moses from his cradle, then ride away with him on his horse, came to Shaylee like lurid bolts of lightning.

She now understood the difficulty of her choice. This man was an Indian, like the one who had shot an arrow into her back, who had taken her beloved son!

She now remembered the sound of Moses crying as the man rode away with him on his horse. Surely her son was even more frightened now that he no longer felt his mother's arms protectively around him, nor had her breast to suckle.

Her heart sank at that thought. Who *would* be feeding Moses?

Who would be holding him?

Would anyone ever again sing lullabies to him?

All of this made her again focus on her task, and the man who lay injured on the cavern floor. She sank to her knees beside him and studied his face.

She was relieved to discover that he wasn't the man who had attacked her.

This man who lay before her was far different in appearance. Except for her husband David, she had never seen anyone as handsome as this Indian.

His skin was of a cinnamon brown color.

He had perfectly shaped lips, high cheekbones, a broad, muscled frame, and waist-length coal black hair, whereas the man who had changed her life forever had been small-boned, with a narrow face and shifty eyes. But what she most remembered about that evil man's features was the livid white scar on his right cheek.

This man who lay unconscious in the cavern had no blemishes except for the wound on his head.

Yes, surely this man in the cavern was the one she was supposed to help, but how *could* she? Like those who had left death and destruction behind at her home, he was an Indian.

What if this man in the cavern was from the same village as those who had taken Moses away? What if he was from the same clan?

What if he had even ridden with them?

What if his looks belied the true man and he was just as evil as the Indian who'd shot the arrow into her back?

She was torn between conflicting feelings. If this injured man *was* one of the gang that had attacked her, she *must* see that he lived. Wouldn't he then lead her to her son? Wasn't that what this was all about . . . finding Moses?

She quickly reminded herself that she must have compassion for this man. That was the true test. If she couldn't show and feel compassion for this Indian, she would never have the chance to see her Moses again.

Confused, yet knowing that she must trust the one above who was giving her a second chance at life, she thought about what first must be done for this injured Indian.

His wound.

It didn't appear to be a fatal one. There was a

bloody lump on his scalp, where blood had also dried in his hair.

But there didn't seem to be much blood loss, for only a few drops stained the cavern floor beneath his head.

Yet she recalled the trail of blood that had led her inside the cavern.

And also she remembered that this man had spent a full night in the cavern already; probably he had been unconscious for that length of time. The blow to his head might be more severe than it first appeared.

"I must do something to get him awake," Shaylee whispered to herself.

Her fingers trembled as she touched the vein in his throat to see how strong a pulse was beating there.

She was relieved when she found it steady and strong. He was not about to die.

"Water," she whispered. "I need water."

Yes, she would bathe his wound. Surely that would awaken him.

That was the important thing at this moment . . . to get him fully awake and lucid. She recalled the voice saying that this man was important to his people.

"Could he be a chief?" she whispered as she raised the hem of her dress and ripped away a portion of her petticoat.

She went to the river and sank the cloth into the water, then hurried back to the cavern and again knelt beside the Indian.

As she began bathing the blood from his head wound, she tried not to have ill feelings for the Indian. She had never been a prejudiced person. In fact, before the attack on her husband, she had felt a deep empathy for all Indians. Time and again they had been lied to and cheated. Many Cherokee had been forced from their homes in Georgia, but she knew that those who lived across the White River from her small cabin had not been uprooted. In fact, the United States Government had shipped many of the Georgia Cherokee to live among the White River Cherokee.

She wondered if this man she was helping was one of those who had been uprooted. Or was he among those who still owned land on the White River?

No, she had never been a person who was prejudiced, but things were different now. An Indian had changed it all for her. And this man was an Indian, too. If she found out that he belonged to the renegades, how hard it would be to be civil to him, much less compassionate.

She stopped bathing the wound for a moment and looked around inside the cavern.

She again saw the turkeys. Surely this man had been hunting before he had been hit over the head.

Yet she saw no weapons.

Perhaps he'd been attacked for his weapon.

Again she slowly ran the cool, wet cloth across his injury, glad to see that she had removed a good portion of the blood already.

She wondered if the cool water would awaken him. It gave her a stab of fear to think that he might never recover.

What then would God's plans for her be?

Standing Wolf felt himself slowly awakening from his deep, injury-induced sleep, as he felt a cool, gentle wetness on his head where pain throbbed and stung clean into the very core of his being.

As he looked up he found sky-blue eyes peering down at him. The sun's rays streaming through the entrance of the cavern allowed him to see long and flowing brilliant red hair framing a face of angelic beauty.

He wondered about the strange glow that seemed to surround her in a haze.

He reached a shaky hand out to Shaylee and when his hand seemed to move right through her arm, he was not afraid, for he believed that he was in the presence of one of the "Spirit People," the *Nunne-hi,* or immortals, whose home was in the distant hills. They were invisible except for when they *wanted* to be seen.

Often Cherokee hunters had witnessed the music, singing and dancing of the Spirit People while hunting near the hills. When the hunters searched for the source, the sound would shift and they would hear it behind them, or away in some other direction, so they could never find the place where the Spirit People lived.

Standing Wolf was surprised that a *white* Spirit Person had chosen to come to his assistance today instead of one who resembled his own people, but he did not question it. He needed help, for although his wound was not life-threatening, it had rendered him disoriented and weak.

While Standing Wolf had been staring at Shaylee, she had been staring back at him, feeling relieved that finally he had awakened. She could see how he studied her, and she knew now, by the way this man reached out to touch her and could not, that she was not present in body, but was only visible to him because he was the one that God had chosen for her to help.

It was strange how he seemed to accept that, as though he knew she was an angel. She wondered how he could know? She certainly didn't have any wings.

Shaylee still couldn't believe that she had been asked to care for an Indian. It was a true test, for she was very torn. She must show compassion to a red man to prove she was worthy of staying on earth to find her son; yet it had been a red-skinned warrior who had destroyed her life and stolen away her child.

It was a time of decision. She could continue helping the man, or step away.

She looked heavenward for answers.

Suddenly Standing Wolf spoke. "Do you have a name?" he asked.

She looked quickly down at him. She hesitated, then answered him.

"Yes, I have a name. Shaylee. My name is Shaylee Whiteside."

She knew that he could hear her because his eyes lit up in response.

Ah, his eyes!

The pupils were jet black.

Surely, she thought, his vision must be as keen as that of the eagle.

"I also have a name," Standing Wolf said, wincing when a pain shot through his head as she removed the damp cloth and laid it on the ground beside him. "I am called Standing Wolf. I am Cherokee. I am of the *Anisahonia,* Blue Clan of Cherokee."

He paused, then again gazed intently into her eyes. He was deeply touched by her loveliness. He felt a spark inside his heart that had lain banked since the death of his wife.

Ho, he wished that Shaylee were real and not a Spirit Person, for in her presence he had once more become a man with feelings for a woman. His heart had begun to sing the very moment he had seen her.

"Your name . . . your hair . . . is beautiful," he blurted out. "You are beautiful."

Shaylee felt suddenly timid in the presence of this wonderfully handsome warrior. His gentleness, his acceptance of her being an angel, made her believe that this man *was* good.

Now she believed that he couldn't have had

any role in what had happened to her. Why hadn't she realized before that the length of time he had been in the cavern proved he had not ridden with the men down the lane that led to her cabin?

Yet she knew that all of these events were somehow connected or God wouldn't have chosen *her* to help the injured man.

She hoped that she would have the answers she sought soon. She wasn't sure how long God would give her to make things right for this injured man!

Chapter Five

Shadows vague,
Cautious shawl,
Shifting time,
Opaque squall.

The forest was so dense, only narrow ribbons of sunshine made their way through the foliage. In the midst of the shadows and trees was a small lane which led to a tiny cabin known by only a few.

When Moon Beam, a young and beautiful Cherokee maiden, heard the sound of horses' hooves approaching the cabin, she grew melancholy, for she knew that it was her brother Short Arrow arriving home. When her brother had been banished from their Cherokee village, she had followed him a short time later. Not because she was forced to go; she had left out of a sense of duty toward her brother who she loved with all her heart.

She had since then cooked for him, kept his cabin clean, and sewed his clothes.

After she saw him enter a life of crime as he allied himself with Indian renegades and white outlaws, Moon Beam remained. But not for him alone. She had fallen in love with one of her brother's white outlaw friends and had learned to close her eyes to what she knew they did.

When her husband had recently died during one of their raids on whites, Moon Beam's heart had been broken. And not only that. The shock had caused her to lose the baby she was carrying in her womb.

After much heart searching, she had decided to return home to her Cherokee people. She only hoped they would allow it, for they knew what her brother was guilty of and might in part cast blame on her because she had allied herself with him.

Tears filled her eyes as she placed a hand over her abdomen. Never had she felt so empty and alone as now. The baby inside her had given her such hope . . . such cherished moments of dreaming of a life without crime, for her husband, as soon as he had been told of the child, had vowed to reform. He had said that he owed it to Short Arrow to ride one last time with him.

It was his last ride, *i-go-hi-di*, forever.

"I must return home," she whispered. She would no longer condone what her brother did. She had pleaded with him to stop. But it was a fever in his heart that burned out of control.

Only a bullet would finally extinguish it.

She didn't want to be there when that happened.

Clasping and unclasping her hands, she eyed her packed buckskin bag, then went to the door. As the breeze fluttered the hem of her fringed buckskin dress around her ankles, she watched Short Arrow ride into view.

She strained her neck to look closer, for she could not help noticing what her brother held in the crook of his left arm. It was something small, and it was wrapped in a blanket. If she didn't know better, she would think he held a baby in his arms.

But, no, it must be something else. It was surely some precious valuable that he had stolen during his raid today. He did this — brought her pretty things to help lift her spirits during her time of sadness.

When Short Arrow saw her standing at the door, her long, black hair hanging so beautifully over her shoulders and down her back, he smiled broadly.

"Come, sister!" he shouted. "Come and take from my arms something special."

She sighed heavily as he rode up and stopped by the hitching rail. His outlaw and renegade friends stopped behind him and looked at Moon Beam.

"I want no gifts today," she said, then reached for her bag and brought it up in her arms. "I am going home, Short Arrow. I can no longer be a part of your life. I cannot bear what you do or the knowledge that you could die as quickly as my husband. I am going home, Short Arrow. Give your gift to someone else."

Short Arrow's smile faded when he glanced down at the bag. He looked with hurt eyes at Moon Beam. "You would leave your brother?" he said, his voice drawn.

"Do not act so surprised," Moon Beam said, stepping outside onto the narrow porch. "You knew that it was my plan, and my husband's, to begin a new life away from you. If he had not died —"

"He had changed his mind about leaving," Short Arrow said tightly. "He would never have been happy elsewhere."

"I do not believe you, my brother," Moon Beam said, a sob catching in her throat. "He would have been happy, because his wife Moon Beam and our child would make it so."

"Whatever you say," Short Arrow said, shrugging nonchalantly. He held the bundle out toward her. "Come. See what I have brought you. It will put sunshine in your eyes again."

"Nothing but my husband and our child could do that," Moon Beam said, stepping from the porch. "I am leaving, brother. Say no more to me about gifts."

Holding the child in one arm, Short Arrow slowly unfolded the blanket from around him.

When the child began to cry, Moon Beam jumped with alarm and dropped her bag to the ground. She felt her breath catch in her throat when Short Arrow unwrapped the baby, giving Moon Beam a full view of him.

"A . . . baby . . . ?" Moon Beam said, feeling a choking sensation at her throat. "You have brought a baby here? You . . . stole . . . a . . . baby?"

"For you," Short Arrow said, his eyes anxious as he awaited her response.

"No," Moon Beam suddenly cried, feeling sick inside to imagine what he must have done to get the child.

She started to run away, but Short Arrow's voice stopped her in mid-step.

"I cannot return the child, so you *must* take him," Short Arrow said. "The child, a boy, is to fill that empty space inside your heart left there by the loss of both your husband and child."

Moon Beam turned and glared at him. "How could you even think I would want a baby like this?" she screamed. "Short Arrow, you have gone too far this time! My brother, you are someone I no longer know." She covered her mouth with a hand. "Surely you killed the parents . . . the . . . *mother.*"

"The father did die some moons ago when we came upon him one day alone on a country road," Short Arrow said, his voice devoid of emotion. "We had watched him. We knew from which cabin he rode and that he left a wife there. The wife? This child's mother? She died today."

47

"No," Moon Beam choked out. "How . . . could . . . you?"

"The child lives, Moon Beam," Short Arrow said dryly. "And he needs a mother." He held the baby out toward her: the child's cries were now only sobs. "You *must* take him. He has no one else."

Beset by so many emotions, Moon Beam exhaled a nervous sigh. She took slow steps toward her brother and the child. Although she was horrified at how Short Arrow had acquired the baby, it was true that the child needed someone . . . *any*one, for Moon Beam most certainly could not leave him in her brother's care.

And she could not deny the pounding of her heart to think that she could mother this child . . . that she could love him now that his mother had been so cruelly taken from him.

Yes, she would find a way to make the wrong done this child right. She would give him much love. And he would never know the viciousness of his mother's death. Moon Beam would devote her life to the child.

But she never wanted to see her brother again, for he was all that was evil on this earth.

As she held her arms out for the baby, she refused to let herself think about the mother from whose arms this baby had been taken. From this day forth, the *a-yo-the* was hers in all respects.

She melted inside when her brother eased the

baby into her arms. "A boy," she murmured, captivated by the child's blue eyes which stared trustingly back at her.

And when she saw the tendrils of red hair on the baby's head, tears filled her eyes. Her husband's hair had been red. And his eyes had been as blue as the baby's. It would be so easy to pretend that the child had been born of her and her husband's love.

It was as though he were there even now, gazing at the child with her, seeing it as theirs. . . .

Then her heart skipped a beat when she saw something else. She reached a trembling finger to the butterfly-shaped birthmark beneath the child's left ear. This was the only thing about the baby that was anything akin to a blemish, for otherwise the child seemed to be healthy.

Her insides tightened when the child began crying again. "He must be hungry," she said, panic seizing her. How was she to feed the child? And how long could the child go without being fed as she sought a way to get nourishment inside his tiny, fragile body?

Short Arrow slid from his horse and stood beside Moon Beam. He enjoyed the sight of her holding the child. He would not allow himself to think of the woman who had to die in order for his sister to become a mother today.

Ho, the deed had to be done the way he had chosen to do it. What did it matter that he had killed both the mother and father, anyhow?

Short Arrow never hesitated at killing when he deemed it necessary. It was just a part of his life now . . . the killings, the maimings, the schemes that bettered his life and took from others.

"A name, sister," he said. "You must give your child a name, for I know that you will leave me and I want to have a name to think about when I imagine you and your son."

"It will be Cherokee," she said, gazing down at the tiny face. "I will raise him in the Cherokee tradition, which means he must be called by a Cherokee name."

"What name comes to you? What feels right for the child?" Short Arrow prodded.

"I have always loved the mighty eagle that soars over White River during the mating season," Moon Beam murmured. She bent low and brushed a kiss across the baby's brow. "I shall call him Soaring Eagle."

"That is a good name," Short Arrow said.

"My breasts are not heavy with milk but I will find someone who will share her milk with my son," Moon Beam said, giving her brother a stern look. "Brother, I am returning home now to live among our Blue Clan of Cherokee. It was not I who was banished. Only you. If they question where I have been, I will say with my husband. They will never know that my husband was an outlaw and that he rode with you. But I will tell them that he was white and that I have given birth to his son, who is also white. I

50

will tell them that he died and that I have brought my son home to raise among our people. How can they not allow it?"

Short Arrow's eyes narrowed. "You cannot return home," he said tightly. "You must stay away. There will be trouble there soon."

"What sort of trouble?" Moon Beam asked warily as she slowly wrapped the blanket comfortably around the baby again.

"To get back at my arch enemy Standing Wolf, I have conjured up the best of schemes," he said. "Chief Bear Sitting Down is to die. *Today.* And Standing Wolf will be blamed, because it will be his knife that will kill the old chief. Standing Wolf has been known to say that he thought the old chief was too set in his ways and that his sorceress wife has too much control of the village. It is known that Standing Wolf is next in line to be chief. When Chief Bear Sitting Down is found dead, and it is Standing Wolf's knife that is found in his heart, will not the people say that Standing Wolf is clearly the culprit?"

"You are wrong to do this," Moon Beam gasped. "Brother, you will be caught. You will be killed for the crime!"

"You do not listen well to your brother," Short Arrow snorted. "It will be Standing Wolf who will be blamed for the crime . . . who will die! Our chiefs have long reigns. They are not easily deposed. Sometimes murdering a chief is the only way for an ambitious man." He chuckled. "In a sense I am doing my people a favor."

"Your people?" Moon Beam said, a sob catching in her throat. "Brother, you lost the right to call them your people long ago. I *will* return home. They *are* still *my* people. I will tell them what you are planning. They will stop you."

He grabbed her by the nape of the neck. "You tell no one or you will die, as well," he snarled. "You have just lost the right to call me brother. You . . . are . . . no longer my sister!"

He dropped his hand away and cleared his throat nervously. "Just in case Standing Wolf can prove that I am the murderer, it is best that you stay far from the village for now," he said. "You can go downriver and stay with friends at a Chippewa village."

Still stunned by his threat, truly afraid of him, Moon Beam slowly nodded, her eyes wide as she took slow steps away from him. "I will go and live among the Chippewa," she murmured. "There both I and the child will be welcome." She swallowed hard. "And . . . safe."

"Moon Beam, I am sorry for what I said about you no longer being my sister," Short Arrow said, his gaze wavering. "You will forever be my sister. And I could never harm you."

"I believe that you could," Moon Beam said, her voice breaking.

"My sister, I will escort you and the child to the river and see that you are safely in a canoe,"

Short Arrow declared, ignoring what she'd just said. "I will say goodbye then, for we will not see one another again for some time. You are better off without me. Many are gunning for me now. You could be caught in the crossfire."

Tears filled Moon Beam's eyes again. "When did life go so wrong for you?" she asked, searching his eyes. "And what about the woman you love? Does she not now carry your child in her womb? Surely you cannot ask her to come and live such a life as this with you."

Short Arrow's eyes narrowed but he refused to respond. . . .

Chapter Six

Omens and dreams,
Awakening pall,
The rain-crows'
Haunting call.

The sun had just risen from behind the distant mountains to light another day. A council was planned with Chief Bear Sitting Down at the village of the Blue Clan of Cherokee. Good Shield, Standing Wolf's best friend, was becoming uneasy. He had addressed the chief more than once outside his closed entrance flap but he had yet to receive a response.

Good Shield tried again, for Chief bear Sitting Down was known to have recently become somewhat deaf. Sometimes, to be heard, one had to shout when talking to the aging chief.

"Bear Sitting Down, it is I, Good Shield," he said, leaning his face closer to the entrance flap that swayed gently in the early morning breeze. "As you requested, warriors are arriving now at the council house. I have come to escort you there."

As Good Shield still waited, he looked nervously over his shoulder at the women who were coming from the river from their morning baths, then at the children in clusters, laughing and playing with each other while their dogs yapped at their heels. All were enjoying the wonderful May morning.

But Good Shield was now even more worried that things did not seem right in his chief's lodge.

And where was the chief's wife?

As Good Shield slowly passed his eyes over the women, he saw nothing of Gentle Heart, the young beauty that his chief had chosen for his third wife; the other two wives had passed on already to the land of the hereafter.

He frowned bitterly when he still saw nothing of Gentle Heart. He wondered what she might be up to, for as far as he was concerned, the woman was evil.

Good Shield had known about Gentle Heart long before his chief had become bewitched by her. Born Chippewa, her shameful exploits with men shamed the good name of her people. The name Gentle Heart was a mockery, for she was anything but gentle-hearted.

But that name had been given to her before people knew what she would grow up to be. The name had been given when she was sweet, gentle, and caring.

But when she became old enough to know that her beauty could get her almost anything her heart desired, especially men, the true nature of the woman surfaced.

She knew just how to twist a man around her finger to get him to do anything for her. Always wanting people to see her as someone special, and knowing that she needed a husband of stature to achieve this goal, Gentle Heart had had her aunt, a known sorceress, cast a charm on the older chief, who had promptly married Gentle Heart.

Good Shield was suspicious of every breath that Gentle Heart took. He was almost certain that she had taken a lover. Although married to a man three times her age, she had the hunger of a young, vibrant woman. It seemed obvious that she would seek sexual encounters with men her own age, especially since her elderly husband was known to be impotent.

"She might even be with a lover now," Good Shield whispered to himself as he gave another troubled glance at the entrance flap.

The woman was certainly not with her husband looking after his welfare!

Good Shield had recently decided that one day soon he would follow Gentle Heart to see if she was unfaithful, and if so, where, and with whom.

But today all he was concerned about was his chief. It was apparent that Chief Bear Sitting Down was not going to respond to Good

Shield, and Good Shield would wait no longer to see why.

He slowly shoved aside the buckskin flap.

Inside, the fire had died down to glowing embers in the firepit, but sunshine streaming through the smoke hole above gave Good Shield enough light to see into the depths of the large skin lodge.

When he saw Chief Bear Sitting Down stretched out on his bed of blankets and pelts at the far side of the lodge, Good Shield was relieved. Surely his chief overslept.

Knowing that his chief would not want to sleep through the council that he, himself, had planned, Good Shield crept into the tepee.

He walked around the firepit, then stopped and stared in horror at the knife that he could now see protruding from his chief's chest.

At this range Good Shield could see that his chief's eyes were locked in a death stare.

Good Shield could even see that what he had thought were red threads in the blanket that lay across his chief were, instead . . . streamers of his chief's blood!

"*Aiee, gah-ween,* no! Let it not be so!" Good Shield cried as he dropped to his knees beside his slain chief.

His heart pained him as he stared at how still Chief Bear Sitting Down lay, and how obscene the knife's handle looked as it protruded from his chief's chest.

"Who would do this?" Good Shield whispered, reaching his trembling fingers to slowly close his chief's eyes. "My chief, who could hate you so much?"

His breath caught in his throat when he suddenly recognized the knife that had killed his chief.

It . . . was . . . Standing Wolf's!

"No!"

Behind him, a familiar voice uttered a cry of alarm that was obviously forced.

He turned with a jerk and saw Gentle Heart standing there, her eyes staring down at her dead husband.

When Gentle Heart moved her eyes slowly to look up into Good Shield's, there was no doubt that he saw an evil glint there. The mourning that she would show to her people would be forced! Pretended!

In truth, Good Shield knew that Gentle Heart was glad she was finally rid of the man she had grown to detest.

More than once he had seen how her husband's mere touch sent shivers of loathing through her.

"My husband is dead," Gentle Heart cried, throwing herself past Good Shield to fall onto her knees beside the still body.

When she knew that Good Shield could not look upon her face, Gentle Heart smiled. She was pretending to be upset over her husband's death, but in truth, she was relieved that it was finally over. The man whom she had so cleverly duped had finally rid them both of the old, stubborn chief.

Gentle Heart gazed at the knife that was still in her husband's chest.

She smiled slyly, for she knew to whom the knife belonged, and why it had been used.

She looked over her shoulder and gave Good Shield a glance.

She could tell by the look in his eyes that he also knew whose knife had downed the old chief.

"You know, do you not, whose knife was used to kill my husband?" Gentle Heart said as she rose slowly to her feet. She lifted her chin defiantly and glared into Good Shield's dark eyes. "Say it, Good Shield. Say whose knife is in my dead husband's body!"

"*Ho,* the knife is Standing Wolf's," Good Shield said solemnly. But he refrained from saying more about it. His mind was active with thoughts . . . with accusations he knew were true.

Gentle Heart hated Standing Wolf. Before she married Chief Bear Sitting Down, she had pursued Standing Wolf even though the Cherokee people and the Chippewa were known enemies and avoided each other at all costs to lessen the chance of war.

When Gentle Heart feared the enmity between their tribes was causing Standing Wolf to avoid her, she had pleaded with him not to let that stand in their way. She had reminded him that she was more beautiful than any other woman in either of their villages and that she had been born of good blood. Her grandfather had been chief. Her Chippewa father *was* chief!

Then when even Standing Wolf turned his back on her, knowing her for the vindictive woman she was, she schemed to marry their chief, instead.

It was now that Good Shield saw her true reason for marrying his chief. She had planned to discredit Standing Wolf for having turned his back on her.

Surely this murder had been planned from the very beginning.

Gentle Heart had probably even asked her sorceress aunt to cast a charm on Chief Bear Sitting Down, even though the charms had not worked when they had been used to lure Standing Wolf into the beautiful young woman's bed.

Thinking that a young woman might make him look younger, and ignoring the fact that no woman as young as Gentle Heart could actually love him, Chief Bear Sitting Down had taken Gentle Heart as his wife.

No one but Standing Wolf and Good Shield knew the true history between Gentle Heart and Standing Wolf. So now, after everyone saw her husband lying there with Standing Wolf's knife in his chest, she would lie and say that not only had Standing Wolf wanted the job of chief taken from Bear Sitting Down, he also wanted the old chief's wife.

"Since it *is* Standing Wolf's knife in my husband's chest, he will be blamed for the murder," Gentle Heart said, slyly smiling into Good Shield's anger-filled eyes.

Good Shield started to grab Gentle Heart and warn her against speaking such an accusation aloud to their people, for she knew it was not true.

But she was past him too quickly and outside, crying out to their people that her husband was dead and it was Standing Wolf's knife that was in her husband's chest!

Good Shield's insides knotted and he curled his fingers into tight fists at his sides as he refrained from going outside and calling Gentle Heart a liar before his people who were now quickly gathering outside their fallen chief's lodge, to start their mourning.

Good Shield's eyes lit with fire when Gentle Heart shouted to everyone that Standing Wolf had been secretly pursuing her behind his chief's back!

Good Shield became sick inside with a loathing never before felt by him as he listened to the blatant lies spewing from Gentle Heart's evil mouth as she shouted how Standing Wolf had asked her many times for secret trysts, which she had refused.

She shouted how Standing Wolf had wanted her husband dead so that he could have her!

Even when Gentle Heart claimed that

Standing Wolf would do anything to be their chief, even kill for the proud title, Good Shield still did not go out and openly call her a liar. This was not the time. She was not only the widow of their beloved chief, she was their "Beloved Woman." She was among those special women who were chosen by each clan to be present at every council.

Gentle Heart's chieftain husband had made certain that she was chosen above all other women in their village when it had come time to vote for the Beloved Woman.

Gentle Heart's title of "Beloved Woman" even gave her the power to serve as counselor to the male leaders of the village. She also had the power to regulate the treatment dealt to prisoners of war.

And even though Good Shield saw that it was best at this time not to speak his mind about the evil woman, he did suspect that she was the one who had stolen Standing Wolf's knife and killed her husband to make it look as though Standing Wolf had done it.

Even when Good Shield heard Gentle Heart go so far as to order her warriors to find Standing Wolf, to bring him to her, that he must pay for killing the chief of their people, Good Shield still did not interfere. He knew that none of their people would believe that Standing Wolf could be capable of doing such a thing as killing their chief, but because she had spoken, they had to do as she told them. She *was* their Beloved Woman, a woman cherished by their fallen leader.

Good Shield was still standing quietly alone in the lodge of his dead chief when he heard the warriors ride from the village to search for Standing Wolf. Good Shield had decided to do his own searching and hoped to find Standing Wolf before anyone else. He must help his friend find a way out of this evil woman's vindictive plan!

He turned, gave his chief one last solemn stare, then ran from the lodge, mounted his brown mustang, and rode from the village.

He set his jaw firmly.

His eyes narrowed.

He *must* find his friend before anyone else found him.

Together they would work this out. They would find a way to discredit the woman whose name belied her true self!

"Woman, you will be sorry you ever breathed the name Standing Wolf across your lying lips!" Good Shield hissed, then sank his heels into the flanks of his steed, urging him into a harder gallop.

Chapter Seven

Omens and dreams,
Endless quest,
Eternity rides,
Destiny's test.

Feeling helpless lying there, Standing Wolf again tried to get up, but he fell back to the cave floor, dizzy and panting.

"You must rest," Shaylee said softly. She looked around for something to make him more comfortable, but saw there were no supplies there.

The most important thing, she decided, was to get a fire going so that Standing Wolf wouldn't be chilled by the damp cavern air, and so that she could prepare one of the turkeys to give him a much-needed meal.

Remembering that she had placed matches in her dress pocket that morning — oh, so long ago — she slid a hand into her pocket and smiled. The matches were still there. She *could* get a fire going. She *could* prepare food for Standing Wolf.

When she saw him looking at her, eyeing the matches in her hand, she held them out. "You will soon have turkey to eat," she said, smiling. "I must go and get some wood. I shan't be long. I'll build the fire just outside the cave entrance. I'll then help you out there so that you can sit in the fresh, warm air."

Worried that his attacker might come back to see if he had survived the blow to his head, Standing Wolf reached a quick hand out to Shaylee.

"No, do not start a fire. It is best that I do not leave the cave just yet," he said thickly. "But I do need nourishment. And surely so must you. Perhaps you can gather some berries. That must do until I am able to fend for myself and return to my village."

"I believe you must have something more nourishing than berries," Shaylee said, remembering that it was her responsibility to help this man. She recalled how God had said that he was going to be unjustly accused. To fight off such accusation, he had to be strong.

She glanced at his head wound. After having washed the blood from it, she could see that there was only a small break in the skin. She was sure he had monstrous headache, but it did seem as though he would fully recover.

"I *can* build a fire in the cave," Shaylee said, hoping he would not object to that. "I shall go farther back. The smoke will slowly filter up through the cracks in the limestone overhead, so it will not be noticeable."

"You seem to understand that I must stay in hiding for a while longer," Standing Wolf said, leaning on an elbow as he gazed into her blue eyes. "You knew I needed help and now you seem to know why. *Hi-ga-ta-ha-tsu?* What led you to me?"

Finding her present circumstances difficult to understand herself, Shaylee didn't know what to say to him. She had never realized that angels were actually assigned jobs on earth.

But she was glad that she had been given the task of looking after this Indian. There was something special about him.

She was sure that was true, or else why would God have sent her to help him?

"I'll go and gather firewood," Shaylee said in order to avoid answering any further questions. It was all best left unsaid until she was given a sign from the Heavens that she could explain everything to him.

Standing Wolf watched her leave. The longer he was with her, the more puzzled he became about her. He believed she had been sent to help him, but why? Why would the Spirit People care about him? Did they know something that he, himself, did not know?

Did it have something to do with the attempt on his life? In time, he hoped to discover the answers. It seemed that if he had truly been meant to die, his assailant would have done more than hit him over the head.

The more he thought about it, the more he believed that his life had been spared for some reason. Only time would tell what that was. And Shaylee was right to insist that he must eat something substantial. The proof was in how weak his knees were and how his head spun each time he tried to sit upright.

After Shaylee had a fire started, she moved aside as Standing Wolf stood up on shaky legs and managed to position himself near the fire.

Shaylee followed him and watched him slowly stretch out beside the fire on a bed of dried leaves that she had prepared for him.

"I shall be only a minute now," she reassured him as she turned and started walking toward the cave entrance. She gave him a look over her shoulder. "I will take one of your turkeys to the river and prepare it for cooking. I shan't be long."

After half an hour the turkey was roasting in the hot coals at the edges of the fire, and Shaylee sat down nearby to tend to it. She was not aware of the aroma of the roasting meat, nor did she feel hunger pangs as she usually would while preparing meat, especially turkey. Cooked wild turkey meat was one of her favorite meals. When she made turkey with mashed potatoes and gravy, she always ate until she could almost burst.

She recalled how her husband used to tease her about how much she could eat.

She felt eyes on her, but they weren't her husband's. They were the handsome Indian's, and although she was no longer able to experience taste, touch, or smell, the feelings that a woman could have for a man were still there inside her heart.

This Cherokee warrior stirred her in a sensual way that only one other man ever had.

She felt not only compassion for him, but also desire, and knew that the latter was wrong, for God hadn't sent her back to earth to fall in love. She was there to help Standing Wolf and to find her precious son.

"Were you hunting for food for your family, perhaps . . . your wife, when you were assaulted?" Shaylee asked, curious.

"No, no family, no wife," Standing Wolf said, turning his eyes from her and staring at the sunlight coming through the entrance.

He wasn't sure why he didn't tell her that he had *had* a wife, but she had died during pregnancy. That had been long ago, when he had been a young man whose heart had been stolen quickly by one of the prettiest Sioux maidens in the area.

Now he was older and wiser. When he chose a wife this time, he would make sure nothing took her away from him.

He could not help wishing that this Spirit Person was real, for when he looked into her eyes his heart sang as it had the first time he had gazed upon the face of his beloved Sunshine!

"My parents died many years ago when their canoe capsized in the river during a fierce storm," he added. "No one of my village has ever witnessed such a storm as that since. Even I, although a small brave of a few years, remember the winds. They blew as if demons had been set loose from the heavens."

"I'm so sorry," Shaylee murmured, feeling his sadness deep inside herself.

She didn't want to be happy that he had no wife, but she was. She was afraid to allow herself to feel anything for this red man, for even if she was sent back to earth again, to live among the living and breathing, she knew that the odds were always against a white woman loving an Indian. It was taboo . . . forbidden!

And Standing Wolf was a man of importance, whose life must be devoted to his people, not to a white woman who might bring heartache not only to him, but to his people as a whole.

Her obligation was to get him well so that he could return to his people for whatever purpose God had planned for him.

"The turkey is ready to eat," Shaylee said, sliding the browned meat out of the coals. She was glad when he sat up and was able to stay sitting.

Although he was still dizzy, and the pain in his head was almost debilitating, Standing Wolf forced himself to sit there and take a drumstick as Shaylee tore it away from the browned turkey.

She watched him bite into it, then was aware of him giving her a quizzical stare. She wasn't eating. Surely he wondered why.

"Will you not eat with me?" Standing Wolf asked, nodding toward the remaining turkey. "You have proved to be a good cook. Taste. You will see just how good."

"I feel no hunger," Shaylee murmured. When he tossed the bone aside and reached out for another chunk of meat, she smiled. "But it is good to see that you are feeding your hunger well."

"After I eat, I want to go to my canoe," Standing Wolf said, not questioning why she wasn't hungry. She was one of the Spirit People. Surely they felt no hunger or thirst, and possibly not even emotions.

Yet he had seen how she had looked at him more than once. There was emotion in her eyes. He could tell that even though she was not someone of this earth, she had feelings for him.

As did he for her, and he was fighting them with all of his being, for he knew that she was there only to guide him through his momentary time of crisis. When he was well enough to fend for himself, he expected her to disappear as suddenly as she had appeared.

"I wish to get back to my people," Standing Wolf said. "I must let them know what has happened. Not only was I downed by a blow to the head, but my valued knife and bow and quiver of arrows were also stolen."

"Do you have a known enemy?" Shaylee asked.

"Yes, I have perhaps the worst of *ha-ma-ma*," Standing Wolf said, tossing another stripped bone into the firepit. "But I am not certain it was Short Arrow who ambushed me. The coward came upon me from behind. If I discover that it was he, I will make him pay for having wronged me."

He looked toward the cave entrance. "I feel stronger now," he said, then glanced at Shaylee. "Would you help me to my canoe? I left it beached on the banks of the river. I am certain it is not far from this cavern."

"I have been at the river," Shaylee said, also glancing toward the cave entrance. Then she frowned at Standing Wolf. "I saw no canoe there."

"The wind must have dislodged it and floated it away," Standing Wolf said.

"Or perhaps your assailant also stole it," Shaylee offered.

Comfortably full, Standing Wolf eased back down onto his bed of dried leaves. "*Ho,* perhaps," he grumbled. "No canoe. No knife. No bow and arrow. Now I have no choice but to stay in the cave until I have the strength to walk the full distance to my village," he said, sighing heavily. "And I cannot send you for help, for I know that you, a Spirit Person, are only known by me."

71

"The mask," Shaylee said. "What does it represent? Why did you wear it?"

He explained about the turkey mask, then drifted off to sleep.

Unsure of what to do next, Shaylee left the cave and went to sit beside the river while Standing Wolf took his nap.

Beneath old sweet-gum trees whose graceful limbs reached out over the water, Shaylee saw several spring lizards lying at the bottom of the shallow part of the river.

She watched them for a while, then gazed Heavenward. "God, am I finished here?" she whispered aloud. "Have I passed the test? If so, will you now lead me to my son? Is he well?"

When she received no response, she realized that she still must stay with the Indian. The more she thought about it, the more she believed that the Lord had purposely led her to this Indian, not only so that she could help him, but also so that the Indian would lead her to her child. Surely she would find Moses at his village.

But Standing Wolf wasn't well enough to travel on foot just yet to get to his village. She must wait, but, oh, the waiting would be so hard, for perhaps her child was only a few miles away in the Cherokee village!

"Moses," she whispered. "I shall never forget you, darling Moses."

Chapter Eight

Ancestors before,
Descendants galore,
Come and go,
To chant no more.

Unable to find any trace of Standing Wolf, Good Shield had returned home and was now lurking in the dark shadows inside Gentle Heart's new log cabin.

He was waiting for her to return from preparing her chieftain husband for burial.

He smirked at the thought of how she pretended to be sad and forlorn over her husband's death. She had even cut her hair and made small slits on her forearms with her knife to show her mourning.

Good Shield wondered just how many people she had fooled with such behavior. Surely he was not the only one who saw through her.

He was almost certain that she was responsible in some way for her husband's death. He had come to her lodge now to question her.

Out of respect for his chief, who even now awaited burial rites, and because his people were so distraught over their chief's death, Good Shield had not yet shown his disdain for Gentle Heart in public.

But when he was alone with her, he would attempt to get some answers.

"If what I believe is true, Gentle Heart will pay dearly," Good Shield snarled to himself, his right hand resting on his sheathed knife.

Good Shield waited impatiently behind a blanket that hung from the rafters in a cabin that had been quickly built for Gentle Heart shortly after her husband's body had been found. No one lived in a place where death had occurred.

As Gentle Heart had joined others to prepare her husband for burial, pretending to care deeply for him, many Cherokee warriors had hurried to prepare her home and had taken her belongings there after making a welcome fire for her in the stone fireplace.

When she arrived now, it would be her first time in the new dwelling, where she would be given time for prayer until her husband's burial.

Good Shield knew that once Gentle Heart arrived, no one would come there to interfere in her time of private mourning.

"No one but Good Shield," he whispered to himself, knowing that he would have all the privacy he needed to get answers from her.

It had been easy to get inside her lodge, for anyone who might have seen him enter would have seen his arms heavily laden with a slab of deer meat, a gift for the mourning widow.

His heart skipped a beat and his breathing quickened when he heard the door open, and then shut.

He leaned his ear closer to the blanket that separated him from the woman he loathed.

His eyes widened and hatred filled him when she actually giggled, then laughed.

He heard her whispering to herself.

"They are all fools," Gentle Heart said. He heard the sound of a blanket slipping off her shoulders.

Good Shield looked down at the floor beside him when the blanket landed there.

Then he listened again to her ramblings, which proved that she was not only a scheming, lying sorceress, but also a crazed madwoman.

"Except for Good Shield, I have them all fooled," Gentle Heart said. He heard the sound of water being poured into a wooden basin. "They'd better be fooled. I will have scars now for the rest of my life because I had to prove something I do not feel, to those . . . those . . . people."

Then when she went quiet, and Good Shield heard her quick intake of breath, he smiled. Surely Gentle Heart had finally seen the slab of meat lying on the hearth. He hoped that whatever blood remained in the meat had run down onto the wooden flooring.

It made him smile to think of her having to walk into the blood to get the meat. Probably she would throw it out of her lodge. He had made sure it was not a fresh kill.

Although still bloody, which made it look new, in truth it was days old. He'd found the deer carcass where it had been left in the forest by an animal that had had its fill of it before leaving it to rot and stink beneath the large pin-oak trees.

Even now he smelled the carcass filling the air with its stench. The only reason Gentle Heart had not smelled it upon her first entry was because she was too busy gloating to notice anything.

But now she smelled and saw the meat.

He could almost feel her eyes moving slowly around the cabin to search for whoever might have brought the stinking offering into her new dwelling.

What he would have liked to have done was to bring meat that had been tainted not by age, but by strychnine, so that after she cooked it and ate it, she would die and the world would be rid of her.

But he was not the sort of man who could take a life so easily, especially someone who could prove his best friend's innocence.

Ho, for now she had the power to order Standing Wolf's death, but soon Good Shield hoped to find ways to discredit her in the eyes of his people.

Making sure he gave her no time to reach for a weapon, Good Shield yanked his knife from its sheath and leapt out from behind the blanket.

"You!" she cried, staring at him wide-eyed. "Only you would have done this. Everyone else treats me gently during my time of mourning. But not you! You have come to torment me with spoiled meat and your accusations, have you not?"

She looked toward the closed door, then glared up at Good Shield. "I shall open the door and scream," she dared. "You will be taken away and made to pay for doing this to me."

"Go ahead and carry out your threat, and I will then carry out mine," Good Shield said in a low voice.

He raised the knife and placed its coldness against the throbbing vein in her throat. "Now it is only you and Good Shield," he spat out. "While I stood behind the blanket, I heard you laughing and mocking our people. That is proof enough to me that what I suspected all along is true. You, not my best friend, caused your husband's death. Who is in this scheme with you?"

"You are as foolish as everyone else in this village if you think I will tell you anything except that I, our people's Beloved Woman, killed *no one,*" Gentle Heart said.

She lifted her chin defiantly as she tried to ignore the cold blade resting so threateningly close to her throat.

"You lie so easily," Good Shield hissed out, leaning his face closer to hers.

"I did not kill my husband," Gentle Heart retorted. "Now go. Leave me to my mourning."

Her eyes slid over to the meat. "And take that stinking mess with you when you go," she said hotly.

Again they looked into one another's eyes, challenging each other.

"You say that you did not kill your husband," Good Shield mused, slowly lowering the knife away from her throat. "Then who did? And what have they done with Standing Wolf? Did you order the same person who killed your husband to kill Standing Wolf after stealing his knife from him?"

Rubbing the raw place on her neck where the knife had abraded the skin, Gentle Heart leered into Good Shield's face. "Standing Wolf is not dead," she said, a laugh lying just beneath the surface. "I would never have ordered anyone to kill him. I want him to live to be banished by his people after he is found. I want him to stand before his people accused of killing the chief. And Standing Wolf will be held accountable for Chief Bear Sitting Down's death. It was his knife that was found in my

78

dead husband's body."

"It was all so carefully planned by you," Good Shield said, taking slow steps away from her, stunned that a woman could be this evil and thus far get away with it. "I will tell everyone that it is all a scheme planned by a woman who was tired of having an old man for a husband . . . a husband whose body was not enough for such a young wife."

Gentle Heart placed her hands on her hips and laughed. "No one will believe you," she said in a mocking tone. "Except for you and Standing Wolf, I have never openly given anyone reason to suspect this side of my nature. And remember that I am still a Beloved Woman who has almost as much power over our people as our fallen chief had."

She stepped close to Good Shield and leaned into his face. "Standing Wolf should never have turned his back on the love I offered him," she hissed. "I told him even then that he would pay dearly for that rejection."

Good Shield shoved his knife into its sheath, then grabbed Gentle Heart by the wrists. "I will find a way to discredit you," he said through clenched teeth. "I *will* prove your role in not only your husband's death, but also Standing Wolf's downfall."

Good Shield ran from the cabin.

He was horrified at everything that had been uncovered during his conversation with Gentle Heart.

Even now her lunatic laughter ran through his memory.

She *was* mad, yet she had guarded her secret motivation well while in the presence of Good Shield's people!

Somehow she had managed not only to trick the old chief into marrying her, but also to fool the Blue Clan Cherokee as a whole.

He knew now that his vow to prove his friend's innocence was not going to be an easy one to fulfill.

But he would not stop at anything to help the missing warrior.

Good Shield and Standing Wolf had been best friends since childhood. Good Shield knew that no one could be as fine, good, noble, and trustworthy as Standing Wolf.

But when a crazy woman and her sorceress aunt were scheming against a man, making everyone see the truth became twice the struggle.

"But I shall succeed," Good Shield whispered to himself.

And he must start now. No more time could be wasted.

He went to Standing Wolf's cabin and hurried behind it. At the back of Standing Wolf's lodge was a dog trot, where Standing Wolf's dog, Winged Foot, lay asleep.

Good Shield stopped and gazed at Winged Foot. He was a bear dog that had been trained to hunt bears. Usually those dogs were ferocious, but Winged Foot was gentle unless cornered, or unless he was in the presence of Standing Wolf's enemies.

Standing Wolf had given him the name Winged Foot because the dog was swift of foot.

Hoping that the dog could sniff out his master's scent, Good Shield opened the gate to the dog trot and knelt down beside Winged Foot.

"Awaken," Good Shield whispered, gently stroking Winged Foot's brown fur. "You have a job that needs to be done."

When Winged Foot awakened and lifted his dark eyes up to Good Shield, Good Shield leaned down over him and hugged him. "Winged Foot, Standing Wolf is in trouble," he said, his voice breaking. "Come with me. Do what you can to help find him. Surely you can sniff out Standing Wolf's scent."

Winged Foot gave Good Shield a long lick on his face, then squirmed away from him, his tail wagging.

Good Shield smiled. Then he ran from the dog trot to his lodge where his brown mustang was grazing on thick grass in a rope corral behind his log cabin.

He had not unsaddled his mount after arriving home from his long search for Standing Wolf. Good Shield grabbed his horse's reins, led him from the corral, then leapt into the saddle and rode off as Winged Foot romped along beside the horse, his nose near to the earth, sniffing.

Good Shield was unaware of Gentle Heart standing at the back of her cabin, where she had just dragged the stinking meat and thrown it into the woods.

Her hands still bloody, the stench of the meat clinging to her flesh, she watched Good Shield ride away with Standing Wolf's dog.

"This is not good," she whispered to herself. That dog was dedicated to Standing Wolf. If anything or anyone could find him, the dog could.

"I must meet with my aunt and see what can be done about this chain of events," Gentle Heart said.

She eagerly rubbed her hands down the sides of her buckskin dress in an effort to remove the sticky blood. "Good Shield . . . must . . . be stopped," she whispered.

Gentle Heart rushed inside her aunt's smaller cabin where the fire in the grate of the fireplace was the only light in the dwelling.

Her eyes adjusting to the semidarkness, Gentle Heart saw her aunt sitting on the floor beside the fire, her shriveled hands working beads onto a new pair of moccasins.

Sitting down before her aunt, Gentle Heart reached a hand out to the old woman's deeply wrinkled face. "Aunt White Wing, I need help," she murmured, then drew her hand away when White Wing looked up at her through slitted eyes.

In the soft glow of the fire only a few of

White Wing's many warts showed. The old sorceress's wiry, long gray hair hung down her back and pooled around her on the filthy floor.

But she was dressed in a lovely beaded dress, for she was skilled at that art and made dresses for the women of the village.

"My niece, what has happened to bring such worry into your eyes?" White Wing asked. She was taken aback when she looked at Gentle Heart's hands and saw how they were stained with blood. She gazed down at the skirt of her niece's dress and saw blood there. She even now smelled its stench.

White Wing looked quickly up at Gentle Heart again. "What have you killed?" she asked throatily. Then her face quivered into a smile, the wrinkles becoming like deep craters around her mouth and eyes. "Are you practicing my ways? Have you made an evil potion?"

"No, I did not kill anything or anybody, and I am not making potions," Gentle Heart said, shuddering as she held her hands out and saw how the blood looked on them.

She suddenly felt as though it was her husband's blood on her hands, for she was no less guilty of his death than the man who slammed the knife into her husband's chest.

She had ordered it done.

That made the deed more hers than Short Arrow's!

But no one would ever prove this.

No one!

"Aunt White Wing, please help me," Gentle Heart begged, glad that her aunt had accompanied her when Gentle Heart had left her Chippewa village to live with her Cherokee husband. Their own people had been glad to see White Wing go, for she had practiced her sorcery one time too many and had set the Chippewa village into a mad rage against her. Now it was the Cherokee people who were the recipients of her aunt's skills with potions and herbs.

"Cast a spell on Good Shield," Gentle Heart softly urged. "Aunt White Wing, kill him."

"Child, tell me what has happened to upset you so much that you now want another man slain," White Wing said. She pushed herself up from the floor. She poured water from a parfleche bag into a wooden basin, then went back and sat down beside Gentle Heart.

She reached for Gentle Heart's hands and sank them into the water, and slowly bathed away the blood as Gentle Heart poured out her feelings and explained how Good Shield was interfering, even threatening her.

"Aunt White Wing, what am I to do?" Gentle Heart asked, desperation in her dark eyes. "I have come so close to having things the way I want them. And now this? Good Shield must die, or I will lose everything all over again."

"Niece, I see and hear your despair," White Wing said softly. "But nothing more should be done that could arouse suspicions against you.

And it *would* look suspicious if something happened to Good Shield at this time. Wait. Surely a better opportunity will come later. And his death is not necessary. You are far more powerful in the eyes of our people than Standing Wolf and Good Shield put together."

White Wing cackled beneath her breath. "*Ay-uh*, niece, wait," she added. "Let Good Shield find Standing Wolf. He will encourage his friend to return to the village to try to prove his innocence. His trust in his friend will be Standing Wolf's true downfall. Standing Wolf will never be able to prove his innocence. And if it comes down to his word against yours, you will be the victor, for never forget that you are your people's Beloved Woman."

White Wing cackled throatily again.

But Gentle Heart saw no humor in anything at this moment, for she knew that the true power behind her standing as the village's Beloved Woman lay awaiting his burial rites. Once his spirit was traveling along the high road with his ancestors, would Gentle Heart's life be in jeopardy?

Gah-ween, no! She suddenly had no reason at all to smile or feel safe under the protective title of "Beloved Woman." She was afraid to ask her aunt to stop and take a good, long look into the future, for Gentle Heart was suddenly not at all sure what it held.

Chapter Nine

Warnings' feel,
Shadows at dusk,
Omens and dreams,
Haunting hush.

Even though it was dusk, Good Shield was determined not to stop this time until he found Standing Wolf. As mist rose eerily from the water, he rode beside the White River in hopes of finding his friend's beached canoe. He glanced down at Winged Foot as the dog sniffed anxiously along the riverbank, then stopped suddenly and began barking.

"Winged Foot, did you find something?" Good Shield asked, his heart thumping wildly at the thought of finally getting somewhere with his maddening search.

When Winged Foot stopped barking and began sniffing along the ground away from the river, Good Shield's hopes rose even more, for he was certain now that the dog had found the scent of his master. Surely within minutes

Good Shield would be able to embrace his friend.

But then his friend would learn the terrible news, not only of their chief's murder, but that Standing Wolf was accused of the crime.

What worried Good Shield was why Standing Wolf had been gone for so long. When he hunted for turkeys, he never stayed away from his home for a full day.

As it was now, he had been gone a full day and night. And whoever had killed Chief Bear Sitting Down would have had to have fought Standing Wolf to get his knife. Standing Wolf would never have given up his knife otherwise.

His thoughts were interrupted and his heart sank when he saw that Winged Foot had led him to a limestone cavern. The dog ran inside the cave, barking excitedly. Being a trained bear dog, surely the dog had tracked a bear to its den.

Discouraged, Good Shield sat on his horse for a moment, then whistled for Winged Foot.

When the dog didn't respond, Good Shield slid out of his saddle, secured his horse, then yanked his knife from its sheath and headed toward the cavern entrance. He had to make sure nothing happened to the dog since he was so loved by Standing Wolf. If Winged Foot got into a fight with a bear, it was up to Good Shield to intervene. This was not the time to be hunting bears, not when Good Shield's best friend's life might lie in the balance.

Suddenly Good Shield stopped.

His breath caught in his throat when he heard a voice.

And now that he was listening more carefully, he recognized the voice.

It was Standing Wolf's!

"Winged Foot did find him!" Good Shield said, smiling broadly as he slid his knife into its sheath.

He stepped just inside the entrance of the cavern, peered through the darkness, and saw a campfire farther inside the cave. Beside it, resting on his haunches, hugging his bear dog, was Standing Wolf.

But it puzzled Good Shield that Standing Wolf was hugging and talking to his dog, yet was looking to one side as he talked, as though someone were there with him.

Good Shield stared in the direction Standing Wolf was looking, but he was too far away to make out what he was saying.

And Good Shield most certainly saw no one else in the cave. He was puzzled by the fact that his friend seemed to be speaking to an empty space!

Then Standing Wolf turned his head and caught sight of Good Shield walking toward him.

From this vantage point Good Shield now saw a great lump on his friend's head. It was apparent that someone had hit him over the head. Could the blow have been so powerful, it had damaged his friend's mind?

"Good Shield, it is so good to see you," Standing Wolf said, clasping Good Shield's shoulder as his friend knelt down beside him. He smiled at his dog, then smiled again at Good Shield. "My bear dog led you to me, did he not?"

"*Ho,* you trained him well, Standing Wolf," Good Shield said, smiling weakly as he looked around and saw no one with whom Standing Wolf could have been talking.

He then focused on Standing Wolf's injury. He gingerly touched it. "How did this happen?" he asked thickly. "Who did this?"

Standing Wolf heard what Good Shield was asking him, but he could not help thinking about something else . . . some*one,* because he was even more in awe of the Spirit Person now than before. It was obvious that neither his dog nor his friend realized she was there.

Not wanting Good Shield to question him out loud about why he had been talking to someone that no one but he could see, and knowing that Good Shield had heard him talking to Shaylee before he made his presence known in the cave, Standing Wolf quickly answered.

"I am alright," he said, as Good Shield lowered his hand away from his head. "I was ambushed. I did not see who did it. Whoever attacked me did it from behind."

It was now that Shaylee was sure that no one

on earth was meant to see her except Standing Wolf.

She moved around in front of Good Shield and studied his face to see if *he* might be the one who'd taken her child from his cradle.

She was so glad to discover that he was not the one, for he appeared to be a dear friend of Standing Wolf's. She would not have enjoyed telling Standing Wolf that his friend was a murdering madman.

But now that his friend was there, he would surely help Standing Wolf get back to his village. She would follow them. And once she was there, she prayed that she would find the guilty party and then her child. It shouldn't be long now. Then surely her patience and her compassion would be rewarded!

"My guess is that it was Short Arrow who did this," Good Shield said. "I have sad news, my friend. Your knife was used to kill Chief Bear Sitting Down. It is obvious to me, and I am sure to you, that the knife was used so that you would appear responsible for the crime."

Although Standing Wolf had never had a fondness for Chief Bear Sitting Down, having differed often about how things should be done to help better the lives of their Blue Clan of Cherokee, he was saddened over the chief's death.

Standing Wolf reached up and gingerly touched his head wound, now understanding why he had not been killed outright, but left badly enough wounded so that he would be disabled while his assailant went into the village and murdered Chief Bear Sitting Down with Standing Wolf's knife.

And now that Standing Wolf was accused of the deed, and he was absent from the village, it might look as though he had gone into hiding.

Ho, it had been planned well, so well that even those people who had always seen Standing Wolf as next in line to be chief might doubt his innocence.

"It does not bode well for me any way you look at it," Standing Wolf said, his voice drawn. "Surely I do appear guilty."

"And with someone like Gentle Heart urging everyone to believe you are the murderer, saying you did it because of your dislike for the chief, and . . . and . . ." Good Shield hesitated to say something that would anger Standing Wolf even more.

"And?" Standing Wolf said, arching an eyebrow. "What else has the sorceress done that you hesitate to tell me?"

"She stood before everyone and told them that you were pursuing her, that your motive for killing the chief was also because you want *her,*" Good Shield said guardedly. "She said everything so cleverly that even now warriors are searching for you as Gentle Heart commanded them to do."

Seething, Standing Wolf found the strength to rise to his feet. He gazed at Good Shield, who rose slowly and stood before him. "The woman I detest with all my heart is trying to make people believe I want her as my wife?" he said, his teeth clenched. "That is a lie I hope to force down her throat."

"You see, do you not, how I concluded that Gentle Heart had a direct role in the chief's death and in your assault?" Good Shield said, his anger no less than Standing Wolf's.

"*Ho,* I do see that what you say is true," Standing Wolf said, doubling his hands into tight knots at his sides.

"Then we must work together to find a way to prove her guilt and in the same breath remove yours," Good Shield said, placing a firm hand on his friend's shoulder.

"But how?" Standing Wolf said, easing away from Good Shield's hand, bending to his haunches again before the fire.

He glanced sideways at Shaylee, who stood so quiet and beautiful beside him. He hungered to bring her into his arms. In her embrace he would find comfort. In her eyes he saw so much . . . such compassion . . . such love.

In this time of trouble, at least he had her there with him. Even though he could not actually hold or touch her, her presence did give him comfort. Her sweet smile made his heart feel less burdened.

Good Shield knelt down beside Standing Wolf. "Right now there is no way to prove your innocence," he said. "But I *will* uncover the truth somehow so that it can be revealed to everyone who doubts you."

Standing Wolf gazed at Good Shield and nodded. "But in the meantime, what am I to do?" he asked. "If I return home and declare my innocence, it will only be my word against Gentle Heart's."

"But there is your head wound," Shaylee said, causing Standing Wolf to look her way.

She looked guardedly at Good Shield, glad that he was staring into the flames of the fire. She took advantage of Good Shield's inattention to speak her mind. "Standing Wolf, will your people not see your head wound and know that someone surely did this to disable you so that you would be out of the way while your chief was killed? Wouldn't they know that this was also done so that your knife would make you appear guilty of the crime?"

"Standing Wolf?"

When Good Shield spoke his name, Standing Wolf looked quickly away from Shaylee and gazed at his friend. "Good Shield, there *is* my head wound for everyone to see," he pointed out, wincing when he reached up and touched the lump on his head. "Surely everyone will realize that someone attacked me in order to take my knife to use for the murder. The wound on my head proves it."

"Gentle Heart will only say that you made up the story to draw guilt away from yourself," Good Shield said, puzzled anew over his

93

friend's strange attentiveness to something in the cave that Good Shield could not see.

"If so, Good Shield, that would mean that I caused my own injury," Standing Wolf said, nervous at seeing that Good Shield had caught him paying attention to Shaylee.

"*Ho,* there are those who might accuse you of that, for it is true that anyone can acquire a head wound if it means avoiding guilt in a murder," Good Shield said, patting the bear dog as he came and settled down beside him. "As I see it, Standing Wolf, you have no choice but to seek refuge at Wind Spirit's lodge. Everyone knows that our head priest's lodge is a sanctuary for all who are accused of crimes until proven guilty or innocent."

"Yes, and I must always remember the sorceress White Wing," Standing Wolf said solemnly. "Being Gentle Heart's aunt, the sorceress White Wing will join Gentle Heart's attempt to prove my guilt. She might even use her sorcery on me . . . worse yet, on all of our people."

"We must find a way to discredit the sorceress as well as Gentle Heart," Good Shield said.

"Yes, the only reason White Wing has been allowed to stay in the village is because of Gentle Heart," Standing Wolf said bitterly. "If Gentle Heart is found guilty of plotting against her own husband as well as the man who is next in line to be the Blue Clan Cherokee's chief, White Wing can be banished along with Gentle Heart because everyone will know that she had to have had a role in the evil scheme."

When Winged Foot rose away from Good Shield and began snarling as he crept on all fours toward Shaylee, she became wary, for she could tell that Standing Wolf didn't want to tell his friend about her.

Good Shield saw the dog's strange behavior and again was puzzled over how both the dog and Standing Wolf seemed aware of a presence that Good Shield himself could not see.

He glanced quickly over at Standing Wolf and was not surprised now to see that he was tense over the dog's behavior.

Shaylee slowly backed away as the dog crept closer to her. But surely the dog wasn't aware of her presence, she argued to herself. Up until now only Standing Wolf was aware of her, and only because she had been sent there to look after him.

When Winged Foot turned suddenly and stretched out beside Standing Wolf, all seemed well again, except for Good Shield . . . who seemed to be looking straight at Shaylee.

Shaylee and Standing Wolf exchanged fearful glances and held their breath. . . .

Chapter Ten

I've known love to be
Fire and ice . . .
Lilacs and roses . . .
Passionate and fragile.
I've know love to be
Starlight and rain,
Beautiful and impulsive.

Both Standing Wolf and Shaylee exhaled a deep breath of relief when Good Shield turned his eyes back to Standing Wolf and away from Shaylee. It was apparent that he saw nothing, and was still only bemused by his best friend's strange behavior.

In Good Shield's heart he feared for his friend. He was truly worried about the blow to Standing Wolf's head and that it might have affected him in ways that would hinder his ability to be chief.

Good Shield placed a gentle hand on Standing Wolf's shoulder. "My friend, what are you going to do?" he asked, his voice drawn.

"What do you want me to do *for* you?"

"Go and have a private council with our Head Priest," Standing Wolf said softly, touched by Good Shield's devotion and true loyalty as a friend.

"I will do that," Good Shield said, nodding. He dropped his hand to his side. "I will explain everything to him. I will tell Wind Spirit that you wish to come to him, but only for refuge."

"Tell Wind Spirit that I wish to seek refuge for only a short time, for I am ready to stand trial before all our people," Standing Wolf said. "But first arrange this with Wind Spirit. I must know that he stands firmly behind me. Then and only then will I come out of hiding and do what must be done to clear myself of this terrible crime against our fallen chief."

He turned a sideways glance to Shaylee, seeing an honest caring and concern in her eyes. He was more and more disturbed that she was not of this earth, but only someone who came to him in his time of trouble.

Surely when all was well in his life again, she would be gone and he would never see her again.

But in his heart and soul she would always be with him.

Always and *i-gs-hi-di*. Forevermore.

"Wind Spirit has always loved you as though you were his son," Good Shield said, then flung his arms around Standing Wolf and fiercely hugged him. "And I love you as though we are *a-na-da-ni-tli,* brothers."

Standing Wolf returned Good Shield's hug for a moment, then stepped away from him. "Go now," he said, his voice breaking with emotion. "I will await your return with an anxious heart."

Good Shield nodded, then ran from the cave, but he returned shortly with two blankets in his arms, and his rifle clasped in his right hand.

"These saddle blankets are for your comfort and warmth," he said. "My rifle is for your protection. The one who attacked you might return to finish what he started."

"*A-a-do,* thank you, my *a-na-da-ni-tli,*" Standing Wolf said as Good Shield spread one blanket before the fire and rolled the other one up for use as a pillow. He lay the rifle close beside the blanket.

"I will go now," he said, turning toward Standing Wolf. Then he left again, and this time Standing Wolf heard the horse and knew that Good Shield was on his way to seek knowledge and counseling at their Head Priest's lodge.

Shaylee moved up next to Standing Wolf and sat down beside him as he settled himself on the blanket before the fire. "We are alone again," she murmured, watching Winged Foot snuggle up next to Standing Wolf. "I was so touched by you and your friend's closeness. Rarely have I seen such devotion in friends."

"*Ho,* it is good to know that I have someone

like Good Shield there for me," Standing Wolf said, smiling at Shaylee.

As Winged Foot tried to get even closer to him to seek affection, Standing Wolf smiled and gazed down at the dog, stroking his thick fur.

"Also it is good to know that I can depend on my dog friend," he said. "It is because of Winged Foot that Good Shield found me."

"At first I found myself afraid of your dog, even though I should have known that he could not sense my presence," Shaylee said. "I wish your dog could see me and that I could pet him. I have always loved animals, especially dogs."

"My dog is a special kind of breed," Standing Wolf said, glad they had something to talk about that helped ease the strain that was suddenly there between them.

"Why is that?" Shaylee asked, drawing the skirt of her dress up around her legs as she pulled her knees up before her.

"He is a bear dog," Standing Wolf said. "He is trained to hunt out bears. I named him Winged Foot because he is swift of foot. Some people fear such dogs as this, for many bear dogs are ferocious. Mine is as gentle as a lamb unless cornered or threatened."

Standing Wolf then reached a hand out toward Shaylee. "I wish I could touch *you*," he said softly.

When she reached her hand out for him, and

it again seemed as though they were both reaching into a cloud of air, Shaylee and Standing Wolf quickly drew their hands back.

More and more, Shaylee was in awe of her feelings for this Indian and felt sad that she had met him under such circumstances.

But perhaps if she had met him in other circumstances, their feelings would not have been the same. Everything now was so unreal . . . so strangely beautiful, surely that was what was causing their attraction to one another.

Had they met at a trading post, or along a path in the forest, would they have seen one another as special?

Or would they have given each other a quick glance and then gone on their way?

"If you were a living, breathing being that I could hold and kiss, I would finally be able to love again," Standing Wolf suddenly blurted out, his heart pounding. Oh, how he wanted her.

"What do you mean by saying 'again'?" Shaylee asked.

"I had a wife," Standing Wolf said, leaning over to slide a log into the fire.

"You were married?" Shaylee asked, eyes wide. "But you aren't now? You said you *had* a wife. Where is she now? What happened?"

"Her name was Sunshine," Standing Wolf said as he watched the flames eating at the log. "We married young. I was eighteen winters of age. She was sixteen. She became with child right away. She did not live past her first two months of pregnancy. Since then I have been in mourning for her."

"But you surely are now in your late twenties," Shaylee said, admiring a man who could love so much that he would mourn his wife for many years.

"*Ho,* my years on this earth now number twenty-eight," Standing Wolf said, gazing at Shaylee. "And I, for the first time since my wife's death, feel that I am free of mourning for her. You are the cause. Only you."

"But I am here for only a short time," Shaylee said, her voice breaking. Her heart ached to know just how much he did care for her.

It would be oh, so hard to say goodbye, but she had known from the moment she'd first seen him that they would have to.

She would cherish the remaining moments with him and not even think of the inevitable.

"The time spent with you will be with me forever," Standing Wolf said.

Again he reached a hand out for her, dying inside when he could not touch her. When she was gone from him it would be as though he was thrown into mourning again, but this time not for his Sunshine.

It would be for Shaylee.

Because of this short time with her, he doubted now that he would ever take a wife, or father children.

His would be a lonely existence. . . .

Touched by his words and the knowledge that he loved her even though he knew it was a hopeless love, Shaylee was at a loss for words. Deep down inside were her own remembrances of a love so special to her. She wanted to share her feelings for her late husband with Standing Wolf, but decided that it was best not to. That was a part of her past that had nothing to do with now and why she was here.

And why blemish his feelings for her by telling him that she, too, had a special love, one which she would never be able to let go of completely?

No, sometimes they were best not said, those words that might do more harm than good.

She chose not to mention her son, either. She was still too uncertain of Standing Wolf's people's role in her son's abduction. She hoped that none of them were responsible.

And the more she thought about it, if she *could* return to earth again and resume life as someone besides an angel, perhaps she would be free to come to Standing Wolf and openly declare her love for him. For she did love him in the way a woman loves a man.

It was the first time she had felt anything for a man since her husband's death.

Afraid she was wishing for too much, Shaylee turned her eyes from Standing Wolf, yet she could still feel his gaze on her, continuing to awaken feelings inside her that she knew were not ordinary for angels!

She wondered if he could see her blushing.

She wondered if angels *could* blush!

Chapter Eleven

We must walk so many paths,
Down the halls of each new day;
To mature and renew our faith,
That indifference will soon decay.

Except for a full moon, the sky was black with
night. Sitting on a blanket beside a soft fire in
the stone fireplace of Wind Spirit's lodge,
Good Shield awaited the Head Priest's response to his tale.

"And so you believe it was Short Arrow who
ambushed Standing Wolf?" Wind Spirit asked
in his cracked voice. He drew his belted skin
robe more closely around his legs as he sat next
to Good Shield on the blanket. His snow white
beard was braided, with one braid hanging
from each side of his mouth, and one from his
chin. His hair was white, coarse, and hung
straight and long down his back.

"*Ho.* As you know, Short Arrow is my friend's
worst enemy," Good Shield said. "I am surprised that he has not tried to seek his ven-

geance against my friend before now."

"A man like Short Arrow has a mind that works in mysterious, devious ways," Wind Spirit said. "But for now let us put Short Arrow from our minds and concentrate on proving Standing Wolf's innocence."

"That should not be so hard to do," Good Shield said. "Because his father was the Blue Clan Cherokee's chief many moons ago, and revered by all who knew him, everyone has always assumed that Standing Wolf would one day be our chief. He was too young when his father died, so someone else had to be assigned the duties of chief. Now it is Standing Wolf's time. We cannot allow anyone to stand in the way of what he deserves."

"Ho, like his father, Standing Wolf is also revered by his people and now at the age of twenty-eight winters, it *is* time for him to be named chief," Wind Spirit said determinedly. "He has not waited patiently for that which was meant to be, to instead be declared a murderer."

"So you believe that it is safe for Standing Wolf to return home to stand trial before his people, to be judged?" Good Shield asked.

"*Ho,* bring Standing Wolf to my home for refuge and he will stand before his people soon after," Wind Spirit said, nodding. "All that is required for his innocence to be declared is for him to go through the proper procedures of a trial. That will stop Gentle Heart's attempts to further discredit Standing Wolf."

"There *is* a connection between Gentle Heart and the way that Standing Wolf has been placed in such a questionable, awkward position, do you not think so, Wind Spirit?" Good Shield asked as he rose from the blanket.

"It would seem so, but only time will give us those answers," Wind Spirit said somberly. He nodded toward Good Shield. "Go. Carry my encouraging words to Standing Wolf. Tell him that he must get all of this behind him quickly so that he can attend Chief Bear Sitting Down's burial rites and then meet in council to be named chief, for he *will* be chief."

"I will go for Standing Wolf and then I plan to do everything within my power to prove my suspicions about Gentle Heart, *and* Short Arrow's role in my friend's predicament," Good Shield said, his teeth clenched.

"Good Shield, I urge you not to hold such hate inside your heart for either Gentle Heart or Short Arrow, until it is absolutely proven that they are guilty of such crimes," Wind Spirit said as he rose slowly to his feet.

Then he embraced Good Shield. "Ride with care in the dark tonight," he warned. "Those who are responsible for our chief's death and Standing Wolf's ambush are still out there somewhere lurking in the shadows."

"I always ride with my eyes and ears open to all sounds around me. Tonight I will travel by canoe so that Standing Wolf's journey home will be easier. He is too ill to ride on a horse," Good Shield said, returning the hug, and then stepping away from Wind Spirit. "Thank you for such late counsel."

"My door is always open to you, my son," Wind Spirit said, then sank back down on his pallet as Good Shield rushed from the lodge, went to the river, and shoved his canoe out into the water.

With determination fueled by his deep desire to help Standing Wolf, he leapt inside the canoe and began paddling hard in the direction of the cavern.

Sorceress White Wing stepped away from the window of Wind Spirit's lodge. She had been lurking there during the whole counsel with Good Shield. She had heard everything. She now knew that Gentle Heart's innocence was being questioned.

Hobbling as quickly as her old legs would carry her, White Wing hurried toward Gentle Heart's lodge, to warn her. . . .

Chapter Twelve

Omens and dreams,
Taunting hush . . .
Mystical things,
Deep within us.

White Wing arrived at Gentle Heart's cabin and did not stop to knock on the door. Breathing hard, she went inside to Gentle Heart's bed and placed a bony hand on her shoulder and shook her.

Gentle Heart awakened with a start. By the dim light of the moon that crept through the window, she saw who stood over her in her bedroom. She also saw concern on the old woman's face.

"What has happened?" Gentle Heart asked, quickly sitting up, the blankets falling away from her. "Why have you come and awakened me in the night like this?"

"Your plan is going awry," White Wing said, then hurriedly explained what she had heard outside Wind Spirit's window. "I was not there during their full counsel, only the last few moments. And I had to strain to hear what was being said, but there was no doubt that your name was mentioned more than once. Good Shield brought your name into the conversation. He is determined to prove that you had a role in your husband's death."

Gentle Heart hurried from the bed. She pulled on a loose and flowing buckskin dress, then sat on the edge of her bed and slid into knee-high moccasins. "I must go to Short Arrow and tell him that things are not going as planned," she said.

She smiled to herself, for deep down inside she knew that the plan was, in a sense, working. If Short Arrow were accused and found guilty of the crime, that would please her as much as if it were Standing Wolf.

She would deny any connection with Short Arrow, and more people would believe her than him, for everyone loathed the vile, scar-faced creature.

She perhaps loathed him most of all, and for good reason. He —

"Gentle Heart, should you leave the village?" White Wing asked, interrupting her train of thought. "What if you are followed?"

"I will be sure that I am not," Gentle Heart said, smoothing down her cropped-off black hair with her fingers. She rose from the bed. "Auntie, please do not fret so much about things. In the end, it will all work out in my favor." She brushed a kiss across her aunt's wrinkled brow, then smiled at her. "Does not it always work out for me so that I get what I want?"

Gentle Heart shrugged as she grabbed a fringed shawl and tied it around her shoulders. "And never forget the power that I have over my people since I am their Beloved Woman," she said, her eyes gleaming.

"You *were* their Beloved Woman, but now that the man who named you so is gone, surely you will be stripped of the title," White Wing said. "Especially if even one person believes that you are even remotely responsible for their chief's death."

"Then I must be sure that does not happen," Gentle Heart murmured. "I must leave now. I must go to Short Arrow and discuss all of this with him. I must be certain he did not leave clues of his guilt which could then prove mine."

"Ha, and what does *he* have to lose if it is proven that it was he who killed the chief and not Standing Wolf?" White Wing said sarcastically. "It is you who will lose, my sweet niece. Only you. Short Arrow has successfully eluded those who have hunted him for one crime or another. So will he elude anyone who comes looking for him for the murder of your husband. Listen well, Gentle Heart. As I look into the future, in my wisdom as one who can cast spells, I see Standing Wolf standing tall over the council, the victor."

"You are surely wrong in what you see," Gentle Heart said, a shiver rushing up and down her spine at the thought that what her aunt was saying might possibly be true. "I have worked too hard for this moment, when I am finally free of the old man. Without him in my life I will be free to live it as I wish."

"And that is with Short Arrow, who is always on the run from those he has wronged?" White Wing said, again laughing sarcastically.

Gentle Heart went silent. She knew not to elaborate on her true plan, not even with her aunt. Telling no one was safer. Even her aunt could not know the truth, for she was old and might be too easily coerced into telling things to the Cherokee people that normally she would not . . . things that could destroy Gentle Heart! It was best to tell no one.

When Gentle Heart still did not respond to what White Wing had said about Short Arrow, White Wing placed a gentle hand on her niece's cheek. "I cannot help worrying about you," she said, her voice breaking. "Standing Wolf has much power in his words. As he stands trial for your husband's death, his words will reach inside everyone's hearts. They will believe him. Then Short Arrow will be hunted down and killed and Standing Wolf will be named chief. I fear that everyone will sympathize with Standing Wolf because of the wrong done him. That alone will be reason enough for them to appoint Standing Wolf chief . . . and to banish *you* from the village, shamed." She swallowed hard. "And what if Short Arrow points an accusing finger your way before he dies? What then, my niece? What then?"

Gentle Heart yanked herself away from White Wing. Her eyes narrowed angrily. "No one will banish Gentle Heart!" she said. "When I leave, it will be when *I* want to leave." She smiled wickedly. "And, Auntie, that will be soon."

"Not soon enough," White Wing said somberly. "You should have told me what you planned so I could have guided you in how it should have been done," White Wing said. She grabbed Gentle Heart in her arms. "Niece, I shall try to use my powers to make things right for you, but sometimes my power is not as strong as that of those who have people who believe in them. Standing Wolf has many allies."

"But not you, *or* I," Gentle Heart said, easing out of her aunt's arms. She placed a gentle hand on her aunt's lined face. "Cast spells, Auntie. Cast spells that will help your niece achieve her goal."

White Wing slowly nodded. "I shall begin tonight," she murmured.

Gentle Heart smiled smugly, then ran from the lodge. She went to the rope corral behind her cabin and hurriedly placed the bridle on her white mustang.

Not taking the time to saddle her horse, she

mounted it, looked stealthily in all directions to see that no one was watching, then rode off into the dark shadows of the night.

When she reached Short Arrow's hideout, and was recognized by the sentries that guarded the cabin, she rode on up to the dwelling and slid from the saddle, not even stopping to secure her horse's reins. She hurried inside and felt her way through the darkness until she came to the bunk that she knew was Short Arrow's.

Ignoring the snores from the others who slept in the cabin, Gentle Heart fell to her knees beside Short Arrow's bunk and fiercely shook him awake.

Short Arrow leaned up on an elbow and gazed in wonder at Gentle Heart, whose face was visible in the moonlight creeping through the windows of the cabin. "What brings you here this time of night?" he asked.

"We must talk," she whispered. She shoved a blanket into his arms. "Come. Let us go outside so that we can speak in private."

Short Arrow hesitated, then swung the blanket around his bare shoulders. He left the cabin with Gentle Heart and stood in the shadows of the porch. "Now tell me why you are here," he said, unable to hide the annoyance in his voice.

For a moment Gentle Heart was taken aback by the way Short Arrow was treating her. She had come like this many times and always before they had gone into the forest and done more than talk.

Although she hated the very ground Short Arrow walked on, at least he satisfied her sexual urges. It was hard for her to go long without a man . . . she needed what a virile man could do for her, what her old, impotent husband could never give her.

She pushed her surprise at Short Arrow's attitude behind her and hurriedly explained why she was there.

"Why, oh, why did you not just kill Standing Wolf instead of only hitting him with your war club?" she demanded.

"You forget so easily? It was our plan to make Standing Wolf look guilty of killing the old chief," Short Arrow grumbled. "If he, too, had died, it would have proven that he could not have stabbed his knife into the old chief's heart."

He laughed sarcastically. "And death would actually be too easy for Standing Wolf," he said. "Does not Standing Wolf stand to suffer more if he is accused of the crime of killing his own chief? He will either be banished or put to death."

"I should have thought more about the plan, then I would have realized that too many people love Standing Wolf to accuse him of anything," Gentle Heart said, sighing heavily. "Wind Spirit. Oh, how I hate that Wind Spirit! He is going to ruin everything for me. He is going to make certain that Standing Wolf is proved innocent."

"I can go and kill Wind Spirit," Short Arrow said, his eyes gleaming.

"No, do not kill anyone else," Gentle Heart snapped back. "There is enough for me to worry about already. I do not want to worry about someone like Wind Spirit coming to haunt me for the rest of my life."

"Your old chieftain husband won't?" Short Arrow taunted, then he took a quick step away when Gentle Heart glared at him.

"I am so weary already of playing the grieving widow," she said. "It was bad enough to play the role of a wife to a man I never loved, but now? To try to show grieving that I do not feel? That alone could cause people to see my role in my husband's death."

She pointed to her hair. "How I hated to cut my hair," she cried. She held out her arms for him to see. "How I hated scarring my arms with a knife."

"All of that is required to make it appear as though you are grieving," Short Arrow said. "And remember this, Gentle Heart, no matter how Standing Wolf's trial goes, you will have achieved your goal of ridding yourself of the old chief, and, at least for a while, making Standing Wolf's life miserable. As he awaits his trial, he must be filled with at least some doubt over what its outcome will be." He paused and forced a smile as he gazed into her eyes. "And you will have everything. Your freedom to marry *me*."

He smiled to himself, glad that this scheming with Gentle Heart was almost over, for he knew that all he had promised her about marriage was a lie. For a woman who was so clever about so many things, she had not seen through his plan.

To him she had just been someone to further his plan to get revenge against his Cherokee clan. Her being married to the old chief had given him an opportunity to strike two blows at once . . . against both Chief Bear Sitting Down and Standing Wolf.

He had never counted on her getting pregnant! He wanted no wife or child to get in the way of a life of violence that excited him more than any woman ever could.

Soon she would know just how much he loathed even the sight of her, especially now . . . now that her body was changing as the child grew inside her womb. In fact, he never planned to meet with her in the forest again. Their trysts had never stirred anything within him; they had only satisfied his sexual needs so that he had not been forced to find female companionship elsewhere.

"Short Arrow, if Standing Wolf can prove that I had a role in this, I will face banishment, perhaps even worse," Gentle Heart said, a sudden true fear in her heart. She gazed intently into his eyes. "You would never tell, would you? Even if forced, you would not tell my role in this?"

"How can you believe that I would betray you like that?" Short Arrow said, keeping his voice steady and low. "And anyhow, who would believe me? I am nothing but a banished warrior. You? You are their Beloved Woman. If they ever do feel that you are, in part, responsible for what happened, they would never do more than banish you, and what does it matter if you are exiled? Would it not be worth it to escape the life you have hated for so long?"

"No matter what, I would not want to suffer banishment," Gentle Heart said, visibly shuddering.

"All will be well," Short Arrow said. "For now, you must return to the village and be strong in the face of whatever accusations come your way."

"*Ho,* and anyhow, no one can prove my role in my husband's death," she murmured. "I will stay at the village until it is time to seek my new life with you." She smiled at how easily that lie slipped across her lips. "I did not see your sister, Moon Beam, in the cabin. Will she be here when I return? I will be glad of the company of another woman."

Short Arrow's spine stiffened. "No. I have brought her a son, and she has gone to the Chippewa village to raise him. But you are a strong woman and you will not miss her," he said, then slid his eyes downward. "You do not

117

have much time left, though, to leave the village before everyone will be able to see your guilt. The proof of your infidelity to your old husband lies right there in the swell of your stomach. Only your loose dresses have hidden it up to now. But what of tomorrow and the day after that? Soon even a dress will not hide your pregnancy."

She smiled wickedly. "I will be long gone before my stomach swells to that size," she said, knowing she wouldn't be going with Short Arrow. She despised his very touch, especially his wet kisses.

But he had served her well. He had killed the old chief and was making Standing Wolf look guilty of the crime, at least for a while.

As far as she was concerned, this was her final goodbye to Short Arrow. She didn't need him any longer. She would return home to her Chippewa people now. As the chief's daughter, no one would dare question her about her pregnancy.

Soon she would have this black phase of her life behind her.

And then she would have to figure out what to do with the child, for she could not see herself in the role of mother for very long!

Chapter Thirteen

I endeavor to sort things out,
Troubled by what I can't understand,
Disbelief, distrust, undecided doubt.

Even though Shaylee could not experience the feeling of being cold or warm, she knew that with darkness came a damp chill. She knew that it must be uncomfortably cool in the cavern. As Standing Wolf ate more of the roasted turkey, also feeding his dog some of the meat, Shaylee added wood to the fire.

She then sat down on the blanket and gazed at Standing Wolf as he continued to eat. The fire's glow was so soft on his magnificent, noble features. And she loved the color of his skin. It was different from the skin of the Chippewa people that she had seen in the local trading posts. Theirs was more reddish copper in tone. Standing Wolf's face had a cinnamon brown tone.

His high cheekbones, his perfectly shaped lips, and the jet black pupils of his brown eyes made him uniquely handsome, as did his broad-muscled frame and his long and flowing black hair.

When he stood, he was tall, athletic looking, and sinewy. While he was with his friend, Shaylee had silently observed that he seemed high-minded, frank, honest, and sincere.

The more Shaylee was with Standing Wolf, the more she believed that he was not a man who would kill easily, or have any role in a heartless murder, or child abduction.

She was beginning to wonder if the one who had ambushed and wounded Standing Wolf could be the same man who had taken so much from her.

It did seem possible, for the crimes had been committed so close together in time.

The crimes were even done in the same area — in the vicinity of the White River. The only difference was that the crimes had been committed on opposite sides of the river.

But she doubted that what she was thinking was true, for that would make it all too easy. That meant that the search would be over for both Shaylee and Standing Wolf at the same time.

"Good Shield should return soon," Standing Wolf said as he tossed a turkey bone into the fire. "He will have paved the way for my return to my village."

"You will feel safe enough to go there?" Shaylee asked.

"*Ho,* because Wind Spirit will be there to help prove my innocence," Standing Wolf said, nodding. He wiped his mouth free of grease with his sleeve. Then, comfortably full, he drew his legs up before him and hugged his knees.

"But how can you be sure that you will be proved innocent?" Shaylee asked, truly concerned about him. She could not envision a man such as he imprisoned, if that was what his people did to those who were guilty of a crime such as murder. She already knew that banishment was used for lesser crimes.

Surely, harsher measures were used to make a murderer pay for his crime.

"I will try to explain the procedure which lies before me upon my return home," Standing Wolf said. He folded his arms across his chest and gazed into the flames as he continued talking.

"When I return to my village I will seek momentary sanctuary at the Head Priest's lodge," he said. "Every Cherokee priest's dwelling is a place of refuge, a place where the innocently accused can be protected. A person is declared innocent until a court can be convened."

"Do you mean you actually have court sessions like the white man, with a judge and jury?" Shaylee asked, truly curious.

It meant a lot to her that Standing Wolf cared enough to explain things to her, for she wanted to know everything about him and his people. Talking about his customs made her feel even closer to Standing Wolf.

She only wished they could reach out and touch one another. She ached to be able to sense everything while with him . . . the smell of his flesh, the touch of his lips, and . . . the feel of his hands on her body.

But she knew that she must enjoy each moment to the fullest, for she did not know when it might be the last. She had no idea when she would be called back to the clouds.

Oh, Lord, she hoped it would not happen until she knew where Moses was and could see that he had been rescued from the murdering madmen!

"No, our court is nothing like the white man's," Standing Wolf said solemnly. "A priest, not a judge, presides over our court."

"The priest that Good Shield has gone to talk to?" Shaylee asked.

"He is the *Head* Priest. No, he will not be the one who decides my guilt or innocence," he said. "There is one other priest in our village. His name is White Buffalo. It is his duty to preside over all cases. He is in full charge of our courtroom."

"When someone is accused of a crime, what happens?" Shaylee asked.

"If the court decides that someone is guilty of an unforgivable breach of law, he is publicly condemned. When there was warring among the tribes, the guilty party was placed in the forefront of a battle line. But now, when there is no actual warring, the guilty one is placed in some other circumstance that will bring him a noble death, one that contributes to the community."

He cleared his throat, then said, "There have been times when a family knew of a member who was responsible for a crime and tried to hide him. When they were caught, the whole family was condemned for the crime. Relatives know they must bring all fugitives to justice to avoid similar punishment."

He shoved a log into the fire, then continued speaking as he gazed at Shaylee. "The brother of a murderer often disposes of him to save the family from becoming the victim of blood vengeance."

"It all sounds so complicated," Shaylee said. "Yet when one studies the courtroom antics of white people, it is no less confusing." She laughed softly. "Sometimes it is nothing but tomfoolery and nonsense how the lawyers go about winning their cases. As for injustice . . . it often prevails if the one accused has no money for a lawyer. But money buys freedom too often when a guilty man should actually be sentenced."

"There are times when death is necessary to rid the Cherokee community of criminals who have seriously harmed our people by their actions," Standing Wolf said. "In the olden days, those criminals were stoned to death, or killed with a weapon. But the most favored treatment, even today, is taking the criminal to the top of a high cliff, where his elbows are tied behind him, and his feet are drawn up and tied. He is then cast headlong over the side and dies on the sharp rocks below."

Shaylee shuddered, then turned her head abruptly when she heard footsteps approaching from the direction of the cavern entrance.

She breathed more easily when Good Shield came into view.

Standing Wolf pushed himself up and steadied himself, then greeted Good Shield with a hug.

"You met with Wind Spirit?" Standing Wolf asked.

"*Ho,* and he encourages you to come to his lodge right away, for he says that you have nothing to fear," Good Shield said. "You are innocent. Your innocence will be easily proved."

Good Shield gazed at the lump on Standing Wolf's head. "Are you strong enough to travel?" he asked. "Are you in much pain? And are your thoughts clear enough for questioning during the court proceeding?"

"I am well enough to travel and to stand before my people to speak in my own behalf," Standing Wolf said. "I am ready to speak words that my people will know are the truth."

"I have brought my canoe to make your travel to the village more comfortable than traveling on a horse," Good Shield said, bending low before the fire as he began shoving dirt onto the flames to extinguish it. "We must leave at once. It is best to travel and arrive at our village under the cover of darkness."

Winged Foot leapt to his feet, his tail wagging as he looked from Good Shield to Standing Wolf.

Standing Wolf bent and hugged his bear dog as he gazed at Shaylee, who stood back in the shadows and became lost to sight when the last glowing embers of the fire were covered and extinguished.

For a moment he was seized by panic. Did his sweet Spirit Person feel she was no longer needed since Good Shield was there to help him?

Had he seen her for the last time only seconds ago?

Without her, life would never be the same, and he knew now how foolish it had been to allow himself to begin caring for someone who could never be an actual part of his life.

"Come," Good Shield said. He placed an arm around Standing Wolf's waist to help him from the cavern. He feared that Standing Wolf might be feigning more strength than he actually had.

Standing Wolf welcomed his friend's assistance, for the more he walked, the dizzier and more disoriented he became. While sitting down, and even standing for only moments at a time, he had not been aware that he was still handicapped by the blow to his head.

It concerned him, for if he was this unsteady and disoriented, how could he stand and make a good defense for himself?

Wanting to prove to himself that he was strong enough, Standing Wolf moved away from Good Shield and walked on his own out of the cavern, with Winged Foot close at his heels.

When Standing Wolf reached the river and saw Shaylee already sitting in the canoe where it lay beached on the riverbank, his heart soared. At least for now she was still a part of his life. He would cherish each moment until she did say a final goodbye.

He boarded the canoe and sat beside Shaylee as Good Shield lifted Winged Foot in.

Good Shield then shoved the canoe into the deeper water and leapt aboard, manning the paddles as he took the canoe out into the middle of the river.

His muscled arms moved rhythmically as the canoe moved silently and swiftly through the water in the moonlight.

Shaylee was feeling a keen anxiousness to see at last the Cherokee village, to know once and for all if anyone among Standing Wolf's people was responsible for the crimes against her and her son.

She glanced at Standing Wolf. She could see how tight his jaw was. She saw the anxiousness in his eyes and realized that he must be apprehensive about his own arrival at his village.

Standing Wolf gazed at her, making her want to scoot closer and cuddle next to him.

If only his arm could slide around her waist! If only . . .

She mustn't torment herself. She knew that what she now had with Standing Wolf would have to be enough.

She turned her eyes from him and saw that the canoe had moved into a fog; the moon's glow was like sparkling diamonds as it shimmered through the mist.

Being enveloped by such beauty, she could not help feeling as though she was part of some joyous fantasy.

The only thing lacking to complete the peace she felt at this moment was her beautiful son!

She gazed at Standing Wolf, thinking that his acquittal, and their ability to touch and to love, would truly complete the fantasy.

"I see the fires of our people through the fog," Good Shield said, breaking into Shaylee's thoughts and bringing her back to the present. She wondered what lay ahead for both herself and Standing Wolf at his village.

Chapter Fourteen

Oh, I've been here, again and again,
Questioning reasons and dimensions,
Hoping to comprehend or perceive
The meaning of this trying tension.

After the canoe was beached, Winged Foot ran off into the dark as Shaylee walked with Standing Wolf and Good Shield into the village. As far as Shaylee could tell, the windows of the cabins were all dark, so no one would be aware of Standing Wolf's arrival.

The moon was now hidden behind clouds, so Shaylee had only vague impressions of the village at this midnight hour. From what she could tell, most of the people lived in cabins, with only a few buckskin tepees scattered here and there at the fringe of the village.

The soft whinny of a horse made her aware of a corral somewhere behind the lodges.

But everything else was quiet except for an occasional yapping of a coyote somewhere in the distance and a loon singing its eerie tune across the river.

Finally they came to a cabin from which fire-light shone. Shaylee followed Standing Wolf and Good Shield into the lodge. Standing Wolf cast her a quick look over his shoulder.

Confident that he would be acquitted in the end, Shaylee gave him a reassuring smile, then stood back.

She watched quietly as the man who must be Wind Spirit looked up and nodded a silent welcome as Standing Wolf and Good Shield sat down on a thick pallet of furs before the fire.

Shaylee studied Wind Spirit and saw that he was quite different in appearance from Standing Wolf and Good Shield. His strangely braided white beard would make him stand out in a crowd, with one braid hanging from each side of his mouth and one from his chin.

He was dressed in a fine white doeskin robe, belted at the waist. His face, the same color as Standing Wolf's, was lined with age, and even his eyes looked aged, but were filled with much intelligence and compassion. She prayed that he had the power to help Standing Wolf in his time of trouble.

She listened to Wind Spirit as he spoke, placing a hand on Standing Wolf's shoulder.

"My *a-tsu-tsa*, it is good that your injury did not keep you from coming to my lodge for sanctuary." Wind Spirit gazed at a lump the size of a hen's egg that protruded through the thickness of Standing Wolf's black hair.

"It is good that you have offered your lodge and your time to this warrior who has been wronged by an unknown assailant," Standing Wolf said, always feeling humbled in the presence of this holy man. "*A-a-do*, thank you for your kindness . . . for your concern, especially now when I know that your heart is filled with sadness over the loss of our chief."

"It *is* a sad time for all," Wind Spirit said, easing his hand away from Standing Wolf, tucking it with his other hand beneath his robe. "But for you, it is the most trying. We must do something about that, and quickly."

"I will stand before our people and profess my innocence," Standing Wolf said. "It will be an easy task for this Cherokee warrior, for I will be speaking the truth."

"And I, as will all who truly know you, believe in your innocence," Wind Spirit said. "But please understand that this Head Priest, who was a close friend of your father's, must follow procedure during your trial or be accused of singling you out for special favors. During your trial, you will be asked the exact questions all accused are asked, and since you are innocent, your innocence *will* be proved."

"There is one among our people who both Good Shield and I believe is guilty of having helped plot the murder so that I would look guilty," Standing Wolf said, his jaw tight.

"Gentle Heart?" Wind Spirit said, his eyes narrowing angrily at the very thought of that

130

woman and the power her husband had given her over the Blue Clan of Cherokee. Wind Spirit, as well as many people of the village, had never approved, but they had accepted her into their lives as their Beloved Woman to please a chief they revered.

But now? Wind Spirit smiled cunningly at the knowledge that her time as "Beloved Woman" was now short-lived, for he would make it so!

"*Ho*, Gentle Heart," Standing Wolf said solemnly. "How can we prove her guilt, for she *is* involved, somehow, in all of this. Anyone who looked closely at this woman when she was with her elderly husband surely saw what both Good Shield and I saw . . . the silent loathing that she felt for him. She rued the day she had ever agreed to be his wife, yet she was, and there was only one way for her to be truly free of him forever . . . his death."

"He was too blinded by her beauty and youth to see her true self," Wind Spirit said. "And I could not bring myself to be the one to tell him how I felt about her. I always tried to please, not disappoint, my chief."

"You never thought she was capable of taking his life to rid herself of him," Good Shield said, sighing. "Nor did any of his people consider this."

"Perhaps we are wrong about her," Wind Spirit said, looking slowly from Good Shield to Standing Wolf. "Perhaps it was someone else who wanted our chief dead, who knocked you unconscious and stole your knife."

"Of course, we would all feel better if she was not a part of the plot against our chief, for it would ease our consciences for not warning him about her," Standing Wolf said solemnly.

"If she *is* guilty, that will have to be proven," Wind Spirit said. "She will have to do something that will make her guilt clear. Give it time. If she has plotted to have her husband killed, and to have *you,* Standing Wolf, accused of the crime, it will somehow be disclosed to all of the Blue Clan of Cherokee."

"What we must focus on now is Standing Wolf," Good Shield said, drawing all eyes to him. "After Standing Wolf is proven innocent, many warriors should go out again to search for the murderer, but this time the search will not be for Standing Wolf. The one responsible must be found to stand his own trial."

Shaylee glanced toward the entrance flap, and then toward Standing Wolf. She felt that now was the time for her to go from lodge to lodge to search for Moses. While Standing Wolf was still in council with the Head Priest and Good Shield, she could surely find the answers *she* sought in this village.

Moving quietly, unseen, Shaylee went from cabin to cabin and tepee to tepee until she had searched all of the beds and cradleboards of the lodges. She came away from them knowing that her son had not been brought to this village.

She was not sure how to feel.

She was relieved to know that Standing Wolf's people had had no role in her child's abduction, yet she was disappointed that she hadn't found him there.

She stood in the middle of the village, where she could see every lodge. The clouds had slid away from the moon, and its glow seemed mystical as it spread its white shroud over everything.

From what she could tell by the things she had seen in each lodge, these people lived decent lives, and if they were all like Standing Wolf, Good Shield, and Wind Spirit, they were good, caring people who would treat a white child kindly.

But Moses wasn't there.

She now had no idea where he might be!

She returned to Wind Spirit's lodge and found Bird Flying, the clan's healer, medicating Standing Wolf's wound. He must be a trusted friend, who would not spread the word that Standing Wolf was there until the right time had come for him to stand trial before his people.

She stood back in the shadows so even Standing Wolf was not aware of her presence in the tepee. She watched Bird Flying and Good Shield leave to go to their own lodges for the rest of the night.

She watched Wind Spirit leave the room, apparently to go to his bed. Standing Wolf stretched out on the pelts before the fireplace with Winged Foot beside the burning embers of the lodge fire.

Shaylee started to go to Standing Wolf to stretch out beside him, to watch him sleep, but she suddenly felt something pulling at her and knew that her time with Standing Wolf was nearly over. She believed that she would rise into the clouds so that God could address her again. She was anxious to see what he had to say to her. Her compassion had been proven, but the whereabouts of her son was still a mystery to her.

She wasn't sure what to expect next, but she believed that she had earned the right to live on earth again. Surely that was the only way she would ever be able to find her son.

And now there was another reason she wished to stay on earth. She hadn't counted on falling in love, but she had.

She knelt down over Standing Wolf. She reached out to try to touch his face before she rose into the clouds, but she was disappointed when she still couldn't.

Suddenly, as though he knew she was there, his eyes opened.

His hand reached out as he whispered her name.

Their eyes held.

"When will you be leaving me?" he asked softly, as though he felt that she was there for only a moment longer. "Is not your time with me over? You helped me. Is not that the reason you came to me from among your family of Spirit People?"

"Yes, in a way, what you think is true," she said, her voice breaking with emotion, for she already missed him and they had not yet said their goodbyes. "I wish I could tell you that I will never leave you, but I have no control over my destiny, *or* yours. It's up to God. *All* of it."

"God?" Standing Wolf said, his eyebrows lifting. "What do you mean? The Cherokee Spirit People are sent to us by the *A-da-ni-do,* the Great Spirit."

"I should have told you long ago that you are wrong about what, or who, I am," Shaylee said, her eyes devouring him, for she felt that God was giving her only a last few minutes with him and she would soon be gone, perhaps forever. "I am not a Spirit Person as you have believed all along. Instead, Standing Wolf, I am one of God's angels. He sent me to you, to help you."

And then she was gone.

Standing Wolf stared blankly at the spot where Shaylee had just been kneeling beside him. He was stunned to know that she could disappear so quickly.

He shoved the blankets aside, stepped around Winged Foot, then went outside and gazed into the sky. "Shaylee?" he whispered, reaching his hands heavenward. "Come back to me, Shaylee. How can I exist without you?"

Chapter Fifteen

Forbidding . . .
Struggles find,
Hidden deep, deeper,
In the mind.

In the mystical light of the moon, with the stars twinkling all around her, Shaylee was weightless and serene, seemingly another star, suspended in a moment of wonder and grace, as she waited to be spoken to.

As before, she found herself fighting to grasp on to remembrances of everything that was important to her, for it seemed that as soon as she was drawn into the heavens, her past seemed less important to her, leaving only the memory of her beloved Moses, the feeling that her arms were, oh, so empty without him.

Now there was someone else she fought to remember with all of her soul.

Standing Wolf.

She already missed Standing Wolf.

Those moments with him had been like an

awakening of her heart, which had lain dormant and sad since the passing of her husband.

She did not want to lose the memory of how it had felt to love again, or how she had hungered to feel Standing Wolf's touch . . . his arms around her . . . his lips on her mouth, kissing her.

"Shaylee?"

That voice, the same voice that she had heard when she had been drawn so magically into the heavens, leapt into Shaylee's heart and stilled her thoughts of things of the earth.

And the voice was still as kind and gentle as before, making her feel so at peace with herself, so joyous.

She listened attentively as it began addressing her.

"Shaylee, I have brought you in my presence again to tell you that while you were on earth as one of my special angels you passed the test of compassion," the voice said softly. "You looked past the color of the man's skin. You helped Standing Wolf in his time of trouble. You have earned the right to choose your future. Do you wish to stay where there is no sadness, no sorrow, no grief, and be with those who passed away before you? Or do you wish to resume life on earth among the living?"

"Could I first ask you a question?" Shaylee asked, wary of questioning the Almighty, for He was all things, the wisest of all.

"Yes, always feel free to ask your Lord anything that you wish to ask," He said, His voice seeming now to be all around Shaylee, as though it were everything . . . the stars, the moon, the beautiful sunshine of a wondrous spring day, the wind whispering through the trees, and the water splashing cool and clear in a shallow brook.

"Please tell me why I have not been shown my son," Shaylee said. "Moses is my everything."

But she quickly thought of someone else; a man. Now he, Standing Wolf, meant everything to her, also. She longed for a life in which both her son, Moses, and Standing Wolf would have a part.

In her mind's eye, she saw Moses lying in a cradle in Standing Wolf's lodge. She saw Standing Wolf sitting on pelts on the floor before his fireplace making beautiful carvings of forest animals on a new bow.

She saw herself sitting beside Standing Wolf, filled with wonder at being with him, as his wife. She could even smell their supper cooking over the open fire. . . .

Her thoughts were interrupted when God spoke to her again.

"Shaylee, your son Moses was not part of the test on earth," He said in a more serious tone. "Do you or do you not wish to enter the golden gate of Heaven, where you will always feel joyous and clear of fears or regrets? Or do you wish to return to earth, where you will experience all feelings of the living? You are young. You can have many years ahead of you as a vital person on earth."

Shaylee was confused that her son was not a part of her test on earth. The part of her that could still feel confusion and doubt made her want to speak more about Moses to God, yet she could tell that the subject was closed. She must make her decision.

It did not take much time for her to decide, for Moses was still to be found, and Standing Wolf was waiting for her.

Any worry that she would be entering a forbidden relationship with an Indian, or that white people would shun her for loving a man with lovely cinnamon-brown skin, was cast aside and of no importance to her.

She knew what she wanted!

She wanted Standing Wolf!

She wanted to find Moses!

Still, there was a part of her that was torn. A part of her wanted to join her loved ones. She could be with David and her parents again!

But she had a son who was still among the living. He deserved to be raised by his true mother!

And if she resumed life on earth, she would have a second chance at not only life, but love. She did love Standing Wolf. She knew that he loved her. All three of them — herself, Moses, and Standing Wolf — could have a second chance at happiness . . . together!

"Lord, will I ever be led to my son?" she blurted out, even though moments ago she was ready not to question Him about anything. She did not want to look as though she didn't trust His judgment.

But she had to know!

Moses, oh, dear, sweet Moses, where was he?

Who was holding him?

Who was feeding him?

Did he cry for her?

Did he . . . miss . . . her?

"In time you will be reunited with your son," God said softly. "Lovely sweet one, have faith. Never doubt that you and Moses will be together again, no matter how long it takes for you to find him. It *is* meant to happen. Just have faith that it will."

Shaylee wanted to question Him further about how long she would have to wait, but knew that she should be thankful for the blessings He had already bestowed upon her . . . that she was one of the chosen ones to have a second chance at life.

It was enough to know that, in time, she would be with her son again.

"Thank you so much for everything you have done for me," she murmured. "And, yes, I do wish to return to earth."

"You are worthy," God said. Then she felt herself being drawn downward out of the sky.

She saw so many things now that were familiar to her . . . the moon-splashed White

River. In the distance, along the river, she saw the Cherokee village. There she would be reunited with Standing Wolf. Her heart soared at the thought.

Chapter Sixteen

Blend our dreams, souls, and spirits,
As one, we'll soar the lofty skies.
Born of freedom, gliding across time.

At the break of dawn, Wind Spirit had left his lodge and blown his shell trumpet, which had awakened and called together all the people of his village.

Every Cherokee village had in its center a circular, fifty-foot-diameter council house that sat on top of a man-made earth mound.

There the old men and head warriors often met to discuss and plan civic and religious matters.

They gathered for social purposes and diversion and feasted and danced with the entire community.

This house was the hub of the village, and the seats within it were assigned according to rank.

As Standing Wolf stood in the center of the lodge, watching everyone filing slowly inside the council house, he avoided their stares and instead gazed at the large room. It was familiar to him not only as an adult, but also as a child, when his chieftain father had brought Standing Wolf into this place of honor with him, to join the council and to learn from it, since he would one day be chief.

The council house had not changed since Standing Wolf had been a lad of two sitting on his father's lap, in awe of everything and everyone in the large house. The side walls were covered with grass thatching and the grass was covered with clay, then more thatch.

The roof logs were covered with a layer of saplings and then successive tiers of bark shingles. A smoke vent had been left in its center where the logs crossed.

The entrance was on the east side of the house with a door and a portico that shielded it in bad weather.

Close to where Standing Wolf now stood, there was a firepit centrally placed, where their clan's sacred fire was always kept aflame.

Several concentric rows of seats along the wall provided places for the lesser officers and the women and children of the village to sit.

Closer to the sacred fire were seats and bedlike ottomans for the chief officers. At the front corners of those seats were five-foot high upright boards. Some of them had carved into them the representation of a full moon.

Others had eagles carved of poplar wood

with their wings stretched out.

On the face of each board were painted chalky white clay figures of mountain lions and a man wearing buffalo horns.

Standing Wolf found himself smiling when he recalled why the seats for the council were sloped toward the back; so that the elderly who came to council would not fall off the seats when they dozed.

His thoughts returned to the present when he saw that everyone that was to attend the hearing was there, including the elders and the priest who would preside over his case.

He glanced over at Wind Spirit and saw how at ease he seemed as he sat on his seat next to the priest who would serve as Standing Wolf's judge and jury today.

When Wind Spirit caught his glance he nodded slightly but did not smile, for he did not want to show partiality toward Standing Wolf. It was best that the priest who would judge Standing Wolf's guilt or innocence was not swayed one way or the other by how Wind Spirit felt about the wrongly charged man in the council house today.

Because of this, Standing Wolf did not return the nod.

Instead he looked quickly past Wind Spirit and found Good Shield sitting among the other warriors. Good Shield was free to smile, which he did. That smile alone made Standing Wolf feel better about things, for his best friend always had a way of doing this for him. They had always been there for one another.

But never had there been anything as serious as this to get through. Never had they faced such a challenge together, but because Good Shield showed such faith and devotion, Standing Wolf felt the burden becoming less inside his heart.

Suddenly a vision came to him that made him start. In his mind's eye he was seeing Shaylee! It was as though she were there with him, holding his hand, smiling at him.

He could almost hear her whisper to him that everything was going to be alright, that her God was there with him to make it so!

He shook his head to clear his thoughts, for a moment shaken. It had all seemed so real, as though it were truly happening.

Because it had seemed so real, he looked quickly through the crowd to see if Shaylee was there. He was disappointed when he saw that she wasn't.

He doubted that he would ever see her again. He wondered whom she would go to next, to offer love and special assistance?

Something drew his eyes to Gentle Heart as she sat only a few feet away among those of importance, glaring up at him.

His eyes narrowed as he stared back at her, and then he put her from his mind when there was a slight stir in the crowd. White Buffalo, the elderly priest who would decide his guilt or innocence, stood up and everyone's eyes went to him.

Standing Wolf turned and faced him. The elderly priest wore a long robe made of white buffalo skin. His coarse gray hair hung almost to the floor. He wore badges of distinction — bands of otter skins with the hair left on — on his head and on both arms above the elbows and both legs just below the knees.

"Standing Wolf, we are gathered here today to hear you speak in your own behalf," White Buffalo said in his deep, resonant voice. "The Great Spirit is here. He also listens. Tell us now. Are you guilty of the crime accused, or are you innocent?"

"I stand before you and my people, to whom I have always given my loyalty and love, and claim my innocence," Standing Wolf said, his voice firm.

"Standing Wolf, can you say without hesitation that you do not lie when you profess your innocence?" White Buffalo asked, observing Standing Wolf carefully as he awaited his response.

"I do not lie," Standing Wolf said, his jaw tight, his chin proudly lifted. "I would never lie as I stand before my people and you, who are judging my guilt or innocence."

"What you have said, is it true in the beloved name, of the great *A-da-ni-do?*" White Buffalo said, leaning his wrinkled old face closer to Standing Wolf's so that their gazes could meet and hold.

"What I have said is true in the beloved name of the Great Spirit," Standing Wolf responded.

"You are saying that you have told me the real truth while in the presence of the powerful Great Spirit, who proclaims his existence without beginning or end, and by his self-existent and literal name in which I adjure you?" White Buffalo continued.

"I have told you the naked truth. I most solemnly swear by this divine, great, adorable, self-existent name which I would never profane," Standing Wolf said, his dark eyes proud.

"Then it is my pleasure to cast aside all doubt of your innocence. Nevermore should blame be cast on you by those who have today brought such doubts before our people," White Buffalo said, shifting his eyes to where Gentle Heart sat in her place of honor amid the elders of the village.

Standing Wolf's gaze followed White Buffalo's.

When he saw the utter contempt in Gentle Heart's eyes, he knew that she was not yet finished with him. . . .

Chapter Seventeen

Winds' rhythm,
Flutters, dances.
Tears and touch,
Elm branches,
Back and forth,
Shallow rifts
Carry voices,
Morning mists.

Shaylee yawned and stretched her arms above her head as her eyes slowly opened.

She sat up quickly when she realized where she was, and then recalled those last moments in the heavens. God had given her His blessing, and then she had felt herself being drawn out of the clouds.

Shortly after she saw the moonlight rippling beautifully in the White River and the Cherokee village in the distance, she seemed to have blacked out.

Now she was just barely inside the entrance of the limestone cavern where she had first met

Standing Wolf. As she slowly rose to her feet, she gazed outside and saw the brightness of the day.

And as sunlight splashed into the cave, she could even feel its warmth as she reached out for it.

Her heart raced as she became aware of other things that for a while had been denied her.

She could smell the fresh mint that grew thick and wild just outside the cave entrance!

She could smell the scent of wet moss that grew up the inside walls of the cavern!

She bent to her knees and ran her fingers through the loose rock on the cavern floor. She emitted a soft cry of pain when one of the rocks scratched the palm of her hand. She then felt a wondrous exhilaration to know that the pain, above all else, proved that she was alive again.

"I can feel!" she cried. "Oh, Lord, I am alive! I can not only feel, I can smell. I have regained all of my senses!"

Her heart skipped a beat, and then she smiled, for she now knew that she would be able to touch Standing Wolf and actually be aware of the warmth of his flesh.

A thrill soared through her to know now that, should he desire to, Standing Wolf could touch Shaylee and feel her.

If he desired to kiss her, she would feel the wondrous warmth of his lips, as he would hers.

She would be able to smell his breath as it

149

caressed her cheeks!

She would be able to feel his fingers running through her long red hair!

They would be able . . . to . . . make love, should he want her that much; for herself, she knew she wanted him, with all her heart and soul.

She turned and walked slowly into the cavern and stopped where they had spent so much time beside the fire. She hugged herself and smiled when she suddenly felt Standing Wolf's presence all around her, as though he were there now with her.

She shivered sensually when she remembered how they had reached their hands out to one another, to no avail.

The next time she was with him, their hands could even clasp.

"Yes, Standing Wolf, I am alive!" she shouted, whirling around like a ballerina and laughing with the joy of knowing that God had been so good to her.

Then she stopped suddenly and her smile faded when another thought came to her.

Her son.

Where was Moses?

How could she go about finding him now that she would be seen and known by everyone?

She would not be able to search inside someone's home without their seeing her.

Now everything she did would have to be

150

done with the knowledge of everyone around her.

But perhaps she would have better luck now than before. She hadn't been able to find Moses before, when she was invisible to everyone except Standing Wolf.

Now, when she could question people, surely she would soon discover where her son had been taken.

She made herself recall God's words. She *would* find Moses.

But she recalled Him also telling her that she would have to be patient.

She *would* hold Moses in her arms again, no matter how long it took.

She *would* make all wrongs right for him.

But this was now, she thought to herself. She suddenly realized she was hungry. And although she seemed to have come out of a deep, long sleep, she was strangely tired.

But the one thing that she wanted even before food or sleep was to go to Standing Wolf.

Oh, how she worried about him. Surely he was standing before his people today as he was being judged.

She had to know.

If he had already stood before his people, had they listened when he said he was innocent?

Or had Gentle Heart, the one who wanted him accused, been more convincing?

"I must go to him now," she whispered. Then she stopped when another thought came to her.

When she *did* see Standing Wolf again, how would she explain why he could now touch her . . . even hold her?

To him she was not real, perhaps even a figment of his imagination caused by the injury inflicted on his head.

"I shall soon know," she whispered.

Yes, and Standing Wolf would know that she was alive.

Then she would explain in detail what angels were, and how blessed she had been to have been one.

Her spine stiffened and her breath caught in her throat when she heard a low growl behind her.

She turned quickly around and gasped when she found Standing Wolf's bear dog standing just inside the cave entrance.

He was looking right at her!

He was baring his sharp teeth at her!

He looked as though he was about to attack her!

Oh, Lord, now that she was a living, breathing person, Winged Foot could see her.

And without Standing Wolf there to convince his dog that Shaylee was a friend, Winged Foot must think her the enemy.

Realizing the strength of a dog his size and seeing how sharp his teeth were, Shaylee was terrified.

Chapter Eighteen

Mystery unfolds,
Traditions past.
Drench the soul,
Shadows cast.

Suddenly Winged Foot stopped growling. His tail began to wag back and forth as he went to Shaylee and snuggled against her leg as though he knew and loved her.

Glad that the threat had passed, Shaylee bent to her knees and flung her arms around the dog's thick neck.

"You do know me, don't you?" she said. She leaned away from him and looked squarely into his eyes. "Somehow you do know me."

She stroked his coarse fur as he panted and his tongue hung lazily from the corner of his mouth. "Surely you even know what Standing Wolf means to me."

The sound of Standing Wolf's name seemed to spark a fire within the dog. In a backward shimmy, he moved away from Shaylee.

His eyes intently on her, he began barking.

The sound was deafening as it filled the spaces of the cavern.

And then he whirled around and left the cave in a flurry of flying rocks, leaving Shaylee staring in confused wonder after him.

He came in again.

He was still barking as he came up to Shaylee and gave her leg a nudge with his nose, then rushed from the cave again.

He continued doing this three more times before Shaylee thought she understood his strange behavior. She had never owned dogs, but she knew that they were intelligent creatures and had ways to communicate their feelings.

Winged Foot was telling Shaylee by his behavior that he wanted her to follow him! Surely God had somehow brought the dog to her for a purpose.

She could think of only one possibility. Winged Foot was going to lead her to Standing Wolf's village.

The one other time she had gone there it had been by canoe. There was no canoe this time. She would have to go on foot.

She left the cave and ran through the forest with Winged Foot, and then across a field of clover where bees buzzed amid purplish white flowers.

Shaylee was seized with an uncanny foreboding when she ran into the dark shadows of the forest again, where there were glens and steep, twisted gorges.

The sunbeams were only scarcely seen as they managed to push their way through the thick foliage of the trees.

There were bluejays squawking somewhere in the distance, their eerie cries echoing all around Shaylee.

Sometimes there was barely enough room for her and the dog to squeeze between the trees to further their journey onward.

After a while Shaylee began to realize her hunger was causing her to become somewhat lightheaded.

And her legs ached from running and even threatened to give way beneath her as they began to feel strangely rubbery.

But as Winged Foot ran onward, panting hard, his tongue hanging farther and farther from his mouth, Shaylee was forced to follow him. Surely they would soon reach the village. If not, she was not certain how much longer she would last.

"I must stop and rest for a minute," she said, aware of sweat rolling from her brow, and of the dryness of her throat.

Winged Foot sensed that she had stopped. He also stopped, whirled around, and came back to her. He grabbed hold of her skirt with his teeth and tugged as his eyes gazed into hers.

"I can't, Winged Foot," Shaylee said, lowering her eyes and breathing hard. "I'm thirsty. I'm hungry. I'm bone tired."

But he wouldn't let up on her. He still tugged at her skirt, and this time he growled.

Shaylee looked up and found him staring stubbornly at her, his teeth still yanking on her dress.

"Alright," she said, trembling as she rose to her feet. "I shall try."

She was puzzled by how he held onto her skirt as they walked together through the forest. Soon she knew why he had been so persistent. It was as though he'd understood her need for food and water. He had led her to a whispering brook, where water ran fresh and clear over a bed of pebbly rocks. And wild strawberries, red and delicious looking, grew in thick vines on the banks of the brook.

"Thank you," she whispered, amazed at the intelligence of this dog.

She gave Winged Foot a quick hug, then went with him to the water and leaned down to fill her hands and drink the delicious liquid in great gulps as the dog quenched his own thirst in the brook.

Shaylee then dove into the fat strawberries, feasting on them and savoring their sweet juice as it rolled down her throat.

Before long, though, Winged Foot was there again tugging on the end of her skirt, and she knew that enough time had been taken for such luxuries as food and water. Winged Foot seemed determined to get her where he was taking her, and she knew where. Standing Wolf's village.

Feeling both exhilarated and anxious, Shaylee hurried along with Winged Foot, and soon saw the village through a break in the trees a short distance away.

Her heart raced at the thought of being so close to Standing Wolf. It wouldn't be long until she could reveal to him that she was no longer an angel.

She was there in the flesh, feeling, seeing, hearing, and desiring!

"I do love you so," she whispered beneath her breath. She hoped that when he realized that she was real, and available, he would also love her.

She ran onward, and when they reached the outskirts of the village, Shaylee became aware of how quiet everything was.

There were no people outside their lodges. Even the dogs seemed too still.

Then she saw the huge council house on the rise of land in the center of the village. She could barely see through the open door, but one glimpse was enough to ascertain that the council house was filled with people.

Her heart skipped a beat when she was able to make out a voice and knew that it was Standing Wolf's.

She knew that he was surely being judged even now.

She wanted nothing more than to go into the council house and stand beside him to voice her own feelings about his innocence.

But she knew that it was not her place to do so. Her presence would disarm him, perhaps so much that he wouldn't be able to think logically about things important to his trial.

But even if she had decided to go and speak up for him, it was obvious that Winged Foot had other plans for her.

Again he had hold of her skirt and was leading her on through the village, and then to a large, two-story, gable-roofed log cabin.

He let go of her dress long enough to nudge open the door made of poplar planks, then came again and grabbed her skirt with his teeth to lead her inside the cabin.

Once inside, he eased away from Shaylee. His tail wagging, he nestled down into thick pelts before the fireplace. She was amazed at how quickly he made himself at home in this spacious cabin.

"This must be Standing Wolf's home," she whispered, inching further into the room.

She was amazed at the generous size of the house hewn from red cedar logs. In one quick glance she saw several wooden chairs in the outer room, as well as small tables on which sat kerosene lamps. Blankets and pelts were rolled up along the wall. Wood storage chests fashioned of clapboards were sewn above to the crossbars with strips of buffalo rawhide.

She gazed in wonder at the supply of weapons that stood against another wall, among them a rifle, a shotgun, a shield, more than one bow, and two quivers of arrows. There was a huge stone fireplace that ran across one whole end of the house, and opposite that was a kitchen.

She wandered into the kitchen. To her surprise she found that he had the same type of wood-burning cooking stove that she had had in her home.

And there were all sorts of domestic utensils on shelves close to the stove — earthen pots, pans, jugs, mugs, jars, and wooden dishes and spoons.

She ran her fingers around a glazed black earthenware pot. There were several of them in different sizes. All were beautiful.

Being in the kitchen, especially so close to food simmering on the stove, made Shaylee aware again of her hunger.

She grabbed one of the wooden spoons and sank it into the pot.

At first she tasted it cautiously, but finding the food delicious, she quickly ate more, until soon her stomach began to feel warm and relaxed.

She gazed into the pot and slowly stirred the small amount of food that was left. It had the consistency of honey. She had recognized a distinct taste of grapes and parched cornmeal. Surely who ever had cooked this for Standing

Wolf had boiled grapes and then mixed them with parched cornmeal. However it had been prepared, it was delicious.

Shaylee went back to the main room of the house and saw something in the shadows that she had not seen earlier. Buffalo-hair cloaks hung from pegs on the wall, the hairs spun as fine as possible, then doubled, with small beads of different colors worked into them.

She glanced down and saw that she was standing on a beautiful carpet of hemp that had been painted with numerous colored figures. She wondered who had made the carpet and cloaks for Standing Wolf, for it must have been done by a woman who had much imagination, time, and patience. Surely only someone who cared deeply for Standing Wolf would labor over these things for so long for him.

"His wife," she whispered, yet she doubted that. She remembered that he had told her how young he and his wife had been when they married . . . and when his wife died.

"His mother," she whispered, nodding. "Yes, surely his mother made these before she died."

She went to a handsome clothes basket made of cane and raised the lid. Inside lay several turkey-feather blankets which had been made by interweaving the long feathers of the neck and breast with hemp or mulberry bark.

She knew that this kind of blanket was warm. It was especially pleasing to the eye.

Again she wondered who had made these for

the man she loved. She hoped to learn to make such things herself. It would be so wonderful to sew, cook, and even clean for him. She had missed having a husband to dote on!

Shaylee became suddenly aware of just how tired she was; the warm food must have made her sleepy.

She yawned and stretched and gazed down at the pelts that lay before the fire where Winged Foot snoozed. It looked inviting to her, as well, but instead she wandered into another room at the far back of the house.

She was stunned to find a three-foot-high, broad bed. It had a white oak foundation and was covered with furs. The bed had a canopy top and curtains which she thought must be to keep out the cold in the winter.

She went over to the bed and pressed the mattress. It was soft, probably made of down from some bird. The blankets thrown across it were made of mountain lion skins and looked so inviting. She was still somewhat chilled from her time in the cave, and the dark, dank forest. She climbed onto the bed and pulled the wondrous warm blankets over her up to her chin.

As she lay there, feeling warm and not at all like an intruder, her thoughts went to Standing Wolf. She wished she could go and stand outside the council house and listen to what was being said. But she knew that her presence there was not the best thing for him. She would wait for him.

She prayed that he would be found innocent and could return to his cabin.

She closed her eyes, smiling at the thought of his reaction when he found her sleeping in his bed.

She opened her eyes lazily when she felt movement on the bed. As Winged Foot came and snuggled down beside her, Shaylee smiled and hugged him to her. "Standing Wolf will be here soon," she whispered to the dog, then fell into a deep, restful sleep.

Chapter Nineteen

The winds whisper your gentle, quiet touch,
Moonbeams dance on the water's edge,
Shining ebony, teasing my dreams,
Destiny cast love's sweet pledges.

Quickly and without question, Standing Wolf had been acquitted of the crime of killing his chief. He now stood proud and tall inside the council house as everyone took turns embracing and congratulating him.

When the final person stepped away from Standing Wolf, Wind Spirit moved to his side. "This show of love for Standing Wolf is good. It is right," he said, drawing all eyes to him. "And now, my people, it is time to appoint a new chief, and you all know that Standing Wolf should be the one. He is the son of a chief we all loved and admired. Had Standing Wolf not been so young when his chieftain father died, he would have then become our chief. He has waited long enough for this honor. Let us go immediately into council. Everyone, all men, women, and children alike, have a vote. One by one, step forth now and speak aloud your choice."

Standing Wolf's heart swelled as each person took his turn, and each and every one, with the exception of Gentle Heart and White Wing, spoke his name.

Out of spite and hate, Gentle Heart voted against him.

As for the old sorceress who sat alone in the darker shadows of the lodge, she had no vote since she was Chippewa by birth and had only come to live with the Cherokee people because Gentle Heart had brought her there.

Now all that remained was the ceremony that would make him chief. Standing Wolf received hugs anew from everyone as they gathered around him to congratulate him.

The warriors whom Gentle Heart had sent out to hunt Standing Wolf came to him one by one, with apologies and hearty hugs.

Gentle Heart sat down beside her aunt and glared at those who were now treating her as though she were nonexistent, as though *her* choice of chief mattered not at all . . . as though she had never meant anything to them, even though she carried the important title of Beloved Woman.

She suddenly stood up and stepped out of the shadows to be seen and heard. "Standing Wolf does not deserve to be chief!" she shouted, causing everyone's eyes to turn to her.

"Appoint someone else! Listen to what I say. I am your Beloved Woman whose word is as powerful as a chief's."

Wind Spirit went to her and stood tall and solemn over her. "That is true *only* as long as the chief who appointed you Beloved Woman is still alive," he said with controlled anger. "Your chieftain husband no longer has the air in his lungs required to speak up in your behalf. And today not only has Standing Wolf been acquitted of murdering your husband, he has also been officially named chief of our Blue Clan of Cherokee. Gentle Heart, you have lost all of your power among our people, for Standing Wolf will never allow you to be the Beloved Woman of our people again."

As Standing Wolf stood quietly by, realizing that he would have to choose a Beloved Woman now to take Gentle Heart's place, all that he could think about was one woman.

Shaylee.

She was the only woman that he would ever want to have as his people's Beloved Woman during his reign as chief.

And he knew that was impossible. She was gone from his life forever.

Even if she was there, smiling at him now, so proud that he'd been appointed chief, he knew that he would not be able to speak her name aloud to his people or say that she would be their Beloved Woman. He had had the privilege of knowing her only because she had been sent from the heavens to help him in his time of trouble. She had called herself an "angel."

Now his life was in order again. He must focus on what was expected of him as chief and forget the sweet face that had filled his heart with love.

Tomorrow he would go through the ceremony of chieftainship, and he had been acquitted of the crime of killing the old chief. Those things should be enough to gladden him even when he remembered Shaylee.

And deep down inside, Standing Wolf would always feel blessed for having known her for even that short time they had been together.

He would never forget her.

She was the woman he loved.

"Standing Wolf?"

Wind Spirit's voice broke through Standing Wolf's thoughts.

Standing Wolf turned and smiled at the Head Priest. "*A-a-do*, thank you, for all that you have done for me," he said, placing a gentle hand on the elderly man's blanket-wrapped shoulder. "Now I must go and speak my goodbye to Chief Bear Sitting Down, who awaits his burial tomorrow."

"*Ho*, go and say your goodbye, then go to your lodge and rest, for tomorrow is not only the chief's burial, but also the ceremony that will formally make you chief," Wind Spirit said. He drew Standing Wolf into his arms and gave him a fond hug. "My son, it is good to have you back among us. May nothing take you from your people ever again."

They embraced a moment longer, then Good Shield walked with Standing Wolf to the smaller council house, where the old chief lay wrapped in his blankets, awaiting the ceremony that would send him on his way to the long road of the hereafter.

"The people showed their love for you today," Good Shield said. "They are proud that you will be their chief."

"Everyone but Gentle Heart and her aunt," Standing Wolf grumbled as he stepped up just outside the entrance flap.

"You must forget them both," Good Shield said, doubling his hands into tight fists at his sides as he recalled how viciously Gentle Heart had spoken against Standing Wolf in council.

He knew to expect worse from her.

She was the sort of woman who would not give up without a last, ugly fight.

"In time," Standing Wolf said solemnly.

He stared at the entrance flap as it swayed gently in the breeze, and then he turned and nodded a quiet goodbye to Good Shield.

After Good Shield was gone, Standing Wolf went inside the dimly lit room, where on one side a small fire burned in a fire pit, the smoke spiraling up through a small aperture in the buckskin covering.

Seeing the wrapped body of his fallen chief lying on a platform, upon which were strewn thick, rich pelts, Standing Wolf went and knelt beside it.

Resting a hand on the wrapped body, Standing Wolf lowered his eyes and said a soft prayer, then lurched when someone grabbed his wrist and yanked his hand from the chief's body.

He turned quickly to find Gentle Heart kneeling beside him, her eyes lit with angry fire.

She squeezed his wrist tightly with her hand. "Get up and leave," she demanded. "Get out of my sight."

His eyes narrowed, his heart pounding with a sudden seething anger, Standing Wolf placed a hand on hers and yanked it from his wrist. "Must I remind you that I have been voted chief of our Blue Clan of Cherokee?" he said, his voice drawn, yet controlled. "If I wish to, I can banish you from the tribe for all of the wicked things I know you have done. It would please me to banish you for your disobedience toward me, the one who is now the true voice of our people."

"You are only chief by vote, not yet by actual ceremony," Gentle Heart said, her chin held high, her flashing dark eyes in silent battle with his.

Unnerved by her continued show of hatred for him, and not wanting to show disrespect to Chief Bear Sitting Down, Standing Wolf rose slowly to his feet.

He gazed with more pity than hate at Gentle Heart for a moment longer, then turned and hurriedly left the lodge.

Carrying her spiteful words with him, Standing Wolf was troubled as he walked toward his lodge. He knew that he had to forget Gentle Heart's harsh words, yet she had a way of sinking her claws deep inside one's belly, twisting, turning, until it felt as though a knife had been thrust into it.

"She will not make my reign as chief easy, that is certain," he whispered to himself. "Some way must be found to prove her role in her husband's death."

He laughed and bent to a knee when Winged Foot came bouncing from around the side of the cabin. Since Standing Wolf's return home, he hadn't placed the animal in the dog trot.

"Where have you been?" Standing Wolf asked, stroking a hand through his dog's thick fur. "You seem excited about something."

Winged Foot sank his teeth into the sleeve of Standing Wolf's shirt and gave it a hard yank.

"You want me to come somewhere with you?" Standing Wolf asked. "*Ha-wa.* Let go and I will follow."

He followed Winged Foot as he ran up to Standing Wolf's front door and stopped. He released his hold on the shirt sleeve and gazed up at Standing Wolf, his tail wagging.

Standing Wolf raised an eyebrow as he gazed at the closed door, and then at his dog. "Is someone in there?" he asked, wondering who could get his bear dog so excited.

He looked up and saw smoke spiraling from the fireplace chimney of his cabin, and also the chimney from his kitchen stove.

He smiled, for he guessed that someone of his village had prepared food for him and started a fire in his fireplace.

He was never without food or warmth in his cabin. Since he had been widowed, the women of the village took turns seeing to his needs, especially his Aunt Blue Bonnet, his father's sister, a widow, who enjoyed doting on her only nephew.

Of late, though, his aunt had not been able to come and go as much, for her legs scarcely carried her anywhere. They were bothered with some sort of aching disease. Even today she had not come to the court proceedings, because she was too weak.

Standing Wolf felt that his aunt was soon to join her brother and husband in the heavens. When she was gone, that would be the last of his close relatives.

Today she had sent him a message that although she could not join everyone in the council house, she would be there with him in heart and spirit.

Shaking off troubled thoughts of his aunt, Standing Wolf opened the door of his cabin.

He saw a fire in the grate as he'd expected, but he smelled something that seemed to be burning. He sniffed and realized that the burning smell was coming from the kitchen.

He rushed in and found a pan on the stove, its contents charred and stinking.

He lifted a corner of his shirt and used it as a potholder, then yanked the pot off the stove.

He glanced down at Winged Foot and eyed him questioningly. "This is why you were anxious for me to come inside my lodge?" he said, laughing softly. "Because someone left food on my stove that was burning?"

He shrugged and walked back into his living room. He realized just how tired he was. He could think of nothing better now than to climb onto his bed and sleep. He would welcome dreams, especially if they were of Shaylee.

He pulled his shirt over his head and hung it on a peg, then yawned, his eyes automatically closing with the yawn as he sauntered into his bedroom.

When he opened his eyes he stopped suddenly and stared in disbelief at his bed.

Shaylee!

Shaylee was snuggled there beneath the blankets, asleep.

His heart leapt at the sight.

He had never expected to see her again.

But there she was, like a sweet, mystical dream!

Chapter Twenty

Hold me, my love,
Tender or passionately.
Just hold me,
Move me, excite me,
Always and forever,
Please, just hold me.
Enduring feelings,
Lazy summer days,
Stay and hold me.
Memories we'll make,
Joy, we'll share,
Remember to hold me.

Standing Wolf could hardly believe his eyes . . .
Shaylee was actually there. He had thought that
she was gone from his life forever. Now to have
been acquitted of the crime of murder and to
see his beloved Shaylee again were two blessings he had not dared hope for.

Then something else caught his attention.
Winged Foot!

From the way he had leapt onto the bed and

snuggled against Shaylee, Standing Wolf was sure the dog knew that she was there.

Standing Wolf also recalled how only moments ago Winged Foot had shown great excitement as he encouraged his master to go inside his lodge.

"Winged Foot," he said softly. "You knew to bring me here because Shaylee was here? How did you know? Does that mean that . . ."

Standing Wolf's breath caught in his throat when Winged Foot suddenly nudged Shaylee, as if to awaken her.

Stunned, Standing Wolf took a shaky step away from the bed. His throat went dry as he watched in disbelief when Shaylee responded, stirring in her sleep. She must have felt the dog nudging her. Winged Foot was able to touch Shaylee. He *did* know that she was there, whereas before, no one but Standing Wolf knew that she was present.

And although Standing Wolf had been aware of her presence then, he could not physically touch her as Winged Foot had just done.

But why? he puzzled to himself, too shocked to move as he continued staring at Shaylee.

How could it be?

What did it all mean?

Was she no longer an angel?

Was she there in the flesh?

Could *he* touch her?

His pulse racing, his knees strangely weak, Standing Wolf crept to the bed and stood beside it.

His hand trembled as he reached out for Shaylee. Then, almost afraid to see if he could touch her, he jerked his hand away again.

When Shaylee showed signs of waking up, her thick, long lashes fluttering against her cheeks, Standing Wolf again reached a hand toward her.

With passion in his eyes, he dared finally to touch her cheek.

When he felt the warmth of her flesh against his fingertips, he flinched as though he had been shot and drew his hand quickly away.

As his own pulse raced, he bent down closer and saw the pulsebeat in Shaylee's throat.

He leaned over her and placed his cheek near her lips. He melted inside when he could actually feel her breath on his flesh!

That could only mean one thing.

She . . . was . . . alive! She was totally, and wonderfully, alive!

Stunned and thrilled by this discovery, he fell to his knees beside his bed and gazed intently at Shaylee. His love for her swept through him in a surge of joy.

"You are no longer an angel," he whispered, his voice breaking with emotion. He sighed deeply. "You are . . ."

Ho, somehow she was now real.

When her eyes opened and he saw the wealth of emotion in them, he knew that she had come to him tonight because she loved him as much as he loved her.

Tears filled Shaylee's eyes when she saw the depth of love for her in Standing Wolf's eyes. He had already realized that she was no longer an angel. Perhaps he had even touched her while she was sleeping!

She reached out for him.

He sat down beside her, then drew her into his embrace and held her.

"I do not understand," he said, his voice filled with wonder. "Tell me how you can be here now with me, how I can touch you, when I could not before."

Shaylee savored the warmth and joy of his arms a moment longer, then drew away from them.

She placed her hands on his cheeks as her eyes moved over his handsome features. She was filled with so many emotions, she found it hard to speak.

But he needed answers, as did she.

She wanted to know how the trial had gone. She thought that it must have gone in his favor, or surely he would not be there now, a free man.

"I will tell you everything I can about how I happen to be here with you, but first, Standing Wolf, tell me, are you free of all criminal charges?" she blurted out, sensually melting when he took her hands from his face and held them.

"The trial is over and, *ho,* I was cleared of all

charges," he said thickly. He smiled into her eyes. "And I have even been named chief of our Blue Clan of Cherokee. The ceremony tomorrow will finalize it."

She slipped her hands free and flung herself into his arms. "I am so happy for you," she cried. "I wish I could have been there for you, but I had other things that drew me away from you for a while."

She again left his arms. "Are you glad that I'm here?" she murmured. "I've not taken too much for granted, have I? You do care for me, don't you? You do want me here with you? Do you . . . want . . . me . . . to stay?"

Standing Wolf laughed easily, his eyes dancing as he gazed into hers. "Do I want you?" he said, gently touching her face with a hand. "For always. That is how long I want you. But I had never thought it could be possible. Your time with me . . . I . . . thought it was . . ."

"You thought it was for only a short while?" Shaylee said, softly interrupting him. "I wasn't sure, myself, if I could truly be with you like this. I . . . had to prove something to someone first. I did, and now I am here. I am here as a living, breathing person. I'm no longer an angel. I can actually feel, smell, eat . . ."

Her stomach growled so loudly Winged Foot's ears twitched.

Shaylee placed a hand on her tummy and laughed softly. "I'm embarrassed," she said, lowering her eyes shyly.

Then she looked up at Standing Wolf again. "I don't know how I can be hungry, for I helped myself to the food cooking on your stove, but I *am* so hungry, I . . . I . . . feel ravenous!"

Her nose twitched. She looked past Standing Wolf at the door, then questioned him with her eyes. "Do I smell something burning?" she asked, her insides tightening when she recalled that she had left the food cooking on the stove.

"There are only ashes left in the pot that you ate from," Standing Wolf said, chuckling.

Shaylee placed a hand to her throat. "I'm so sorry," she said. She was glad that he saw humor in her carelessness.

"That does not matter," Standing Wolf said, gently touching her cheek, marveling anew over being able to touch her sweetness. "Everyone makes mistakes." He brushed a kiss across her brow. "Even angels."

"Angels," Shaylee said in a whisper, remembering how it had been before she was an angel.

She had spent much time in her kitchen and was now recalling that fateful morning when everything in her life had changed.

She could remember it now, as though she were there again, living it, how Moses lay in his cradle beside the kitchen table as Shaylee ate her breakfast of oatmeal and toast.

The kitchen window had been open to let in

the morning breeze.

The smell of lilacs blooming on a bush just outside the window had wafted into the kitchen.

It had been a beautiful day, so beautiful she had planned to take Moses for a walk in his buggy later on in the afternoon when her chores were finished.

"He loved that buggy ride so much," she found herself murmuring aloud. She realized that Standing Wolf had heard her when she felt him take her hand and hold it lovingly as he asked about what she had said.

"Who are you thinking of?" Standing Wolf asked, bringing Shaylee's tear-filled eyes up to his.

"My son," she replied, a sob lodging in her throat. "My baby. My Moses."

Standing Wolf's heart skipped a beat. "You have a son?" he asked, his voice wary. "And . . . a . . . husband?"

Shaylee lowered her eyes. The same sadness that always gripped her when she thought of David was there again, paining her. "I *had* a husband," she said, her voice breaking. "He was murdered."

Then she looked anxiously into Standing Wolf's eyes. "Perhaps the same men who murdered my husband also took my child!" She grabbed his arms. "Standing Wolf, I must find my son, Moses. I must!"

Standing Wolf felt the desperation in her

tight grip, and he heard it in her voice. He actually felt her pain at losing her husband. He knew the pain of losing a wife.

And he, too, had experienced the pain of losing a child. Although his child had not yet been born, the pain and the loss were still felt inside his heart.

But this woman's child was surely still alive!

He gazed at her stomach when it growled again. Then he looked into her eyes again. "I want you to tell me everything, but first I am going to get you some nourishment," he said, hurrying to his feet. He smiled. "Back at the cavern, I remember how you only watched when I ate."

"Yes, that was when I was an angel," she murmured, smiling up at him.

"But you are very real now," Standing Wolf said.

"Yes, I am real," Shaylee said, her voice breaking with emotion. "Very real."

"This Cherokee warrior is very glad," Standing Wolf said, sighing. "I am going for food for you." He reached a hand out for her. "Come with me. Let me introduce you to my aunt."

"I would rather wait here for you in your lodge while you get the food," Shaylee murmured. "Your people, perhaps especially your aunt, have had enough to absorb these past few days without having to question you about a white woman who has suddenly appeared in your lodge . . . and in their new chief's life."

Standing Wolf bent to his knees beside the bed and swept Shaylee into his arms.

His lips trembled as he touched hers with them.

Then when her arms twined around his neck and she returned the kiss with joyful bliss, everything within Standing Wolf knew that he could never love anyone as much as he loved this woman, so much that he hated letting go of her for even a moment.

The taste of her lips was like honey.

Her hair and her body smelled heavenly . . . like lilacs.

Her body was pliant and sweet in his arms.

Her arms around his neck, proving how much she wanted him, were like a magical elixir, making him hunger for more than food at this moment.

He wanted her.

All of her.

Shaken by his feelings, having been without a woman he desired with all his being for far too long, Standing Wolf stood up, then gazed for a moment into Shaylee's blue eyes.

Then, breathless with wonder, he turned and rushed from the room.

He was aglow with happiness over how things had turned out for him. He had wanted Shaylee so badly, but had given up ever seeing her again.

And then suddenly there she was. In his bed.

And she was touchable!

They had not only held one another, they had kissed, a kiss that had left his knees weak and his heart pounding!

Ho, she had come to him because she had deep feelings for him.

He could not believe it was happening, but he now knew that they could have a future together. They would be man and wife. And then there would be children.

Many of them!

The children would bring many bright moments of sunshine into this world that was too often gray and foreboding.

"But her son?" he whispered as he headed towards his elderly aunt's lodge. "Moses. She called him Moses. I will find her Moses for her!"

Hating having to awaken his aunt, Standing Wolf quietly lifted her entrance flap.

He smiled when he smelled the delicious food that was cooking over the slow flames of her fire. His aunt was a woman of goodness and heart, a woman who in the past always made certain that she had food over her fire for anyone who ventured there in need, or just for a social visit.

She was no longer able to prepare the food herself. The women of the village kept her lodge filled with the wonderful aroma of food warming over her fire!

Until recently, when her fingers began to

ache too much to work, his aunt had kept him fed, had sewn his clothes, and had woven rugs for his floor.

Since his parents' deaths she had been his everything, a woman he loved with all his heart. She never failed to make him feel special, beloved.

Tiptoeing into the one-room log cabin where his aunt slept, Standing Wolf knelt down before the embers in the grate, where more than one pot of food was simmering.

Most enticing of all was his Aunt Blue Bonnet's delicious succotash.

As a child he had often watched her make succotash out of brown beans mixed with hominy. He had shelled the black walnuts for her and had watched her place large pieces of the walnuts in the succotash. The mixture was then thickened with pumpkin.

Ho, even though his aunt would have had someone else make the succotash from her recipe, the delicious food would delight Shaylee no less.

He would also take Shaylee his aunt's special hominy drink. He smiled as he recalled the times when he had helped her prepare this favorite drink. After he had shelled corn for her from their cobs, she would soak the corn in lye until the skin came loose and was removed.

He had then helped his aunt beat the dried corn in a corn beater, after which they had sifted the powder from the remaining kernels.

The powder was then cooked and thickened a little with cornmeal.

It was called "crack corn," and was especially delicious after it had been kept until it had soured.

"Nephew? Is that you standing beside the fireplace?"

He turned and gazed at her as she sat up in her bed. She wore a long gown knitted from wild hemp, with a long fringe of colorful beads and feathers reaching the ankles.

Women of her status were permitted to weave colorful beads and feathers into their clothing. When her fingers had allowed it, she had spent days weaving for others.

Her thick gray hair was twisted into a bun above her head. Shadowed grooves showed on her aged face in the fire's soft glow. Her eyes were sunken, only brown slits now, and she could barely make out things around her.

"*E-tlo-gi*, Aunt Blue Bonnet, you can hardly see, yet you always know it is I who comes into your lodge," Standing Wolf said, kneeling beside her bed.

"My eyes are weakened by age, but my sense of smell has strengthened," Blue Bonnet said, laughing her husky laugh. "Sweet nephew, do you not know by now that I always *see* you by your *smell?*"

"I hope you smell something that pleases you," Standing Wolf said, chuckling low as he leaned over and gave her a gentle hug.

"Everything about you pleases me," Blue Bonnet said, wrapping her arms around him, then fondly patting his back.

"Your words are too kind," Standing Wolf said, leaning away from her. He gently touched her lined face. "Sister to my *e-do-da*, I love you so much."

"No one could love anyone as much as I love you," Blue Bonnet said, patting his knee. "You have always been like a son to me."

"As you are like a mother to me," Standing Wolf said softly.

"And the wound on your head? Does it still pain you?" she asked.

"It does pain me sometimes, but I have had so much on my mind, I do not have time to think about it," he said.

"Nephew, let me say how happy I am that you were acquitted today in the court of law, and that you have been voted in as our people's chief," Blue Bonnet said, framing his face between her gnarled hands. "I hope you understand why I was not there. My feet, legs, and fingers ache so much. It is even too hard for me to make my way from my bed to my rocker beside the lodge fire, let alone go to the council house."

"*Tsi-ga-ta-ha*, I know," Standing Wolf said thickly. "And I understand. All *did* go well for me today, *e-tlo-gi*. And I will now be chief and watch over our people."

"Like your *e-do-da*, you will be a good

leader," Aunt Blue Bonnet said, a tear running from the corner of her eye as often happened at the mention of her brother, who she still missed with all her heart.

She knew, though, that sometime soon she would be reunited with him. When she was taken on that long road to the hereafter, she would be walking on it hand in hand with her beloved husband and her wondrous brother.

She rejoiced at that thought and looked forward to the moment when she finally took her last, painful breath of life.

"Sweet aunt, I have kept you from your sleep long enough," Standing Wolf said. He took one of her hands and kissed its palm affectionately, then slid her hand beneath the warm blankets and pelts. "Tonight I have come for food. If you will not miss it, I will take some back to my lodge."

"You cannot eat it here and sit with your aunt for a while longer?"

"Someone waits for me in my lodge," Standing Wolf said, so guardedly that he knew his aunt had noticed.

"Who will sit and eat with you in your lodge?" Blue Bonnet asked, leaning forward so that her eyes were close enough to Standing Wolf's face that she could make out his features. "It cannot be Good Shield. If it were, you would not have spoken so guardedly about it."

"No, it is not Good Shield," Standing Wolf

said. He inhaled a quivering breath, for he wasn't sure when would be the best time to tell his aunt about the woman he had fallen in love with. She was white. His aunt had no good feeling for whiteskins, for she had seen them take too much from their people.

"The person who waits for me is even more special to me than my best friend Good Shield," he said. He swallowed hard, then continued. "Aunt Blue Bonnet, this person who awaits my return to my lodge is a *a-ge-ye*."

"A woman?" Blue Bonnet said, raising an eyebrow. "Hmm. That is good, my nephew. You have mourned your wife's passing long enough." She smiled. "Now tell me. Which tribe is this woman from?"

Standing Wolf went quiet. A part of him hated telling her . . . a part of him was too proud not to!

"Auntie, the woman is *u-ne-ga,* white," he blurted out.

Her gasp of disbelief told him that he had been right to be wary of telling her. . . .

Chapter Twenty-one

Sleep, old one,
Dream of
freedom,
Lost loves,
And ghost trails —

Chief Bear Sitting Down was now buried. Standing Wolf had gone through the ceremony that had made him the official chief of his people.

The mid-morning sun was bright.

The air was filled with the pounding of drums as the Blue Clan of Cherokee people participated in a "Friendship Dance," a ritual that was always held after the burial of one of their loved ones.

Both men and women participated, but men led and did the singing, carrying either a drum or rattle.

A woman with tortoiseshell rattles fastened to her calves followed behind the leader and kept time with his singing by stomping her feet to shake the rattles in rhythmic sequence.

The drum was made of a small section of hollowed buckeye trunk. The open end, or "head," was covered with woodchuck skin held down by a hickory hoop.

The outside was carved and painted.

The drumhead had been soaked in water and the hoop had been pounded down over the skin until the skin rang when struck lightly. The drumsticks were made from pieces of hickory or black walnut, less than a foot long, and each had a small knob on the end.

Shaylee sat beside Standing Wolf on a platform at one side of the circle of people who were also watching instead of participating in the dancing.

As she continued to watch the dancers moving in simple rhythmic walking steps that kept time with the drums, Shaylee became lost in thought.

Last night, as she had sat waiting for Standing Wolf to return with the food, Shaylee had become uneasy, so uneasy she had almost fled in panic.

She had been afraid that Standing Wolf's elderly aunt might have spoken against her because she was white, for Shaylee knew that the older Indians had no good feelings for whites.

Then when Standing Wolf came back to his lodge, carrying his aunt in his arms instead of food, Shaylee felt that everything she had wished for was slipping away. The old woman's eyes revealed just how much she abhorred the very sight of a white woman in her nephew's lodge.

After a while, after they talked, and Standing Wolf explained to Blue Bonnet how Shaylee had helped him, how Shaylee's tiny baby was even then at the mercy of some crazed renegades and outlaws, Blue Bonnet's heart softened toward Shaylee.

It was Blue Bonnet who had asked Shaylee to join in the two celebrations today, the burial rites that would send one chief along the road to the hereafter, and the ceremony that would bring a new chief into the lives of her people.

She had even invited Shaylee to join in the Friendship Dance, which was always held after a burial to help the people forget their sorrow.

Yes, Shaylee felt blessed again today. She could sit with Standing Wolf on one side of her and his aunt on the other, and when his people glanced at her it was not with mistrust in their eyes, for everyone knew and trusted Blue Bonnet's judgment. Without her approval, they might not have been as quick to accept their new chief's choice of wife, especially since they had just buried a chief who had been blinded by a woman's youth and beauty.

Blue Bonnet had even confessed today that she was happy Shaylee had come into her nephew's life, for Standing Wolf's eyes were now smiling for the first time since his wife's death those many moons ago.

But there were two who did not join in every-one else's acceptance of Shaylee. Gentle Heart and her sorceress aunt gazed at her even now from the circle of observers.

Shaylee knew that Gentle Heart and White Wing saw her as someone who stood in their way. After all, Shaylee had helped Standing Wolf in his time of trouble.

Shaylee felt sure that Gentle Heart had had a role in what had happened to Standing Wolf, yet no one could prove it.

Not yet, anyhow.

Shaylee had heard Good Shield tell Standing Wolf that he was going to watch Gentle Heart and catch her doing something that would prove her guilt.

That couldn't happen too soon for Shaylee, for she didn't trust anything about Gentle Heart, or White Wing. There was a genuine evil in the eyes of both of them.

Shaylee's gaze moved back to the dancers, for many of them were now singing while circling around the fire. She listened carefully to them as they sang, *"Wah! Ha-hi-u, Ha-hi-u, Hah-hah-hah, Ha-hi-ei."*

The songs consisted of an individual melody sung with a series of words and poetic phrases that represented sounds of nature.

She saw how each dancer now seemed to be using different items as they danced — pine boughs, sticks, eagle feathers, wands, pipes, masks, and robes.

As she continued to marvel at the beauty of their dances, Shaylee's thoughts drifted back in time, to the burial earlier in the day, and how the chief's body had been carried to its place of interment. The body had been laid alongside a large rock, and a wall about eighteen inches high was built on the other side to enclose it.

A covering of wood and an arch of stone had been laid over it as a roof, stones then being heaped over the whole to create a small tomb. His personal belongings had been buried along with him.

Afterwards, as she walked back to the village beside Standing Wolf, he had explained to her that his people believed that at death the soul entered a mystical, but living, body, that was smaller than the earthly one. The body that the soul entered grew smaller each year until at last it vanished and ceased to be.

Now, she again focused on what was happening around her as the pungent aroma of old tobacco permeated the air, mingling with the smell of food that was cooking over a large out-door fire.

Shaylee felt that the dance today held a gripping power as great as any opera in the white society, for its drama and music directly expressed the most important realities of Cherokee existence.

Now the older men circled around inside the circle of people, their wives joining the circle, and after them the young men and women.

Round and round the circle went, gradually picking up speed and volume as more people joined in the "magic ring."

Shaylee jumped when she felt Standing Wolf's hand in hers.

She looked quickly over at him and smiled wanly when he nodded toward the dancers, then stood and urged her to her feet.

"I will be too clumsy," Shaylee said as she stood up beside him. Ignoring her protest, Standing Wolf led her toward the dancers. "I have never danced a step in my life, Standing Wolf. I have never been one who enjoyed dancing."

"You are now a part of the Cherokee, and dancing plays a big role in our lives," Standing Wolf said, leading her amid the dancers, where she had no choice but to start moving in time with the music or be trampled by those who danced and sang.

Dressed in clothes given to her by a maiden of her own age and size — a short, sleeveless, close-fitting deerskin dress belted at the waist with a broad, woven belt, and fastened at the bosom with roaches of bone — Shaylee found herself picking up the beat of the drums. Her feet, shod in moccasins, moved automatically to the rhythm.

Standing Wolf, dressed in full buckskins, held Shaylee around the waist and smiled as he saw how quickly she learned the dance of his people.

His eyes lingered on her, for he could not help gazing with admiration at how his people's clothes looked so right on this petite, beautiful white woman. Besides the buckskin dress, she wore a hide handkerchief around her neck which was tucked down into the bosom with a bell attached to it.

He knew the clothes of the women well, for he had seen his wife dress in them each morning, and today what Shaylee wore was no different than Sunshine's attire. Under her dress was a petticoat woven from wild hemp. This extended down to her knees and had a long fringe that reached the ankles.

As with all Cherokee women, no leggings were worn, but Shaylee's deerskin moccasins came to her knees and had small bells attached at the ankles. Those bells were tinkling now and filled the air with their soft music with each of Shaylee's movements.

Standing Wolf smiled as he recalled the previous night and how she had reacted to the food he had brought to her after he had taken his aunt back to her lodge. To Shaylee, the food and drink had seemed bitter.

He had explained to her how the Cherokee ate a lot of soured food and drinks and how they did not notice it when they ate the succotash and drank the hominy drink.

Soon the bitterness no longer bothered Shaylee, for her hunger outweighed every other consideration.

He wondered now how she would react when she knew of another special food of his people — pudding made from the blood of butchered animals.

As he continued dancing with Shaylee, feeling lighthearted and gay, his mind strayed to the burial ceremony. The Head Priest had passed around a piece of tobacco, meant to enlighten the people so they could bravely face the future. Then a strand of sanctified beads had been handed from person to person to comfort the hearts and souls of those who were finding it hard to say a final goodbye to their fallen leader.

Standing Wolf had been one of those mourners who had found it hard to say goodbye. He found it hard to accept the way the old chief had died.

His life had been needlessly taken by some murdering fiend, and why? What had it gotten anyone?

Some *could* say that it paved the way for Standing Wolf's chieftainship. But everyone knew that was not the motive behind the murder.

There was only one person who had wanted him dead. Gentle Heart. She was now rid of an old man who had become an object of hatred in her life.

Ho, one day he would find a way to prove her guilt.

But for now, he had much to do. He would

send his men out time and again until they found the one who had actually sunk the knife into their chief's heart.

And he would try to help find Shaylee's son.

Soon he hoped to make this woman who had come to him so mystically his wife!

He again thought of the old chief. He looked heavenward and spoke to Chief Bear Sitting Down in his thoughts, telling him to sleep, oh, mighty warrior, dream of quests, Indian princesses, warm furs . . .

A tug on his arm brought Standing Wolf back to the present.

He gazed down at Shaylee and stopped, aware now that everyone else had stopped dancing and were disbanding and moving to the large outdoor fire for the feast.

"You were lost in thought," Shaylee murmured. She searched his eyes. "What were you thinking about?"

"Chief Bear Sitting Down," he said. "I was wishing him well."

"He is in a better place now," Shaylee said, remembering how often those words had been said about her husband by the people of the beautiful Baptist Church up the road several miles from her house.

"*Ho,* but he was a man who enjoyed living," Standing Wolf said, his voice solemn.

He turned away from Shaylee and found Gentle Heart and White Wing standing back from the others, their heads together as they talked, their angry eyes gazing back at Standing Wolf.

As always, they unnerved him. He knew what they were capable of. Soon he hoped to prove it to everyone.

Good Shield stepped from the crowd, blocking Standing Wolf's view of the two women. He came toward Standing Wolf and Shaylee with two wooden trays of food. Winged Foot was trotting along beside him, his tongue hanging out, his tail wagging.

Standing Wolf was glad that Good Shield had distracted him from thinking about things that bothered him, for now was not the time to labor over ugly things. This was a time of celebration, celebrating the beginning of their old chief's long journey to the stars, and the beginning of a new chief's reign.

As Standing Wolf waited for Good Shield, Shaylee turned and gazed at Blue Bonnet. She had been carried and placed with the other women her age, who were drinking and eating, and laughing.

When the older woman turned and caught Shaylee looking at her, she smiled. The gesture warmed Shaylee through and through.

Shaylee knew that it could have been so different. She could have been resented so much that she would never feel welcome at the village.

But God was still looking out for her and had made sure that hadn't happened.

She turned her eyes heavenward and said a silent prayer of thanks, and then again thought of Moses, hoping that God would be as generous about helping her find him.

"Here is food for my woman," Standing Wolf said, handing the wooden platter to Shaylee. "Good Shield has brought us bear sausage and —"

"Bear sausage?" Shaylee said, paling at the thought of eating bear meat.

"There is also *u-la-tli-ya-ay*," Standing Wolf said, sensing that Shaylee was again having trouble with the food of his people. "It is a root that grows in clusters like beets. When it is washed and cut into small pieces it is nourishing. As is *tse-wi-na*, also a small root resembling a turnip. After it is washed and boiled, it is quite refreshing to the taste."

He gestured toward the many other vegetables, meats, and berries. "The food is good not only for your stomach, but also your soul," he said, pleading with his eyes for her to take the platter and eat.

Knowing that she had more than just food to adjust to, Shaylee smiled weakly and took the platter.

Standing Wolf gently took Shaylee by an elbow. "Come and sit beneath a locust tree as we eat," he said, glad when she nodded and went with him.

Good Shield sat beside Standing Wolf, savoring his food as he glanced first at Shaylee and then at Standing Wolf.

Standing Wolf felt his friend's eyes studying both him and Shaylee. He looked at him questioningly.

"Will Shaylee now be our people's Beloved Woman?" Good Shield blurted out as he set his empty platter aside.

Taken aback by the question, Shaylee gazed at Standing Wolf as she breathlessly awaited his response.

"To be a chief's Beloved Woman, the woman must first be his wife," Standing Wolf said, his gaze resting softly on Shaylee. "Is your love for me as strong as what the stars feel for the midnight sky? Although we have only recently met, I know that my love for you is true and everlasting. Will you be my wife? Will you be my people's Beloved Woman?"

So much had happened so quickly in her life. Shaylee knew how she wanted to respond to Standing Wolf's questions, yet she was a little fearful of what he was asking of her.

Oh, yes, Lord, how she loved him.

And how she wanted to be his wife.

But to be given the special title of "Beloved Woman"?

His people did seem resigned to having her in their village as a part of their chief's life.

But would they be able to go further in their acceptance of her?

Would they truly accept a white woman as their Beloved Woman?

Suddenly afraid, afraid she could not have what she so desperately wished for, after all, Shaylee dropped the plate of food to the ground, jumped to her feet, and ran away from Standing Wolf.

She was keenly aware of how quiet everything became behind her.

She could almost feel the people's eyes on her, staring.

She could almost feel Standing Wolf's shock at her behavior. She could even feel his hurt!

"Oh, what have I done?" she whispered, now realizing that her reaction to his questions could not be worse.

Tears rushed from her eyes. Blinded by them, she became disoriented and did not know which house was Standing Wolf's.

She stood wiping her eyes, her heart pounding, then became aware of something tugging at the skirt of her buckskin dress.

She looked down and through her tears saw Winged Foot's teeth latched onto the tail end of her dress. His eyes were soulful as he gazed up at her.

"You beautiful, wonderful dog," she sobbed out, then went with him into the lodge that she knew was Standing Wolf's.

She bent and hugged the bear dog as he let go of her dress. Afraid that she had just managed to lose everything she wanted with all her heart, she went to the bed and flung herself across it.

Her body racked with deep sobs, she buried her face in the blankets that still held the smell of Standing Wolf.

"Standing Wolf, I'm sorry! Sorry!" she said between sobs. "Oh, how I love you. And . . . all . . . I can do . . . is disappoint you."

"You did not disappoint anyone."

His voice, and what he said, his *nearness* as he moved onto the bed beside her and took her in his powerful arms, made things suddenly right again for Shaylee.

She clung to him, then became deliciously swept away into the clouds, but not by God's command this time.

By Standing Wolf's tender, joyous kiss!

Without even realizing how it happened, Shaylee soon found herself silkenly nude beside Standing Wolf on the bed.

She reached out a hand and ran it down the full length of his body, reveling in the wonders of his cinnamon-brown flesh, unclothed and pulsing with desire for her.

"I want you," Standing Wolf whispered huskily into her ear, his hands warm and wonderful on her breasts. "White Swan, tell me that you want me as much."

"I have never wanted anyone as much as I want you," Shaylee whispered back, her fingers now running through his thick, long black hair. "Make love to me, Standing Wolf. Please? Make love to me now?"

Then she gazed questioningly into his eyes.

"You called me by the name White Swan," she murmured. "Why?"

"Do you think the name is beautiful?" he asked, his eyes twinkling.

"White Swan?" she said, forking an eyebrow as she wondered about it. "Yes," she then said. "It is so very pretty."

"It is an Indian name that I have given you because you are as beautiful as a swan. And your skin is as soft and white as swan's down."

A gentle, joyous warmth filled Shaylee. "You always make me feel so special," she said, trembling sensually.

"Because you are," he said softly.

"I do love my new name," Shaylee said; then her eyes wavered. "I remember you telling me when we first met how much you liked the name Shaylee. You said that *it* was beautiful. Don't you think so anymore?"

"*Ho,* I will always think the name Shaylee is beautiful," he said. "At times I will call you Shaylee and at times I will call you White Swan. Will that confuse you?"

She laughed softly. "No, it will just make me feel extra special because I will be a woman with two beautiful names."

As he placed soft kisses across her brow, his hands swept down her body until his fingers found the place that was wet and ready for him. In slow caresses he readied her even more, until she groaned and pressed her womanhood even closer to his fingers.

201

When one of his fingers slid up inside her, waves of pleasure splashed across Shaylee's flesh.

She ran her fingers down the full length of his back, and then shuddered when she swept them around to where his thick, throbbing manhood lay against her leg and her fingers wrapped around it.

When she began moving her hand on him, Standing Wolf slid his lips from hers and opened his mouth over the sweet, smooth column of her throat. He could feel the pressure rising heatedly within his loins. The pleasure was so intense he had to work at not crying out with rapture for all to hear.

His teeth clenched as he fought to keep himself from surrendering to a world of euphoric intensity, for he would not do so without his woman receiving her pleasure at the same moment he found his.

He reached down and eased her hand away from him.

And then he rose above her.

His eyes hot coals of passion as he gazed into hers, his heart throbbing as though many drums were beating inside his chest, his hands on her breasts, softly kneading them, he shoved into her in one deep thrust and moaned with the onslaught of pleasure that overtook him.

"Please kiss me again," Shaylee whispered, her cheeks hot, her pulse racing, her body on fire with needs she had almost forgotten existed. "I love you so, Standing Wolf. And, yes, I want to be your everything!"

"My woman, my White Swan," he whispered huskily, then brought his lips down onto hers in a hard, passionate kiss. Their bodies moved in unison, their passion peaking.

Their sealed lips muffled their groans of rapture so that only Winged Foot could hear as he watched from the foot of the bed, his tail thumping.

Chapter Twenty-two

Silence cries to be heard
Screaming her ugly words,
Beneath a mystical surface
Lies such anger, unheard.

Glad that she had learned how to ride a horse when she was a small child, Shaylee proudly rode today beside Standing Wolf as they left a raft ferry that had taken them across the White River to the side where she had lived with Moses in their small cabin.

In order for Shaylee to be able to help her father with the chores on their small farm in Boston, he had taught her to ride so that she could go out on occasion on horseback and check the small herd of cows in their pasture.

Then when she had married David, she had helped him haul firewood home behind her horse after he had spent a full day cutting down trees and chopping the wood into smaller pieces that fit her cook stove and fireplace.

That all seemed so long ago, she thought.

Her childhood had gone by in what seemed one blink of an eye, and then her marriage to David had been so short-lived it seemed now as though it had never even happened.

But her memories helped keep David alive, and her need to find Moses was what drove her today back to her home to start the search for her son.

She recalled again the pain of the arrow piercing her back and the horror of lying there helplessly as the redskin renegade carried Moses off on his horse.

She cringed when she recalled the torches being thrown onto her home, and how only moments later she had been whisked away to the heavens above.

"Shaylee, are you still comfortable with what you have chosen to do today?" Standing Wolf asked. "You feel this is the right way to begin your search for your son?"

"Something tells me that it is," Shaylee said, yet the smile that she gave Standing Wolf was not as sincere as she wished it to be, for in her heart she truly wasn't sure what was the best way to go about finding Moses.

Perhaps it was just that she needed to go back to her home one more time, even though she knew she would find it in ashes.

But no matter why, it did seem important to begin at her cabin, where she had last held her son, where she had rocked him and sung lullabies to him.

She needed to feel close to him in this way, and then she could let go of that part of their past and begin anew when she did finally find him.

"Standing Wolf, thank you for coming with me," she blurted out. "You could have easily chosen to go with your warriors as they begin their search for Chief Bear Sitting Down's murderer. You don't know what it means to have you with me. Your presence alone is such a comfort to me."

"I would not be anywhere or with anyone else," Standing Wolf said, the fringes of his buckskin shirt stirring in the gentle breeze, his long hair fluttering down his straight, muscular back.

He smiled as he looked at Shaylee. Although he had found her beautiful when she wore the clothes of a white woman, he found her even more beautiful in the dress of his people. The buckskin dress, with its fancy beadwork and fringes, clung to her like a glove, defining her delicate, sweet curves. As she sat in the saddle of blankets, the dress was hiked up past her knees, revealing the flesh of her shapely legs down to where the moccasins came up to hide her ankles.

His gaze went to her flaming red hair and how it shone in the sunlight, an extension of the sun in its fiery color. He could smell the sweet river-water scent of her hair and body and recalled with a throbbing heart how they had shared a morning bath downriver so that they would have total privacy.

It made flames ignite in his loins as he recalled what else they had shared, their lovemaking this morning even more intense and meaningful than last night. Today Shaylee seemed more relaxed and better able to enjoy the lovemaking than their first time together.

He looked forward to tonight after they made a campfire beneath the stars and had eaten their evening meal. He would show her again the intensity of his love for her. He would, for a moment at least, make her forget the sorrow she felt at her son's loss.

The knowledge that a man of his own skin color could be so heartless made anger leap into his heart.

He would search until he found her son, and when he found Moses, he would find the man responsible for causing so much pain in Shaylee's life.

Shaylee had caught Standing Wolf studying her, especially her red hair. She knew that it fascinated not only Standing Wolf, but all of his people.

Shaylee sighed and looked away from him. "It isn't far now," she said, kicking her heels, sending the brown mare into a brisker trot.

As Standing Wolf rode beside her, she became achingly aware of things familiar to her — the country road cut out of the wilderness that would shortly become the lane leading to the remains of her cabin and the land where David had spent so many hours tilling the soil.

She looked to the side of the road and saw the bright-colored iris that grew wild throughout the forest, recalling the times David had brought a bunch home for a bouquet for their dinner table.

She smiled when she recalled placing bees-wax candles on the table those nights, instead of the smelly tallow she usually used. They had pretended to be rich those times, when in truth they were dirt poor.

Yet in a sense they had been richer than those who could boast of having more money than they could ever spend in a lifetime. Hers and David's riches had come from their love.

She shivered dreadfully when she rode past the spot where David had been ambushed and killed. She looked quickly away, or she would again see him lying there in a pool of his life's blood. She had found him herself when she had gone searching for him after he did not arrive home when expected.

Feeling stronger now that she had someone to hold her and make her see hope in the future, Shaylee rode onward. She turned her horse to the right and onto the lane that led to what had been her home for too short a time.

In her mind's eye she could not shake the image of horsemen riding in a dust cloud up the lane toward her home. How paralyzed with fear she had been, and how desperately she had tried to get her firearm to protect Moses, only to be struck by the dreadful arrow.

Standing Wolf sensed that Shaylee was suffering, for she would suddenly shiver, as though someone had splashed cold water on her, and then she would gasp softly and wince.

He was beginning to think that this was a bad idea, returning to the scene of the crime, where everything was coming back to her and hurting her all over again.

He wished to reach out and grab her reins and turn her horse in another direction, but knew that it was already too late. Up ahead, at the end of this rocky lane, he saw the black rubble of ashes that had once been her home.

He tried not to envision her being hit with an arrow, or her son taken away by a renegade.

But he could not help remembering all that she had told him about that fateful day. It was as though, now, it had all happened to him, for anything that touched his woman's life also touched his.

"Oh, Standing Wolf, if only I could find some clue that would help me find my son," Shaylee said, her eyes misting with tears as she drew rein before the ashes.

But before she or Standing Wolf could dismount, they heard the arrival of a horse and buggy behind them, coming down the lane they had just traveled.

Shaylee turned and saw the couple arriving in a buggy. As they drew closer, she recognized them. It was the couple who had purchased her parcel of land. The woman was a pretty thing in her lacy dress and beautiful bonnet.

The man showed his wealth by the way he was dressed in a fancy black suit and stiffly starched white shirt where a diamond glistened from the folds of his ascot. He wore a top hat and gloves, and he sat on a soft leather seat, his horse a magnificent black steed that showed it had been trained to trot just perfectly.

Shaylee inched her horse closer to Standing Wolf's and exchanged quick glances with him, then nervously smiled at the man and woman as the buggy came to a stop a few feet from her.

"Good day to you, young lady," Clarence Edwards said. He tipped his hat to Shaylee and then gave a distant, cold look at Standing Wolf as he replaced his hat on his head.

Again the man centered his attention on Shaylee. His eyes were disapproving as he swept his gaze over her and noticed her Indian attire.

"Mr. Edwards, Mrs. Edwards, it's good to see you again," Shaylee said tightly, taking a dislike to this man whose prejudices were worn in his eyes. His wife's lifted chin proved that she felt the same as her husband.

"We've met before?" Barbara asked, peering more intently at Shaylee. "I don't believe I remember you."

"No, I doubt that you would," Shaylee said, sighing heavily. "We met only once. That was at the auction of my husband's property."

"What property?" Clarence asked, his voice tight as he looked slowly from Shaylee to Standing Wolf, and then again at Shaylee.

"The land adjoining my cabin," Shaylee said, a sob lodging in her throat as she looked past the horse and buggy at the land that had been precious to her husband. "The land my husband farmed before he was murdered."

Clarence's eyes widened. He stiffened his spine and gaped openly at Shaylee. "Why, my word, it's *you*," he said, his voice lowered in pitch. "Shaylee. Shaylee Whiteside. I . . . we . . . thought you had perished in the fire. We came today to see who was trespassing on our land, for we took it upon ourselves to lay claim to all of this property when we believed you and your son . . ."

"Yes, my house was set a fire, but my son and I survived," Shaylee said, choosing not to explain how she happened to be one of the living and breathing again.

She would never tell another soul, except perhaps Moses when he grew up and could comprehend the magnitude of what had happened to his mother.

"We were going to have the rubble removed today," Clarence said, nervously drumming the fingers of one hand on a knee. "But I see now that we no longer have the right to do that. This small parcel of land still belongs to you."

"No, legally you don't have the right to my

land, but still I give you permission to do with this land whatever you wish, for it is no longer of use to me," Shaylee murmured, her fingers tightening on her reins. "I only came to take a look, to. . . ."

She stopped before saying why she had truly come today, not even sure now why she had. This visit had not proved anything to her, or served any purpose, except to start the pain anew inside her heart.

"Where is your child?" Barbara asked. "And . . . what . . . are you doing dressed like an Indian, riding and associating with one?"

Hearing the contempt in this woman's voice when she uttered the word "Indian," Shaylee grew angry. She knew now to expect the same reaction whenever any white person saw her with Standing Wolf.

It made her sad to know that there was such prejudice against the red man, since they were truly the first people in America.

And it made her even more determined to allow people to see her with this man who would soon be her husband. She was proud of him. She was proud to be a part of his people, their heritage.

Finding the couple contemptible, Shaylee decided not to waste any more words on them. She turned and gazed at the burned rubble, smiled at Standing Wolf, and nodded toward the lane. Understanding her silent message he rode off beside her.

"This land is truly ours?" Clarence shouted after her. "You won't come back later and lay claim to it?"

Still Shaylee ignored them, smiling at the thought that they would always wonder whether or not the land would be theirs forever.

"Do you wish you had not gone there today?" Standing Wolf asked softly.

"I'm very glad that I did," Shaylee said, sighing resolutely. She smiled at Standing Wolf. "Now let's truly begin the search for my son. What I am leaving behind no longer matters."

"Sometimes it is hard to let go," Standing Wolf said, knowing how he had not been able to forget his young bride until now . . . until Shaylee.

"I know," Shaylee murmured. "And there is one thing I will never give up — my determination to have my son with me again."

"And you will," Standing Wolf said, his jaw tight. "I will not rest until the child is in your arms again."

"And also your arms, Standing Wolf, for you will be his father," Shaylee said, her voice breaking at the thought of Moses having a father. "You will be the best of teachers for Moses. I want you to teach him everything Cherokee. When he is old enough to have a pony of his own, he will ride with the young Cherokee braves."

"When we find him and bring him into our

lodge, I will give him a blanket, the kind that is made solely for our young braves, to warm him on the long, cold nights of winter," Standing Wolf said. "This sort of blanket is made out of mountain lion skins which transmits to the children the powers of acute smell, strength, and cunning, and which gives them the first rudiments of war."

Shaylee paled. "War?" she said, her voice drawn. "I thought your people no longer participated in warring."

"One never ignores the possibility of war, especially with whites always a threat to our people's existence," Standing Wolf said dryly. "One must always be prepared, although we are now a tribe of peace. Early on, the Cherokee warriors acted as intermediaries among all tribes and became known as the 'Peacemakers of the Plains.' There were even Cherokee guides who rode with white parties who passed through hostile Indian regions to guarantee their safe journey. My uncle, who is no longer of this earth, was one of those guides. I remember seeing him in the special clothes that he wore when he was a guide. To distinguish who they were, all guides wore a distinctive hunting coat trimmed with red yarn fringes."

As they rode onward beside the White River, Shaylee edged her horse closer to Standing Wolf's. "You are of the Blue Clan of Cherokee," she murmured. "Why are your people called that?"

"Our clan was named after a bluish plant that is gathered from swamps and used for food and medicine," Standing Wolf said. He understood that Shaylee needed this small talk to fill her mind as they rode onward and discovered nothing of her son's abduction.

Yes, he knew that it would take much time and searching for answers to be found.

It might take days, weeks, and months.

But their search would never end until Moses was reunited with his mother. Standing Wolf had promised her that her son would be with her again. And he would.

"The bluish plant is called *sakoni,* or *sahoni,* and is a kind of narrow-leafed grass producing berries that look like young cucumbers. The root of this plant is a powerful elixir for my people. It is used to protect our children from disease, and it is customary at the appearance of each new moon, to bathe all of our children in a liquid made from the plant's boiled roots."

He gave her a soft smile. "I spoke earlier of the blankets made solely for the young braves of our people," he said. "There are special blankets for the young female children, as well. The skins of fawns are used, since they are a shy and timorous animal."

"That is sweet," Shaylee said, laughing softly. "I shall remember to make such a blanket for our first-born daughter." Then she frowned. "Yet to make such a blanket, a beautiful fawn would have to be killed." She shook her head quickly back and forth. "No, I can't do that. Our daughter will have to have some other blanket for her bed."

"I thought you would feel that way," Standing Wolf said, smiling and nodding at her. "For you are a woman of good heart, as are the women of my village. Rarely do any of them ask for such a blanket for their daughters."

"I can think of one who would," Shaylee said, knowing that she had a bitter edge in her voice. "Gentle Heart. She would probably even laugh as the fawn was slain for the blanket."

Standing Wolf chuckled. "You are a very astute woman," he said, then went quiet when he saw the raft ferry waiting to take passengers to the other side of the river.

He looked at Shaylee. "It is best to return now to the Cherokee side of the river," he said. "There we will resume our search. It was a red man who took your child. He would live on that side of the river."

"Or hide there," Shaylee said sarcastically.

"*Ho,* I am certain he is in hiding with those others who ride with him," Standing Wolf said. Then they both went quiet as they boarded the raft ferry, remaining in their saddles as they headed back to the other side.

Shaylee was suddenly filled with gloom and despair, for she now knew that the search for her son would not be an easy or short one. She hoped that she could keep remembering what

God had said to her, that she *would* be reunited with Moses again.

"But when?" she asked softly as she gazed heavenward.

Chapter Twenty-three

Hold me, my love,
Tender or passionately.
Just hold me.
Move me, excite me.
Always and forever,
Please, just hold me.
Enduring feelings,
Lazy summer days,
Stay and hold me.
Memories we'll make,
Joy we'll share.
Remember, to hold me.

The sun was waning in the sky. Shaylee's bones ached from having been on the horse for a good part of the day. As she and Standing Wolf made their way back toward the river after searching the forest, she wondered if she could go much farther. She had never been on a horse for so long. She wasn't even sure if she could go again tomorrow to search for her child.

She ached as she tried to slide her right leg only an inch to stretch it.

When she found Standing Wolf watching her, she smiled weakly at him.

"It's been a long day," was all she offered, not wanting to labor over just how long or how miserable she was. She believed that an Indian warrior would want a woman who was strong, not weak and spineless.

From having read about Indians, she knew that their women were expected to do many things for their warrior husbands that had no part in any white woman's chores. Although Shaylee could carry her weight in tubs of wash water, she knew she had much more strenuous chores ahead of her as Standing Wolf's wife.

And she would prove to him that she was capable of doing anything he expected of her. As she was doing now, she would just grin and bear the aching bones and muscles.

"We will rest the night and if you wish, we can return to the village for a day or so before resuming the search," Standing Wolf said, recognizing fatigue when he saw it.

He also recognized bravery and determination in a woman. This woman, whose fiery hair matched her spirit, was determined to prove that she was strong in the face of all obstacles.

He admired this about her, as he did so many other traits. Her devotion to her son especially.

"No, I don't want to return to your village just yet, but I do look forward to a night of rest beside a campfire," Shaylee said, trying not to moan when a sharp catch in her right side made her flinch.

She slid a hand to her side and slowly rubbed it as she gazed ahead at the White River. "I also look forward to soaking myself in the delicious water of the river," she murmured.

"We will stop, make camp, catch our evening meal, and as it cooks over the fire, we shall bathe together in the river," Standing Wolf said. He sidled his horse closer to hers and reached a hand out to brush back some damp ringlets from her brow.

"I shall wash your hair for you," he added, then ran his fingers through her hair and lifted it from her shoulders.

A sensual thrill rushed through Shaylee at his touch. His fingers now moved around and he brushed a hand across her breasts. "I would like that," she said, her pulse racing at the thought of them together in the water again.

She could never get enough of him. Now that passion had been awakened in her heart again, she wanted Standing Wolf each waking moment.

All he had to do was look at her and her heart began a nervous hammering inside her chest.

Her eyes widened when she suddenly heard something through the trees a short distance away. She smiled quickly at Standing Wolf. "Did you hear that?" she said, already tasting roasted turkey. "Did you hear the turkeys gobbling? Surely they are down by the river."

Expecting him to be excited since he was such a skilled hunter, and recalling how he had been hunting turkeys on the day he'd been ambushed, she was surprised when he only smiled at her in a strange sort of mischievous way. She had thought he would grab his rifle from the gun sheath at his horse's right side to go and kill their supper before it got away.

She peered through the trees when she heard the turkey call again. "It sounds so close," she murmured, then gave Standing Wolf a questioning stare. "Aren't you as hungry as I am? Lord, Standing Wolf, it makes my mouth water just to think about a good meal of turkey, and *you* show *no* signs of even thinking about getting one for us."

Standing Wolf was enjoying her reaction to what he knew was not a turkey's gobble. There was such a sweet innocence in everything she did. As each moment passed, he loved her more dearly.

"Come," he said, nodding toward Shaylee. "We shall go and find the gobblers."

"It's about time," Shaylee said, sighing resolutely. "I truly thought you were going to ignore them."

She rode onward with him as she sent her horse into a gallop toward the river.

Then, puzzled anew, she gave Standing Wolf another wondering stare. "Won't the noise from the horses' hooves frighten the turkeys away?" she said, drawing a tight rein as she thought of that possibility.

Her horse came to a halt, as did Standing Wolf's.

"And why haven't you taken your rifle from the gunboot?" she asked, raising an eyebrow.

"We will go the rest of the way by foot," Standing Wolf said, sliding out of his saddle. "Come with me. Lead your horse."

Shaylee dismounted awkwardly and tugged on her reins so the horse would follow her. "I still can't figure you out," she said as she gazed over her shoulder at the rifle that still rested in its sheath. "How on earth are you going to kill a turkey without your firearm?"

Again Standing Wolf only gave her a mischievous grin, then stopped and wrapped his reins around the low limb of a beechnut tree. "You want to see the turkeys?" he said, forcing himself not to laugh out loud at the amusement of what lay ahead.

"Yes, but more than that, I want to *eat* one," Shaylee said, following his lead, securing her horse's reins on the same tree limb.

When she still saw that he didn't get the rifle, she stamped over to his horse and took it herself from its sheath. She went to Standing Wolf and shoved it into his hands.

Standing Wolf still only smiled, then nodded toward the river when the gobbling sounds erupted again from the riverbank. "Do you see turkeys?" he asked, giving Shaylee another quick smile.

Shaylee moved on ahead of him toward the river, her footsteps cautious, her eyes searching the brush that clung to the riverbank. Surely the turkeys were hidden somewhere there. They certainly hadn't been frightened away, because she still *heard* them.

When she reached the river and the gobbling sounds were all around her, and she still saw no sign of turkeys, she turned and gave Standing Wolf a puzzled stare. "I don't understand," she murmured.

Suddenly frogs leapt out around her feet, startling her. She gazed in wonder down at them as they multiplied on all sides of her, and then she gasped when she heard the sounds that were coming from them. It most certainly wasn't the normal sort of croaking sounds.

"Now do you see why I did not need the firearm to kill our supper?" asked Standing Wolf, laying his rifle aside. "Come with me. Help me to gather frog eggs."

"Frog . . . eggs?" Shaylee said, again looking at the many frogs who sang songs that sounded like turkeys gobbling.

"These are 'turkey frogs' " Standing Wolf finally explained. He clapped his hands to frighten the frogs away. "I have brought you here not to eat turkey, but instead turkey frog eggs."

The frogs had hopped away to hide in the

tall, thick grass away from the river. Standing Wolf bent and pointed out the tiny sand hills among the rocks. Each was filled to over-flowing with tiny eggs.

"Goodness gracious," Shaylee said, her eyes widening. "I have never heard of such things as turkey frogs."

Standing Wolf then pointed out the tiny black tadpoles darting about here and there in the shallowest part of the river's edge. "The Cherokee children come to the river and gather tadpoles and take them home for pets," he said. "The children put the tadpoles in bowls so they can watch them. Dirt is sprinkled in the bowls each day to feed them."

"When my Moses is old enough to enjoy tad-poles —" she began, then stopped abruptly when she realized where her thoughts had taken her. Sometimes she still felt as though Moses was with her, for it seemed inconceiv-able that he wasn't!

No one could have been more protective of her child than Shaylee had been.

"Your Moses *will* have tadpole pets," Stand-ing Wolf assured her, drawing Shaylee's eyes quickly to him. "Having hope . . . is the best way to get through the sadness of what has happened."

"I know," Shaylee said, her voice breaking. "Sometimes I just need to be reminded. Thank you for being here, to do that for me."

"I will always be here for you," Standing Wolf

said, their eyes holding.

Then he looked away from her. "Let us now gather eggs so that your stomach will not start its grumblings," he said, chuckling.

"Yes, let's," Shaylee said, laughing softly at how quickly he could add humor to a situation. She held the skirt of her dress up and made a pouch for the eggs as Standing Wolf gathered them and placed them in it.

Giggling, feeling like a schoolgirl, Shaylee went with Standing Wolf, and as he built a fire on the beach out of fallen cottonwood branches and twigs, she carefully unloaded the eggs from the pouch of her dress.

"We will allow the coals to get hot, and then we will bury the eggs in those coals," Standing Wolf said, standing up and offering Shaylee a hand. "But while the fire burns down to coals, we will bathe."

Passion was born again between them as they undressed and dropped their clothes to the ground away from the fire.

Their eyes moved slowly over each other's nude bodies, and then Standing Wolf reached out and cupped her breasts in his hands.

Shaylee closed her eyes and sucked in a wild breath of pleasure as Standing Wolf kneaded her breasts, and then put his mouth on one and flicked his tongue around the nipple.

But realizing how she had perspired during the long day on the horse, she knew that he had to be tasting the salt of sweat on her flesh. Only wanting him to taste her when she was fresh and clean, Shaylee leaned away from him, her eyes misted over with passion she was momentarily denying herself.

"I'd rather bathe first," she murmured, her eyes holding his. "I want everything to be perfect when we make love."

He took her hand, kissed its palm, and then, laughing, ran with her into the river.

Although they had no soap, the river water was clean and refreshing against their tired flesh.

Shaylee leaned her head back and allowed her hair to sink further into the water, sucking in a breath of rapture as Standing Wolf kissed the hollow of her throat, then moved behind her and ran his fingers through her hair as he washed it.

"That feels delicious," Shaylee murmured as his fingers kneaded her scalp. She sighed with pleasure when his fingers lowered from her hair and swept down her back, lower and lower, stopping as he swept his fingers around to caress her where her passions seemed centered.

Wanting even more than that now that she felt clean and ready for Standing Wolf, Shaylee turned and faced him. Her own hands now strayed, searching beneath the water, until she found his manhood swollen and responding to her touch as she moved her hand on him.

Feeling too close to the ultimate pleasure,

Standing Wolf reached down and moved her hand away. Then he swept his arms around her and drew her against his hard-muscled body.

Their bodies strained together as their lips met in a frenzy of kisses. Shaylee lifted a leg around him, sucking in a wild breath of pleasure as he slid his manhood inside her and began his rhythmic thrusts.

Shaylee moved her lips from his. She laid her head on his chest and let herself be transported once again to that place where only lovers went.

Standing Wolf's body was fluid with fire as he continued to shove inside her. His hands cupped her buttocks and held her closer to his heat. He held his head back and groaned as he felt the beginning of the spasms that would send his seed into the womb of the woman he would love forever.

They clung and savored the wondrous moment after they found the peak of passion.

"I shall always love you," Shaylee whispered. "I am so glad that I was led to the cave where I found you."

"White Swan, when I first saw you I truly did not believe that you could be real," Standing Wolf said, now sweeping her fully into his arms and carrying her from the water. "Never had I seen anyone as beautiful."

He slid her to her feet, then framed her face between his hands as he looked adoringly down at her. "Never shall I see anyone as beautiful again," he said huskily. "For always there will only be you."

With their bodies pressed together and the sun lowering behind the distant mountains, they kissed again, then fell apart when the cooler breeze of evening made them aware of still being unclothed.

Laughing and talking, completely in tune with one another's feelings, they got dressed. Then Shaylee sat down beside the fire as Standing Wolf arranged the frog eggs amid the warm coals at the edge of the fire.

Standing Wolf got a blanket from his horse and spread it beside the fire, then sat with Shaylee on the blanket as they waited for the eggs to cook.

They talked and laughed some more; then as the moon rose high in the sky and the stars twinkled against the dark heavens, they ate the eggs by the light and warmth of the dying coals in the firepit.

"I'm amazed at how long the fire's coals are warm," Shaylee said, gazing into the glowing embers.

"When burned, cottonwood preserves its redness longer than any other wood used in fires," Standing Wolf explained.

"I love it here," Shaylee said, sighing. In the dark she could see the eyes of deer and antelope as they gazed at her and Standing Wolf from the sand bars and banks where they had come down for water.

She looked to her right, where willows hung their branches over the water, and saw several elk eating leaves from the lowest branches.

Then suddenly Shaylee was reminded of more dangerous animals that were part of the night when she heard the howling of a wild wolf pack somewhere in the distance.

She shivered and looked quickly at Standing Wolf.

She was glad when he brought his rifle closer to his side.

"The fire will keep them away," he offered. "Always know that you are safe while with me."

Shaylee scooted closer to him and snuggled, yet knew deep in her heart that no one was ever truly safe. All she had to do was remember the viciousness of her husband's ambush, and how quickly things had changed for her the day the outlaws and renegades rode down the lane to her house.

She closed her eyes tightly as she tried not to remember those things, but they were always there, tormenting her.

Moses, she thought to herself. *My darling, your mother will never give up looking for you.*

"You have been so strong," Standing Wolf said, sensing that Shaylee was again transported back in time to that fateful day of her son's abduction. "So shall you continue to be."

Shaylee smiled weakly as she gazed up at him, then flung herself into his arms. "Please help me stay strong?" she said, tears sliding from her eyes. "Please? Will you?"

"You know I will," Standing Wolf said, lifting her onto his lap facing him. He wove his fingers through her hair, then placed his hands at the nape of her neck and brought her lips to his.

His kiss was all that Shaylee needed to make her feel at peace with herself and the world.

She now knew that she had been led to Standing Wolf by God not only to help *him*, but for him to help *her*.

She smiled, thinking that God was wise in all ways, for Standing Wolf was perfect for her at this time in her life. She cherished the very thought of being with him, of being loved by him, of *loving* him.

"My woman . . ." he whispered against her lips. "My forever woman."

She smiled and kissed him again.

Chapter Twenty-four

Omens and dreams,
Dawn's blush . . .
Abandoned fosterling's
Desperate rush.

Hoping to get in another full day of searching before returning to the village, Shaylee wondered if she could last another day on the horse. She and Standing Wolf had broken camp at dawn and were already quite a distance from the river.

They wove their way through a dense forest, where the sun would struggle through the thick foliage overhead, and then Shaylee and Standing Wolf would be riding where the trees thinned out and the sun could flood the forest floor with its beautiful glow.

They would then again ride on the open prairie where masses of flowers lay before their feasting eyes as if a rainbow had fallen from the sky and spread its varied colors in narrow bands across the land.

A chill coursed through Shaylee when they entered the forest again and the dampness and sour smell of rotted leaves seemed to wrap themselves around her.

But she didn't complain to Standing Wolf about any of these discomforts, especially how today her body seemed twice as sore as yesterday. She never wanted to give up her part in the search for her son. When he was found, and he would be found, she wanted to be there to grab him into her arms, to hold him next to her heart forever.

Her breasts were aching unmercifully, too, and she knew that was because she needed her precious baby's lips there, suckling milk from them.

She tried to put all of this from her mind and concentrate on the things around her, and how Standing Wolf had grabbed his rifle from its gunboot, and how his jaw had tightened.

"Did you hear or see something?" Shaylee asked, her spine stiffening.

"I do not hear, but *ho*, I see something," Standing Wolf said, his eyes narrowing as he peered to his right.

He drew a tight rein and then reached over and grabbed Shaylee's reins to stop her horse.

He talked in a whisper only loud enough for Shaylee to hear. "We must go the rest of the way on foot," he said, sliding from his saddle.

"What do you see?" Shaylee asked, also in a whisper as she slid from the saddle and inched closer to Standing Wolf.

She looked all around her and saw nothing, then followed his gaze and saw that he was studying the ground at his right side.

"Someone has been here not long ago on horses," Standing Wolf said. He bent to a knee and moved his hands over the leaves that were scattered about. He nodded and looked quickly up at Shaylee. "As I thought there would be, in the damp ground beneath the leaves, there are fresh hoofprints."

Shaylee's heart skipped a beat, then she sighed heavily. "But they could have been made by anyone," she said. "I just can't get my hopes up, Standing Wolf. Surely we won't be lucky enough to find the murdering cowards this easily."

"Luck is not how I find those I search for," Standing Wolf said as he stood beside Shaylee. "I know tracking well. And I know the minds of these renegades. Were I to want to go into hiding, this shadowy, elusive forest we are now riding through would be my choice. People who are traveling usually avoid such dark, dank forests as this. Even if it lengthens their journey a half day, they will avoid riding where shadows dance all around them . . . shadows possibly made by unsavory characters such as those who came to your home and took so much from you."

He reached his hand to the lump on his head that was now all but gone. "Those responsible for my ambush and the old chief's death might also be hiding where they feel no one will venture," he said. "Today, though, I focus only on finding your son's abductors. My warriors are searching for those who downed me and killed Chief Bear Sitting Down."

"I will forever be grateful to you for helping me find my son when, in truth, your people might be questioning your judgment about helping a white woman instead of joining your warriors on *their* search," Shaylee said, taking his hand and squeezing if affectionately.

"You are not just any white woman," Standing Wolf said, bringing her hand to his lips and softly kissing it. "You are *mine,* and I am my people's chief, whose decisions are always believed right."

He eased his hand away from hers and peered ahead through the thickness of the trees. Shaylee could see his nose twitch as he seemed to smell something.

"We are near a campsite," he said, his hand tightening on his rifle. He gazed at Shaylee, and then the horses. "Secure them and then we will go see who we have found."

Shaylee nodded and wrapped the reins of both horses around a low tree limb, then moved stealthily beside Standing Wolf as they went onward.

Standing Wolf leaned low and whispered into Shaylee's ear. "Careful not to make any sounds now. Not even a whisper. And walk lightly as does the stealthy panther over the leaves."

Her pulse racing, the excitement of the moment making her forget her aches and pains, Shaylee nodded and lifted each foot as lightly as possible.

Her spine stiffened and she felt a sudden leap of fear when she heard laughter up ahead. Her eyes widened when the distinct smell of coffee brewing and meat cooking over an open fire came to her.

Standing Wolf reached over and grabbed Shaylee's wrist to stop her. He nodded toward a thick stand of brush only a few feet ahead of them.

She returned the nod as he dropped his hand from her and used it to steady the rifle. He would be prepared to fire should someone suddenly lunge out from hiding.

Shaylee moved quickly beside Standing Wolf and was soon behind the thick forsythia bushes, their yellow blossoms profuse and beautiful. Her eyes widened and her throat constricted so much she thought she might choke when from that vantage point she caught sight of those who sat around the fire, laughing, joking, eating, and drinking. She recognized the very renegade who had taken her son from his cradle and ridden away with him on his horse.

Too paralyzed to do or say anything, Shaylee continued staring at the livid white scar on the renegade's face.

Then her heart sank when she realized that,

yes, she had found the renegade, but not her son!

She looked quickly at the men with him and knew they were the ones who had ridden with this renegade that day.

But what had they done with her Moses? she wondered despairingly as tears came into her eyes.

Desperation seized her as a terrible thought came to her. Oh, Lord, what if they had found her son a nuisance and they had . . .

No! She would not think that way. The renegade had stolen her baby for a purpose! Surely he had taken Moses to someone.

Perhaps he had even sold the baby to a childless couple, or just given him away to save himself the bother of caring for him.

Standing Wolf could hardly believe his eyes. He was staring at his arch enemy Short Arrow, the very man he'd always suspected of stealing Standing Wolf's knife to kill Chief Bear Sitting Down. He had not seen Short Arrow since the day he had caused Short Arrow's banishment. He had hoped that day that he would never come face to face again with the man he loathed with all his being.

His thoughts were interrupted when Shaylee reached over and grabbed his arm.

"Standing Wolf," she gasped out, her face pale. "Those are the men who came to my home and . . . and . . ."

Her voice broke when she found it difficult to

finish what she had to say.

She lowered her eyes, took a deep breath for courage, and then looked at Standing Wolf. "These are the ones," she said solemnly. "The very renegade who took my son. The one with the scar on his face. He is there beside the fire." Her voice broke again. She swallowed hard. "But, Standing Wolf, I don't see my son. What have they done with him?"

She wiped the tears from her eyes and exhaled a heaving breath as she started to rush away. Standing Wolf reached out and grabbed her.

"Let me go," she said, her eyes pleading with him. "Come with me. Help me get answers. Force that scarred man to tell me where Moses is. I can't stand not knowing!"

Standing Wolf laid his rifle on the ground and placed gentle hands on her shoulders. "The man you have pointed out to me is my own worst enemy, who is called Short Arrow. I believe he is responsible for ambushing me, and possibly for killing our chief. And, no, my woman, we must not be hasty about this," he said, his eyes imploring her. "There are too many men with Short Arrow. We must hurry back to the village and gather together many warriors. Then we will return. We will surround them. They will hand over their weapons. They will be interrogated. You will then know where your son is, and with whom."

"But once they break camp, won't they go on

their way?" Shaylee said, so afraid of losing Short Arrow and never finding him again. She was surprised by what Standing Wolf had said about the scar-faced man. That he was the very man who had committed such crimes against the Blue Clan of Cherokee.

"I can't chance that, Standing Wolf," she blurted out. "I've come this close to finding my son. I just can't chance losing sight of that heartless renegade again."

"It is too dangerous for you to stay here alone," Standing Wolf said, glancing at the rough bunch again. They had a side of ribs cooking over the fire. Each took what he wanted by cutting off some of the ribs with his knife. They looked carefree, even though they left so much grief behind wherever they traveled. And Standing Wolf was not at all surprised that Short Arrow was a part of them.

"But don't you see?" Shaylee pleaded. "I must."

"And if they do leave, what then?" Standing Wolf asked, his voice drawn.

"I will have no choice but to follow them," Shaylee said. "And I know now that you are good at tracking. I shall find a way to leave something for you to follow to make the tracking easy for you."

Seeing her determination, and understanding the love she had for her child, Standing Wolf saw that he had no choice but to agree to her plan. And without her he could make better time back to his village and return with help even more quickly.

He shoved his rifle into Shaylee's hands. "Protect yourself," he said tightly. "Stay out of sight. And use this firearm if you feel threatened in any way."

Shaylee lifted her chin proudly as she gripped the rifle. "I shall," she murmured, then leaned into his kiss as he lowered his mouth to her lips.

As he turned and ran away from her, leaving her there with weak knees and a pounding heart, she looked heavenward and silently questioned God with her eyes, wondering if this was His plan. Was she, alone, to rescue her son, or would she get in the worst trouble of her life?

Chapter Twenty-five

Souls sense hidden things,
Silence, loneliness,
Sound their screams.
The forest's shadows go deeper,
Living things grow meeker.
Warnings feel shadows at dusk,
Omens and dreams, haunting hush.

Good Shield had not gone with the warriors, having stayed behind to keep an eye on Gentle Heart. Hoping to find her doing something that would discredit her and prove her guilt, Good Shield had followed her from the village, far downriver.

He believed she was traveling to meet with someone, perhaps the very person who had stabbed the knife into Chief Bear Sitting Down's body.

But his hopes were dashed when all that Gentle Heart did was to begin undressing, proving that she had come so far from the village only to be assured of privacy during her bath.

Disgruntled, thinking that he had wasted valuable time following her, he turned his back to Gentle Heart.

His thoughts moved to Standing Wolf and the white woman. They were on their own search. For a child. *Hers.*

And then Good Shield thought of Standing Wolf's position in this . . . how he had fallen in love with a white woman and so quickly. Good Shield saw the goodness and the loveliness of the woman, yet he still wished his best friend had chosen a woman of their own race.

He saw a rough road ahead for a forbidden union such as theirs. Their peoples had never mixed without the disapproval of both the white and Indian community.

The splashing of water drew Good Shield around. His spine stiffened and his eyes widened as he stared in disbelief at something that had until now been hidden beneath the looseness of a buckskin dress. As water dripped from the dark nipples of Gentle Heart's breasts, Good Shield saw that her stomach was . . .

"She . . . is . . . with . . . child!" he whispered, knowing that the child could not be her late husband's. It was a well-known fact that Chief Bear Sitting Down could not father a child.

"Then whose child is it?" Good Shield whispered. His pulse raced when he realized that finally he had found a way to prove to his people that this woman had wronged her husband. She had been unfaithful to her husband, which was a reason in itself why she might have wanted him dead. To be free to marry the father of her child!

Seething with anger, yet bursting with pride that he finally had a way to discredit this woman, Good Shield stepped out from behind the thick bushes. His fists on his hips, his legs spread, he glared at Gentle Heart.

Gentle Heart froze. When she saw who was there and realized that he had seen the proof of her pregnancy, she felt trapped.

"You spied on me?" she screamed, her hands doubled into tight fists at her sides. "You watched . . . me . . . bathe?"

"*Ho,* I have been watching you, you sorceress . . . liar . . . killer," Good Shield hissed out. "You will no longer get away with murder. Come. You are going back to the village with me. You are going to show everyone your betrayal of your husband! The swell of your stomach is proof of too many things, sorceress. You can no longer deny having a role in your husband's death!"

A look of panic came over Gentle Heart's face. She momentarily stiffened, and then turned and stumbled into the water. She began swimming in wild, erratic strokes to the center of the river.

"Do you think you can get away from me? Never! You will stand before our people, guilty!" Good Shield shouted.

He ran and dove into the river and swam after her.

When he reached her, he grabbed her around the waist and turned her to face him. He took his knife from his sheath and held it at her throat.

"Tell me whose child you are carrying, for surely that is the person who killed my chief!" he shouted, his eyes narrowing as she gave him a defiant look.

"I tell you nothing," she hissed.

"You *will* admit the truth, sorceress," Good Shield said, leaning into her face as he took the knife away from her throat. "You will admit it to everyone, for I am taking you back to our village, where you will face everyone with the truth."

"I won't go!" Gentle Heart screamed, yanking at his arm, which now held her in a tight grip as he began bodily carrying her from the river.

"You *will* go," Good Shield said, throwing her ashore as he reached the riverbank.

He laughed as she tried to scamper away, her wet feet slipping and sliding on the dew-dampened grass.

"There is nowhere you can go, or hide, to get away from the truth that is waiting to be told to my people," Good Shield said, climbing, dripping, from the river.

He slammed his knife back into its sheath at his right side, then raked the fingers of both hands through his long black hair and drew it back from his eyes.

Lying helplessly on the ground at Good Shield's feet, Gentle Heart gazed pleadingly up at him. "Do not make me do this," she said, her voice breaking. "I will leave the village willingly. Please do not make me show my pregnancy to everyone. I will be ridiculed."

She grabbed his leg and screamed up at him. "I do not think I can stand being ridiculed!" she cried. "I am a Beloved Woman. I . . . am . . . revered by everyone."

"You might have been by a few, but never did you fool all of our Blue Clan of Cherokee," Good Shield said heatedly. "It was only because of our chief, your *husband,* that you were allowed to sit in council pretending to be someone you were not. You were only named Beloved Woman because of our chief, who was blinded by your beauty."

He threw his head back and laughed raucously, then glared at her again. He shook her away from his leg. "You have been a shameful mockery of a Beloved Woman," he said, his voice tight.

As she scooted farther away from him on the ground, Good Shield kept creeping toward her, his eyes filled with loathing.

"You *will* stand before our people to be judged," he said. "Your infidelity will make it clear that you had a role in your husband's death."

He bent down and grabbed her by the wrists, yanking her to her feet before him. "Admit it to me now and I will see that your ridicule from our people is not as harsh as it might be should the truth be forced from your lips while you stand before everyone," he said.

"I . . . cannot . . . do that," she said, a sob lodging in her throat. "I will never admit to anything."

"No, I doubt that you will," Good Shield said, dropping his hands away from her. "So it will be enough for me, and our people, to see the proof of your infidelity."

He grabbed a blanket and shoved it around her shoulders. "Come," he said. "We go now to the village. Once there, you will drop the blanket away from yourself and allow everyone to see what I have discovered."

"I cannot enter the village dressed . . . dressed . . . in only a blanket," Gentle Heart said, trembling as she clutched the blanket around her shoulders. "Allow me to dress, Good Shield. Please?"

"Your soft voice, your pleading, will get you nowhere with me," Good Shield said. He nodded toward their village. "Walk, *a-ge-ye,* or I will carry you."

Gentle Heart peered down at her clothes, then down at the blanket that covered her nakedness. She sighed resolutely and walked away with Good Shield.

No more words were exchanged between

them and soon they were walking toward the center of the village as people came from their lodges, staring disbelievingly.

Soon the people of the village were standing around Good Shield and Gentle Heart, silent, their eyes filled with questions.

Good Shield stood stiffly beside Gentle Heart, but just as he reached out to grab the blanket away from her, he stopped. He saw Standing Wolf riding into the village at a fast gallop.

He looked past him for Shaylee, his heart skipping a beat when he saw that she wasn't with Standing Wolf. Something must have happened to her.

Yet he didn't leave Gentle Heart's side to go to Standing Wolf. He waited patiently for him to bring his horse to a halt behind the circle of people.

Standing Wolf had seen the crowd even before he had entered the outskirts of the village, and as he came closer, he was able to see Gentle Heart and Good Shield standing amidst them, the center of attention.

And now, as Standing Wolf slid out of the saddle and began making his way through the crowd, he saw that Gentle Heart was dressed in only a blanket, her face tear-streaked from crying.

A hush came over the crowd as Standing Wolf stepped up to Gentle Heart and gazed questioningly down at her, his eyes moving slowly over her scantily attired body.

He then turned and questioned Good Shield with his eyes.

In response Good Shield grabbed the tail end of the blanket and gave a yank, leaving Gentle Heart totally nude, the round curve of her belly drawing all eyes.

Gasps of disbelief, some even of horror, came from the crowd. As though they were one entity, the people inched forward, staring at the proof of a woman's betrayal of a husband who could not father children.

Standing Wolf stared disbelievingly at the swell of her stomach, then he spat at her bare feet.

"*Ho!*" Gentle Heart screamed as she folded her arms frantically over her large breasts. "I am with child!"

But she said no more because she didn't want to confess to anyone that a child had never been part of her plan. It was a mistake that had just happened . . . a mistake almost as bad as allying herself with Short Arrow.

She dared everyone with a bold, lifted chin. "Who among you women who are young and vital would not seek ways to fulfill the hungers of the body?" she cried.

"Was it fair that I should lie cold and untouched in my husband's blankets? No! It was not fair! I am a woman with needs!"

"A woman who is desperate enough to break vows and be with another man is a woman who would also kill to be with that man, would she not?" Standing Wolf said, grabbing Gentle Heart's arms away from her breasts, holding them out so that the proof of her pregnancy was even more pronounced. "You have confessed one transgression today, Gentle Heart. Confess the other. Tell us the name of the man who stole my knife and plunged it into the heart of our chief!"

Gentle Heart's lips were pursed tightly together as she glared up at Standing Wolf.

"Is the man's name Short Arrow?" Standing Wolf roared out, his spine stiffening when he saw Gentle Heart's eyes widen.

"Short Arrow?" Good Shield said, drawing Standing Wolf's eyes to him. "Have you discovered some proof that you have not told me about?"

"No, no absolute proof, but it is absolutely true that it was Short Arrow who abducted Shaylee's child," Standing Wolf said dryly. "Shaylee and I found Short Arrow's camp. She pointed him out to me as the one responsible for her son's abduction."

He paused and glared at Gentle Heart again. "And more and more I believe it was Short Arrow who slammed the knife into our chief's body," he said thickly. "He had debts to pay, and I believe his vengeance was achieved." He gazed at the crowd. "And, my people, I believe Short Arrow planned with someone we know very well how he might achieve his vengeance by killing the chief and clearing the way for this woman to go to him."

"Stop!" Gentle Heart cried. "You are wrong. I would never want to be a part of Short Arrow's life! Never! Marriage to Short Arrow was never planned. Nor was the child! It just happened. He, alone, is guilty of . . . of . . ."

She went pale as she realized just how close she'd come to saying too much!

"You need say no more, sorceress," Standing Wolf hissed, realizing that she had just stopped herself from admitting truths that would condemn her forever in the eyes of the Cherokee people. "Is not what she said proof enough that she and Short Arrow are allies in crime? Is not her pregnancy enough to prove her disloyalty to her husband? What say you, people, about this woman?"

"Guilty! Guilty! Banishment! Banishment!" the crowd began crying, waving fists in the air. "Leave, Gentle Heart. Carry shame with you for the rest of your life!"

Standing Wolf smiled smugly, even though he knew that he did not truly have proof enough to hold Gentle Heart for the murder of her husband.

"No!" Gentle Heart cried. "I had nothing to do with my husband's death. It was Short Arrow. He did it to free me and to place guilt on Standing Wolf. I did not ask him to set me free."

Gentle Heart glared at Standing Wolf. She

had so badly wanted to destroy him . . . to punish him for rejecting her. But it was enough now to know about Shaylee's child. Now that Standing Wolf had pointed an accusing finger at Short Arrow, Gentle Heart knew whose child Moon Beam was raising as her own.

It was good to know something that Standing Wolf did not know. Perhaps one day she could use this information to her own benefit.

For now it was enough that Standing Wolf had no idea where the child was, or with whom. That meant that he would not be able to lessen the pain in the heart of the white woman he obviously adored!

"Gentle Heart, you have said that Short Arrow is guilty of killing Chief Bear Sitting Down," Standing Wolf said, puzzled that she had admitted so much. "Yet you say you were not involved. Because you will not confess to the crime, and we have no proof, you are free to go," Standing Wolf said. "It is best that you leave now. You have lost the respect of all who know you in my village. And since there is no absolute proof of your role in your husband's death, you will be punished only by banishment."

He then turned and glared at the sorceress White Wing, who had stepped into view. "There is one among us who still has feelings for Gentle Heart and she will not be allowed to leave with her!" he shouted. "White Wing must stay as Gentle Heart leaves. It is a true punishment, indeed, to separate these two women who took joy in scheming so many evil things together."

Gentle Heart and White Wing exchanged lingering stares.

Neither woman begged for the other.

Gentle Heart spun around on a bare heel and left, the blanket she now clutched around her shoulders her only claim to having been a part of this band of Cherokee.

Tears rolling down her leathery old cheeks, White Wing watched Gentle Heart depart.

Standing Wolf looked into the crowd as they all watched the separation of the two women. "Neither one of these women deserves anyone's pity!" he said, seeing pity in some of the women's eyes as they watched Gentle Heart depart the village.

"White Wing!" he then said, facing her. "Go to your lodge. Stay until you are told you can leave. And do not try to follow Gentle Heart. If you do, you will be stopped and locked away forever in your lodge."

Her eyes glittering, her old jaw set tightly, White Wing turned and walked through the crowd toward her lodge.

Standing Wolf waited until she was inside and her door was closed, then motioned with his hands for his people to gather more closely around him.

He then went into more detail about Short Arrow, and how Shaylee was even now watching him until Standing Wolf returned with many warriors.

He then chose the warriors who would ride with him.

Wind Spirit came among them. He gave each warrior a small root that, through a ritual, had been given the power to confer invulnerability on those who might enter into battle.

Each warrior chewed some of the root, then spit its juice on his hands and rubbed it on his body; these actions were meant to make the enemy's bullets and arrows slide off like drops of water.

Shouting war chants, Standing Wolf, Good Shield, and many warriors rode from the village.

Chapter Twenty-six

Dreams, visions,
Tease and play,
Confusion's game
On display.

The outlaw friends continued to sit and talk after their meal, resting around the fire and telling jokes that sent them into bouts of laughter, while Shaylee waited for Standing Wolf to return with his warriors.

As the moments passed she became more afraid that he might not get there in time, for surely these men would be on their way soon.

Would they attack some other innocent person, or would they return to their hideout? Shaylee wondered. Clearly, this was only a temporary resting place. There had to be a lodge hidden somewhere, where they took things they stole.

She wondered if that was where she would find her son.

If so, who was there caring for him?

Just as she thought of Moses, she was re-minded of her breasts and how they were aching again. As she touched one through her dress, she winced, for the breasts were now not only hurting, they were swollen, tight, and hot.

She closed her eyes and gritted her teeth as the pain worsened.

"I must get cool water on them," she whis-pered to herself. She turned and looked desper-ately around for a creek or any water that might be used to bathe her breasts, to soothe and cool them.

She turned to the men again. She was afraid that if she left for even a few moments, they might decide to leave and she would lose track of them.

The feverish ache suddenly transcended all other concerns. If she could splash water on her breasts, surely they would feel somewhat better, at least for a while.

And if she found her son today and he was able to feed from her breasts, she would be fine again. Her breasts were filled with milk, that needed to be released.

But until that was possible, she *must* get them soothed with cool water or she did not think she could bear another moment of the pain.

Sighing, Shaylee gazed for a moment longer at Short Arrow, hating him with every fiber of her being. Then she turned and tiptoed through the forest, her eyes searching for the shine of water.

When she found a small stream that wove, snake-like, beneath the trees, she ran to it and fell to her knees beside it.

Desperately, she pulled the dress over her head, then lowered her hands into the water and filled them with the refreshing liquid.

She sighed with relief as she poured the water from her hands over her breasts and felt a momentary relief from the painful heat.

She repeated this several times until she felt that she must get back to where she could watch the renegades.

"I must hurry," Shaylee whispered, quickly pulling her dress over her head. Just as the dress settled down around her, she heard the snapping of a twig behind her and she knew that she was no longer alone. She sucked in a wild breath of fear.

But then she smiled, thinking that it was surely Standing Wolf. He might have returned with his warriors and found her gone. Expert at tracking, he would have discovered her by the stream in moments.

Relieved that he had finally returned from his village, Shaylee smiled and turned to the man she loved.

Her breath caught in her throat when she saw how wrong she had been.

It was the very man she loathed with every ounce of her being . . . the very man who had altered her life so drastically.

It was Short Arrow, and he had an arrow

notched onto his bow, its sharp point aimed directly at her.

But soon Shaylee knew that this man's reaction to her was something she had not anticipated. His eyes were wild with fright as he stared at her, and he took a step away from her, his hands visibly trembling as he tried to keep the arrow steady.

"You!" Short Arrow gasped out. "How can it be? I know your face. I know the flame of your hair! I even recognize your eyes! You cannot be alive. I killed you with an arrow."

Realizing now that he recognized her, Shaylee found his predicament humorous.

"You are surely bewitched!" Short Arrow said, his eyes moving quickly over Shaylee. "Or . . . are . . . you a spirit person? Someone who is not alive, but who appears to me today to torture me into thinking that I have gone insane?"

She could almost enjoy these moments when Short Arrow was so confused, even thinking that he might have gone insane.

But she realized that she was totally alone with this madman, and she was seized by panic.

"Where did you take my son?" she screamed. "Did you harm my Moses? Please tell me. Where is he? Who is he with?"

Soon realizing that this woman was real enough, Short Arrow's first thought was to kill her again and to do it right this time. He had an idea.

"Come with me," Short Arrow said, motioning with his pointed arrow toward her.

"Where?" Shaylee asked, relieved to know that he wasn't going to kill her right there. That might give Standing Wolf time to get back and save her. "Where are you taking me?"

"You want to see your son?" Short Arrow asked, his eyes dancing as he saw how anxiously she nodded her head.

"Please, please take me to him," Shaylee begged, even as she wondered what he was up to.

Was he going to take her to Moses and then finish them both off so that they would no longer be a bother to him?

Or was he sincere? Perhaps he had tired of the child, and was happy to give him back to his mother.

"*Ho,* I will take you to the child," Short Arrow said, the lie slipping across his lips easily. In truth, he was going to take her to his hideout, tie her up inside the cabin, and then set fire to the place and let the fire finally finish her off. His mistake last time was not to have placed her *inside* the burning house.

Realizing that if she had gotten this close to their hideout, others might penetrate the forest as well and find his cabin. He planned to burn the place and move deeper into the wilderness.

"Thank you," Shaylee said, trying hard to believe that he was being honest with her. "I will forever be grateful if you take me to my son."

Forgetting her aching breasts, or that Standing Wolf might be almost there with his warriors, Shaylee walked with Short Arrow back through the forest until they reached his campsite. She was anxious to get to the hideout to see if her son was there.

When the men saw her, they leapt to their feet and drew their firearms, then slid them back into their holsters when Short Arrow explained who she was, and why she was there.

"I have promised to take her to our hideout, where I will reunite her with her son," Short Arrow said. There was a keen questioning in his friends' eyes, but they knew not to question his reason in the presence of the woman.

Shaylee was very aware of the looks in the men's eyes. Obviously, they were doubtful about what Short Arrow had said. Why?

Did it mean that her child wasn't where Short Arrow said he was?

Or did it mean they could not understand his taking her to their hideout, being kind enough to give her child back to her?

Or, the worst scenario of all, did it mean that Moses was already dead?

Or was it all just a ploy to get her to the cabin?

If so, why? she thought desperately.

She looked guardedly from man to man and saw quiet amusement in the depths of their eyes.

She now knew that everything Short Arrow had said was a lie and that she was being taken to their hideout for some evil purpose.

Perhaps they were going to take turns raping her.

Or perhaps she would not even make it there, but be killed before she got there.

Shaylee looked quickly over her shoulder, desperately wishing that Standing Wolf and his warriors would appear from out of nowhere.

"Do you have a horse?" Short Arrow asked.

She wanted to say no, so they would not be richer by one more horse after they killed her, but she was afraid of being forced to ride with one of the men, so she decided it was best to tell them about her horse.

"Yes, I have a horse," Shaylee said, fighting to keep her courage. She would not show her fear to these madmen.

"Find it!" he shouted at one of his men. "Then bring it to me."

Soon Shaylee was on her horse, her hands tied behind her, as she was led through the forest. A part of her was scared, yet another part of her could not let go of the hope that just possibly she was being taken to her child.

The hope that she held onto was the only thing that made her fear bearable.

And there was Standing Wolf.

She would not give up hope of his finding her.

Chapter Twenty-seven

Clouds, gray skies,
Storms and such,
Omens' and dreams'
Daunting touch.

As Shaylee rode onward through the forest, she kept searching for a break in the trees where she might see a cabin. The timber all around was full of noises — animals rustling about, and far behind her, beaver in the river, thumping the water with their broad tails. That sound echoed through the forest like the popping of a gun.

But all she could see were trees upon trees, the shadows darkening on all sides of her.

She winced when in the distance she heard a growl of thunder in the heavens as though an omen of what was to come.

Had God allowed her to live only to let more misery and heartache into her life?

Was Heaven the only place where she would be reunited with her beloved Moses?

Again she heard the slight rumble of thunder in the distance. She gazed heavenward and tried to see the sky, but the foliage was too thick.

Her gaze was distracted when Short Arrow fell back and rode among his men. As he spoke in a low tone to them, so low that she could not hear him, the men's eyes, as well as Short Arrow's, were on her.

She gathered from this that Short Arrow was sharing his plans for her with the men. It seemed that he was the leader of this pack of renegades.

Swallowing hard, Shaylee looked quickly away from them and focused again on the forest ahead of her. It seemed an eternity since she had been ambushed by Short Arrow. Her behind was already aching almost as much as during the long ride with Standing Wolf.

And again she was aware of her aching breasts. They were even heavier with milk than before, and their feverish heat made her sick to her stomach.

Distressed by it all, she finally hung her head, but fought off the desire to cry. She wanted to appear strong to these fiends, and not only for them, but herself.

Courage.

She needed the courage that Standing Wolf admired in her.

"We are almost there," Short Arrow said as he rode up and sidled his horse closer to hers.

"Then, white woman, you will have your son."
His lips formed a smile. "Does that make you
happy?"

Seeing ridicule in his eyes as he smiled mockingly at her, Shaylee knew that he was toying
with her, and that she had been foolish ever to
believe that this renegade would take her to her
son.

"Have you killed him?" she blurted out, her
anger replacing her need to cry.

"Kill a mere baby?" Short Arrow said, again
mockingly. "Do you think this Cherokee is
heartless enough to kill a baby?"

"Yes, I do believe that you could be capable
of the most heinous crime of all," Shaylee
hissed out. She looked quickly away from him
when the men suddenly broke away from Short
Arrow and Shaylee and rode on ahead of them.

Shaylee watched them ride into a clearing a
short distance away, where a small, precariously
leaning cabin sat in the middle of the cleared
land. If Short Arrow hadn't given her reason to
believe that she wasn't being taken to her son,
she could have become excited by the sight of
the cabin.

Now it only caused a keen apprehension to
sweep through her, for she now felt that she
might find her death, instead of her son, at the
cabin.

But before she died, would she be ravaged by
these madmen? she wondered, a shiver of dread
rushing across her flesh. Had she returned to

earth to be defiled in the worst way by the worst of men?

Her one great hope was Standing Wolf.

Surely he had already been to his village and was on his way back to the spot where he had left her.

She hadn't been able to leave anything for him to follow as she had promised to do.

She only hoped that his skills at tracking would be enough for him to find and rescue her.

Shaylee's eyebrows rose when she saw how quickly the men were taking their belongings from the cabin and roping them to the backs of their steeds, or stuffing them into their saddle-bags.

Numbness grabbed Shaylee as she realized why these men were taking what belonged to them from the cabin.

They had no more use for the hideout.

Shaylee's breath caught in her throat when Short Arrow yanked her from her horse, causing her to fall clumsily on her back on the ground.

"Get up and go to the cabin," Short Arrow said as he loomed tall and threatening over Shaylee.

Fear filled her heart, for it was apparent that the men had finished taking their things from the cabin. They were all on their horses, silently watching Shaylee.

She knew now that she was going to be left

behind, but that seemed too simple for these men who killed so easily.

She was probably going to be shot, or perhaps her throat would be cut with a knife.

She knew they would not leave her there to be found by someone.

Yet she wouldn't beg for mercy. She would accept her fate now, as she had before.

But it was hard for her to understand any of this, especially why God had sent her back to earth, only to be killed again so soon by the same man!

Another rumble of thunder in the distance made Shaylee gaze heavenward. The storm was still far off, yet the thunder made everything that was happening now seem even more ominous.

An omen?

No, she thought not.

It was just another spring storm taking its time getting there, nothing more, nothing less.

Short Arrow grabbed Shaylee's wrist and half dragged her into the cabin, then shoved her onto a rickety wooden chair.

Although she was scared to death, she wouldn't let Short Arrow realize it. She would never beg this creature for anything again. She just held her chin high, tightened her jaw, and gazed into empty space as Short Arrow secured her wrists behind her, and then wound the rope over and over again around her and the back of the chair.

He laughed as he tied her legs to the legs of the chair, and then stood up over her. In his eyes there was a wicked glint, and in his smile a keen mocking.

Shaylee had looked up at him for a brief moment, then again stared straight ahead. She was secretly relieved that he was only tying her to a chair and leaving her in the cabin.

She found it hard to believe, though, that he would leave her there for someone to find and question.

But if he was going to kill her, he wouldn't have tied her to the chair.

Yes, Standing Wolf would soon find her. She would be rescued.

She would then lead Standing Wolf to these villains and she would laugh in Short Arrow's face as Standing Wolf sentenced him to death!

But Shaylee's hopes were dashed when Short Arrow pulled a match from a buckskin pouch at his waist.

The color drained from her face when she realized what he planned to do.

He wasn't going to leave her there to be found alive.

He was going to set fire to the place to be sure she never said another word to anyone!

Still she would not beg or ask for mercy. Whatever her fate would be, would be.

It just made her so sad to realize that her life was going to end this way. She had seen such promise in her tomorrows with Standing Wolf.

Standing Wolf, she thought desperately.

If he was anywhere near, surely he would see the smoke. He would smell it!

Yes, she still had hope.

She . . . would . . . not . . . die!

Her heart pounded as she watched Short Arrow leave.

When the smell of smoke wafted into the opened windows at the sides and the back of the room, she knew that Short Arrow was setting fire to the cabin from all sides.

She could imagine him standing there, gloating, as the cabin became enveloped in flames, knowing that she, the one person who could accuse him of so much, would not be able to tell anyone anything.

Shaylee's breathing grew more rapid as the smoke became thicker inside the cabin. "Moses," she whispered, her voice breaking.

She now feared that she would never see him again; nor would she ever be held by Standing Wolf again, listening to the sweet words he whispered into her ear.

She could not help questioning God in her heart! She could not help feeling betrayed!

Then she became aware again of the thunder in the heavens, but this time it was much closer.

She could hear the cracking of the bolts of lightning and saw their lurid flashes as the heavens became coal black with clouds.

When the men began screaming from fear as

the lightning worsened around them, bouncing on the ground close to them, threatening to strike them, even slicing into trees and toppling them around the men, Shaylee laughed. At least before she died she was getting pleasure in knowing these men were afraid!

And then she became aware of something else. The horses were bolting into the forest.

Shaylee was then aware of silence. The lightning and thunder had stopped, as though a magical wand had been waved.

And miracle of miracles, rain was now pounding the roof of the cabin as it fell in torrents from the heavens!

Soon every flame had been extinguished!

Shaylee was stunned. Now only small puffs of smoke remained of the fire, and the storm had gone as quickly as it had come.

A brilliant sunset now cast its orange glow all around her.

Shaylee could hear robins warbling their evening song in the branches of the trees.

She lurched in her chair when suddenly an eagle perched just outside the door of the cabin on a hitching rail, its dark eyes staring inside, meeting Shaylee's wondering gaze and holding it before taking flight again.

It was as though the majestic bird had come there for a purpose, as though trying to tell her that she would be alright.

She became choked with emotion when she realized who had sent the lightning and thunder and rain, and then the lovely eagle.

She smiled heavenward and said a quiet thank you, then relaxed and waited for Standing Wolf to find her. She was certain now that he would.

She felt guilty at having questioned God.

She said a quiet, sincere apology, then hung her head and drifted off into a peaceful sleep as she continued waiting for the man she loved.

Chapter Twenty-eight

Ruins unbearable,
Frontier's fears,
Seclusions lonely,
Lullaby of tears.
Predestined days,
Suggestions' power,
Unreal fates,
Condemned hour.

Shaylee awakened in a sweat, her dreams tumultuous.

Laughing, Short Arrow had been there aiming his arrow at her.

She had seen her baby through a wall of fire.

She had heard David's voice crying out for her as though from a deep, dark well.

And when she had dreamed of Standing Wolf, the same wall of fire had been between him and Shaylee, the heat too intense for either of them to get through.

And then she had awakened.

Her heart pounding, she looked around and

soon realized where she was, and how she had gotten there.

Short Arrow.

She swallowed back a sob when she saw the blistered walls of the cabin, and recalled that he had brought her here to die a horrible death.

With a pain in her heart, she recalled how she had hoped to find Moses in the cabin, only to realize even before she arrived that she had been duped by one of the most evil men that walked the earth.

Her heart skipped a beat and her breath caught in her throat when she now suddenly realized something else. As she moved her legs and arms, the ropes fell away. Somehow they had come loose. She was free!

Her eyes filled with tears of joy as she rose from the chair, for no one had to tell her how she had been freed. An angel had surely been sent from the heavens to look out for her. She could not see the angel, but she smiled heavenward and whispered a quiet thank you anyhow, then stumbled with weak knees to the door.

She wasn't sure how far she could go. But she must try to find Standing Wolf.

"My horse," she whispered, raking trembling fingers through her long red tresses as she gazed around her. The horse was nowhere in sight.

She trembled as she looked into the dark, ominous shadows of the forest. She remembered how far she had traveled to get to the cabin, and knew that she must backtrack over the same path. She hoped she would meet Standing Wolf before long.

"He's probably blaming himself," she whispered to herself.

Yes, he would surely blame himself when he realized that something had happened to her, for he would think that he should have insisted on her returning with him to the village.

But no matter what he might have said or done, she never would have gone with him. She hoped he realized that and did not carry guilt in his heart. She would reassure him when they were together, that what had happened to her had been of her own making, for it had been Shaylee who had decided to stay behind while Standing Wolf went to his village for help.

In the future, she would not be so hasty to do things her way, but would take the time to weigh decisions in her heart and mind and do things that would not endanger her, or Standing Wolf.

Yes, she had much to learn about living in this wilderness where murderers stalked the shadows.

She forced herself to concentrate on taking one step after another. It seemed to be the hardest thing she had ever done in her entire life, for never had she been so bone tired as now.

And her breasts were still like heavy, heated, painful weights!

She was tempted to sit down and wait for Standing Wolf to find her. But she knew the importance of putting as much space as possible between herself and Short Arrow. Should he decide to go back to the cabin to see if she had died in the flames, he would not rest until he found her and made certain that she was dead.

With this fear prompting her, she stumbled along, stopping only occasionally to lean against a tree for a short rest.

Hunger and thirst soon tormented her. Water seemed the more important of the two, for the smoke from the fire had terribly dried out her throat. She was even having trouble swallowing.

Nevertheless she walked onward, almost frantic now as she searched between the trees for the shine of water. But none was in sight. She couldn't even see the horse's tracks any longer. By looking so hard for water she had strayed from the path made earlier by the horse's hooves. She wasn't sure if she was making progress, or going in circles!

Frustrated, yet still determined, she kept trudging onward. Then through a break in the trees, she saw a stream. Surely she had found a tributary of the White River. If so, she could follow the creek and finally reach the Cherokee village!

Thirst driving her onward, Shaylee broke into a run towards the creek.

And then she stopped abruptly. Her heart soared with relief when she saw Standing Wolf. Her bronze dream was on the other side, his magnificent, muscled steed splashing into the creek.

Standing Wolf's sleek, long black hair blew in

the wind as he rode his horse through the water. Then he saw her. His heart pounded like drumbeats inside his chest as his gaze swept over her. He knew now that she had suffered. She was disheveled. Her face was black with ash. Her beautiful red hair was tangled and hung wildly over her shoulders. He could not get to her quickly enough.

As though in a trance, Shaylee watched the water splashing upon Standing Wolf's bare and beautiful bronze legs, for he wore only a breechclout and moccasins.

Then as his steed reached the other side, pounding the edge of the creek bank, her eyes met Standing Wolf's. It seemed as though they blended together in soul, so much so that she wondered if she was truly experiencing this, or if she might be having a spirit dream.

A crow screamed in the forest, echoing all around. The startling sound confirmed the reality of the moment.

"Standing Wolf!" she cried, holding her hands out to him. Then she fell to the ground, crying exhausted tears.

Standing Wolf brought his horse to a halt beside Shaylee and quickly dismounted. He fell to his knees beside her. He lifted her fully into his arms and cradled her close.

"You found me," Shaylee sobbed out, her voice almost gone now from the dryness. She placed a hand to her throat and coughed.

Sensing what was wrong, Standing Wolf carried her to the creek bank and knelt down beside it. He held her in his arms and with his free hand brought water to her lips until she had quenched her thirst.

She looked past him, to the other side of the creek. "Where are the others?" she asked, still amazed that he had found her when she had strayed so far from the trail.

"After I lost your tracks, I sent my warriors in many different directions," Standing Wolf said, now gently pushing some of the locks of hair back from her eyes. "I chose to come this way, and now I know my decision did not come solely from my own thoughts. They were planted there by the supreme being who brought you to me in the cave."

Shaylee sighed, then closed her eyes. "Yes, and I'm so glad. Standing Wolf, I'm so very, very tried," she murmured. "And . . . and . . . I am in such pain."

"You . . . are . . . in pain?" Standing Wolf choked out. "Where do you hurt? Did someone harm you? How did you get so far from where I left you?"

"Short Arrow . . . he . . . ambushed me," Shaylee said, her voice breaking. "He took me . . ."

She continued until she had told him everything that had happened since they had said their goodbyes. After it was all said, Standing Wolf knew that he had to find Short Arrow for more than one reason. No one wronged his woman twice!

"You say there is pain, yet you said that Short Arrow did you no actual harm," Standing Wolf said, his gaze moving slowly over her, seeing her total disarray but no visible injuries.

"The pain I have is only because I need my baby suckling at my breasts," Shaylee said, wincing when sharp pains again attacked her breasts. "Because my baby cannot suckle the milk from them, they are swollen, hard, and filled with heat. What can I do, Standing Wolf? I . . . hurt . . . so."

He held her close and rocked her in his arms. "I will take you home with me, and our healer will see to your pain and relieve you of it," he said thickly. He gazed into her eyes. "Are you too ill to ride with me on my steed?"

"No, please take me," she said, a sob lodging in her throat. She gazed softly up at him. "Oh, how glad I am that you found me! Standing Wolf, oh, Standing Wolf, thank you, thank you."

"Never feel a need to thank Standing Wolf for anything," he said, holding her in his arms as he stood up and walked toward his horse. "I will always be here for you. You are my woman who will soon be my wife." He stopped and looked with keen love and gentleness into her eyes. "My woman, do you know how I cherish the very nearness of you?"

She smiled and kissed him, then winced with added pain as he lifted her as gently as possible onto his saddle of blankets and then mounted behind her.

After getting her comfortable in his lap, holding her next to his thudding heart as she snuggled against him, he guided his steed into the creek and splashed to the other side, then headed in the direction of his village.

He went over everything that she had said about Short Arrow, then smiled when he thought of the renegade becoming frightened by the bolts of lightning and riding off like the coward he was.

When he thought of how Short Arrow had tied Shaylee inside the cabin and set fire to it, he longed for vengeance.

But all that mattered at this moment was that he had found Shaylee, and he would never allow anything like this to happen to her again. He would guard her with his life.

The one thing that ate at his insides was that Shaylee had not found her son. He now feared she never would, especially since it was Short Arrow who had decided the child's fate. The renegade had proven time and again just how twisted his mind was and that he was capable of anything.

Ho, now that Standing Wolf knew that the renegade was responsible for Chief Bear Sitting Down's death, and had twice almost succeeded in killing Shaylee, Standing Wolf vowed that he would somehow, some day, find Short Arrow and finally put a stop to his madness!

Chapter Twenty-nine

I could follow him
Always and forever,
If he beckoned me,
To know his love
On thick, soft furs.
Ah, passionate ecstasy!

As God pulled the curtain down and the last rays of the sun swept the treetops along the bluffs, Shaylee lay amid thick, soft, warm furs awaiting the healer's arrival.

Bathed and dressed in a loosely flowing robe that gave her aching, hot breasts more freedom beneath it, Shaylee was not in as much misery as earlier. But she still hoped the healer had something that would eliminate the pain altogether. But she doubted it. Her son was the only true remedy, his tiny lips releasing the milk from her breasts.

Smelling beautifully clean of river water, Standing Wolf sat down beside Shaylee on the pallet of furs. Winged Foot lay near the fire on the floor. His eyes closed as he went quickly asleep.

Standing Wolf reached out and drew Shaylee next to him. He gently held her as they awaited the healer's arrival.

"There is another way besides the healer's cure which could relieve you of the pain in your breasts," he said.

"There is?" she murmured, anxious to hear, for she did not want to let Standing Wolf know the doubt she felt about his healer being able to help her. "How, Standing Wolf? What else can be done?"

"There is more than one newborn child in my village," he said, watching her eyes as he made his suggestion. He almost knew her reaction before she said it, yet he felt he should reveal all options to her. He loved her so much, he wanted to do everything he could to help her.

"Yes, I'm sure there are several," Shaylee said, noticing how he was hesitating. "But what —"

He slid a gentle hand over her lips, stopping her question. "One of the babies could suckle at your breast. With the release of the milk, much of the pain would disappear."

Shaylee was taken aback by his suggestion. She could not imagine another child at her breast; it would bring too sharp a reminder that it was not hers.

"No," she blurted out.

She turned her eyes away from him and bit her lower lip at the mere thought of a child other than Moses at her breast. To her it would be the worst misery of all; she could not bear to see another child suckling where her own child's lips should be.

"I couldn't do that," she said. "It might take the pain from my breasts, but it would torment my heart to know that it was not my Moses."

"I understand," Standing Wolf said. He placed a finger beneath her chin and brought her face around so that their eyes could meet and hold. "And I was wrong even to suggest it. I should have known the pain it would cause you to feel another child's lips on your breasts when you do not know the fate of your own."

"He has to be alive," Shaylee said, tears flooding her eyes. "I just know he's alive."

She didn't say that she knew this because God had promised her, for deep inside herself she wondered if Moses *was* alright.

She had never met anyone as heartless and mean as Short Arrow. It was so fitting that he had been banished from the Blue Clan of Cherokee, for surely there was not one bone in his body like them.

These people, who had taken Shaylee in as though she were one of them, were kind and generous, almost to a fault.

Because of their trusting nature, they had often been duped by whites. She was glad, though, that this clan of Cherokee had not yet been displaced by the United States Government. Although the government was pushing on all sides as it gave whites permission to settle in the White River basin, at least the Blue Clan of Cherokee had much of their original land, so much that they had even given some to other clans of Cherokee that had been banished by the government from Georgia.

Now, *those* were the true losers, for she knew that many of those families had been rich landowners whose plantations were large and profitable. They had even owned slaves!

"Tell me about the process that your healer might use on me," Shaylee said. "I've heard white people refer to your healers as 'conjurers.' Some have called them 'medicine men.'"

"That is because Cherokee priests can be both leaders of religious services *and* healers," Standing Wolf said, glad to have something to talk about to pass the time as they awaited the healer's arrival.

He knew she had not rejected his suggestion because she did not want an Indian at her breasts. She was not a prejudiced person.

One day, when they had children, the chances were that their child could be more in his image than hers.

In his mind's eye he could even now see her holding their child with much love and adoration in her eyes as his cinnamon-colored flesh contrasted with the silky white of Shaylee's breast.

Ho, it was an image that made his insides glow with a pleasant warmth, as though their child were already a part of their lives!

"Some Head Priests serve as doctors on war parties. At home some practice healing for every kind of ailment, while others specialize in treating specific illnesses," he said. He smiled at her. "Usually our Beloved Women are treated by priests. When you and I say our vows, *you* will become our people's Beloved Woman."

"I will?" Shaylee asked, her eyes wide. "Even though I am white?"

"The color of the skin does not matter," Standing Wolf said. "You will be my wife. I am my people's chief. My people will accept you as their Beloved Woman as they accept you as my wife."

"I am so touched by how they have accepted me into their lives," Shaylee said, placing a gentle hand on Standing Wolf's cheek. "I'll try hard never to let them down."

"You never shall," Standing Wolf said, glancing through the opened door. When he still didn't see Dancing Star, their clan's healer, he continued, "You mentioned how whites call our healers medicine men, saying our healers and priests practice magic and deception. Those who say those things do not believe our healers can heal anything of significance."

"That is why white people use this derogatory term to define white men who run traveling medicine shows," Shaylee said softly.

"*Ho*, I have heard that said," Standing Wolf said stiffly. "And that is something we Cherokee turn our backs on."

"And with such dignity," Shaylee said, cuddling close as he drew her next to him again.

As they gazed into the soft flames of the fire, Standing Wolf continued to talk, for he knew that he was helping to take her mind off her misery until Dancing Star came and used her medicine on her.

"In Cherokee our healers are called *ku-ni-a-ka-ti* which is a combination derived from *ku-ni,* an arrow, and *a-ka-ti,* which means going along, or following a course," Standing Wolf said. "The title was chosen because the healers follow the course of the arrow in healing the wound made by it."

"In other words, White Swan, the treatment is applied directly to the wound or precisely above the spot where the pain is most intense," he said. "*Ku-ni* is a kind of slim cane that grows on the mountainside. It is heavy and has a hard texture, and since arrows are made of it, they are called by that name."

"Standing Wolf?"

Dancing Star's soft voice drew Shaylee's eyes to the door. Neither she nor Standing Wolf had heard her approach.

Standing Wolf slid gently away from Shaylee, rose, and went to Dancing Star. He took a buckskin bag from her and with a gentle hand on her elbow led her to Shaylee.

"This is Dancing Star, our people's healer," he said. "She has come to help you."

"The healer?" Shaylee said, surprised it was a woman.

"I have come to take your pain away," Dancing Star said, falling to her knees next to Shaylee.

"As a rule, male healers treat only men, and female healers treat only women," Standing Wolf explained. "There are things that happen to each that only a healer of like sex can treat."

He nodded toward Shaylee's breasts. "As in your case," he said softly.

Shaylee's pulse raced as she gave the healer a nervous smile, for she was apprehensive about having a Cherokee healer help her instead of a white doctor.

She quickly brushed those thoughts from her mind, for she felt as though by thinking that, she was no better than those white people who called the Indian doctors charlatans.

She had even heard them referred to as witch doctors, a term she had most definitely not used while discussing Standing Wolf's healers with him. That was a shameful way to describe those who worked to help people in pain.

Dancing Star smiled at Shaylee as she reached a gentle hand to her face, then moved her fingers through Shaylee's long red hair. "The color of flames," she said, in awe of Shaylee's hair. "It is rare to see hair of such color."

"My mother's hair is the same color," Shaylee murmured, glad that the medicine woman was starting off their relationship with small talk instead of jumping right in and doctoring her. She was becoming more relaxed by the minute.

"The sun has blessed both you and your mother," Dancing Star said, settling down beside Shaylee, sitting with her legs crossed. She smoothed her long doeskin robe out around her. Then she nodded at Standing Wolf. "Bring my bag to me. Sit beside me and your woman. Your presence will make her more comfortable as I try to eliminate her pain."

Shaylee was so glad that Standing Wolf had been asked to stay. She smiled at him, and then watched Dancing Star as she began taking things from her bag. The healer was in her early twenties. She had a kind face and intelligent eyes. Her hands were gentle. Her fingers were long and lean, almost fragile. Shaylee felt at ease with her.

"All healers use a combination of action and prayers," Dancing Star said. "The two are inseparable. And *faith* is vital on the part of both healer and patient. You must believe absolutely that your pain can be removed."

Dancing Star reached for one of Shaylee's hands and held it. "Do you believe?" she asked softly.

Shaylee found it remarkable that again her faith was being tested. But she did have a strange sort of calm in the presence of this woman and she *did* feel that Dancing Star could help her.

"Yes, I believe," Shaylee said as Dancing Star's hands reached Shaylee's waist, guiding her down onto her back on the pallet of furs. "I truly believe you will help me."

"Then I shall," Dancing Star said. "I must now lift your gown. To heal the pain in your breasts, I must be able to touch them."

Shaylee could not help it when a splash of color rose into her cheeks. Not many had actually seen her unclothed. Forcing herself to forget being timid, Shaylee lifted the gown up until it lay in folds just past her breasts.

She barely breathed as she waited to see what Dancing Star was going to do next. She had taken several small buckskin pouches from her bag and had laid them at her left side.

Shaylee kept glancing at them, and then at Standing Wolf, and then into the healer's kind eyes.

"Before I came to you tonight I gathered hickory bark from a tree and burned it to coals," Dancing Star said. "I warmed my hands in the same fire that burned the hickory bark. I will now press both of my hands tightly to the location of your pain. While I do this I will pray to the great red spider above to come and take away the redness, swelling and pain."

Trying hard not to question what Dancing Star had chosen to do to heal her, Shaylee gave

Standing Wolf another quick glance.

When he smiled and nodded at her, everything in her relaxed and she closed her eyes and held her arms out as Dancing Star began chanting while pressing her hands against Shaylee's breasts.

The pressure was almost too much for Shaylee to bear, but she knew that oftentimes with healing came more pain.

Shaylee's heart pounded even faster as Dancing Star held her hands against her. She found herself wanting to cry out and tell her to please stop!

But Shaylee recalled Dancing Star saying that Shaylee had to have faith.

It seemed that perhaps this time Shaylee's test of faith might fail her, for she felt no better.

She hurt even more than before Dancing Star had placed her hands on her breasts!

Shaylee's eyes flew open suddenly as she felt Dancing Star lift her hands away from her after the healer had spoken the same prayer four times and was now blowing on her breasts.

When Dancing Star finally stopped, she placed a gentle hand on Shaylee's cheek. "By blowing on your breasts I have transferred the answer I received from the above being," she said. "Now I will do one more thing and you will feel much better soon."

Shaylee wanted to ask Dancing Star what she was going to do next, but again made herself remember the word "faith" and said nothing, only waited.

She watched her take a small pine branch from her bag, then dip the branch into one of the small pouches.

When Dancing Star brought it out again, it was dripping with some liquid.

"This medicine made from hickory bark I will now sprinkle on you," Dancing Star said, holding the dripping branch over Shaylee, shaking the medicine onto her breasts.

Dancing Star closed her eyes and chanted again, praying to the coldest waters to come and cool the fever and ease Shaylee's discomfort.

"Coldest waters, come and carry this woman's heat and pain away!" she cried again and again.

Shaylee could not believe it, but almost immediately she began to feel the heat and pain easing somewhat. She looked with awe at Dancing Star, then smiled and waited as the healer pulled her dress down over her.

"Thank you," Shaylee murmured. "Oh, how can I ever thank you enough? I . . . feel . . . so much better already."

"Tomorrow, when the sun rises beautiful in the sky, all of your pain will be gone," Dancing Star said, gathering her pouches and placing them in her bag.

Dancing Star then lifted the bag and rose to her feet. She placed a gentle hand on Standing

Wolf's shoulder, exchanged smiles with him, then left the cabin and closed the door behind her.

"It's a miracle," Shaylee said, sitting up, feeling so relieved she wanted to shout with glee.

"Dancing Star is a woman of many miracles," Standing Wolf said, taking Shaylee's hands. "I will go now and get food. We shall eat, then sleep. I can almost feel your weariness." He smiled. "And the sooner you go to bed tonight, the sooner you will find yourself well tomorrow."

She sighed. "And what else will tomorrow bring?" she asked, never knowing what to expect since so much in her life had changed.

"Our wedding ceremony," Standing Wolf said, drawing Shaylee's eyes quickly to him.

"Tomorrow?" Shaylee gulped out. Her face and eyes lit up with excitement. "Truly? We will be married tomorrow?"

"If you will still have this Cherokee chief as your husband," Standing Wolf said, enjoying her excitement.

Shaylee flung herself into his arms. "Yes, yes!" she cried. "I want you so much. I want you forever!"

His heart soaring, Standing Wolf held her tenderly.

Chapter Thirty

Seasons, signs,
Ancient times,
Drifting glimpses
Tease the mind.
Voice your meaning,
Share all wisdom,
Catch my dream
In your prism.

The search for Short Arrow and his men was postponed so that everyone could witness their chief taking a wife.

Soon to be Standing Wolf's wife, Shaylee sat outside the village council house with the women on one side of the circle of Cherokee as Standing Wolf sat with his warriors on the other side. Pride and love shone in his eyes as he tried to be attentive to those who talked with him, while all the while his eyes glanced more often than not at Shaylee.

As Shaylee caught his glance, she smiled at him. She found it hard not to look at the man who would soon be her husband. She so badly wanted to sit with him, but knew that sitting apart was required before the marriage ceremony.

But once they were married, they would finally be alone. All the celebrating was done prior to the actual ceremony.

First the warriors had played their favorite game. Called *Chungke,* it was both an athletic and a gambling game. Near the council house fine sand had been strewn across a large square of cleared ground to make a slick playing surface. Only one or two men from each side played at any one time. The game was played with a stone that had scooped-out sides and resembled a large, thick discus, and eight-foot-long throwing poles that tapered at each end. These were religiously maintained and preserved from one generation to another until entirely worn out. They were the property of the village, not the players.

The *Chungke* players had stood side by side about six yards from the end of the playing field. One of them hurled the stone on its edge in as direct a line as he could toward the middle of the other end of the field.

The players then ran forward a few yards and threw their poles at the stone, scoring higher the closer they came to it.

Players had been running and throwing all evening long, wagering as prizes their ornaments and wearing apparel, except for their breechclouts.

Standing Wolf had then feasted with his warrior friends in a dwelling on the left side of the council house, while Shaylee had feasted with the women in a dwelling on its opposite side.

During that feast, Shaylee had been introduced to many new foods. One of them was called "broadswords" which she had enjoyed more than any other she had eaten.

Dancing Star, who was quickly becoming Shaylee's special friend, had explained how the broadswords were prepared so that she could cook this dish for her new husband. To make broadswords, women gathered corn blades when they were green and tied them together by the ends and hung them in the shade to dry. They then made the corn blades limber by dipping them in hot water. Corn balls were then flattened in the palms of their hands and wrapped in the corn blades, tied with thread, and dropped into boiling water to cook.

Dancing Star had said that hickory, oak, or cucumber leaves could be substituted for the corn blades.

Shaylee had also enjoyed a fish soup. Dancing Star had also explained how it was prepared, saying that trout was gutted, strung on a stick, and hung over either an inside or outside fire and turned now and then until it didn't drip anymore. It was then placed in a dry buckskin bag and left on a shelf until needed.

The same sort of soup simmered over the fire

in Standing Wolf's cabin even now, for them to enjoy when they were alone . . . after they made love, Shaylee hoped.

Now, as dancers performed, Shaylee watched, yet her mind kept drifting. Early this morning, before the sun rose, Standing Wolf had left their cabin to prepare himself for the wedding ceremony. Shaylee stayed in the cabin, where several Cherokee women came to prepare her.

Some had worked bear grease into her hair, to make it glossy, then had sprinkled her hair with red and yellow earth.

The rims of her ears had been pierced and strung with metal ornaments.

She now also wore multiple strings of beads around her neck which were made of sea shells and turkey bones, the strings overlapping in such a way that almost her whole chest was covered.

She reached up and touched another necklace that lay amid the beaded ones. It was a special gift from Dancing Star. It was called a Squash Blossom necklace. With twelve turquoise settings, one for each month of the year, the necklace was shaped in a design resembling the flower of the squash plant. Dancing Star had explained its special meaning to Shaylee, that it represented fertility to the Indians. It was said that whoever wore the necklace would bear many healthy children. Shaylee had been touched deeply by the gift, for with all of her heart, she wanted to give Standing Wolf many children. She only hoped that Moses would be there to be her future children's big brother!

Her dress was made of beautiful soft white doeskin and decorated with spun white opossum hair dyed red and yellow. Bear hair had also been used, to obtain a black thread that had been spun together with the dyed oppossum hair.

Shaylee wore no leggings, but wore knee-high moccasins covered with beads the same color as the spun hairs on her dress.

Blood root had been used to make Shaylee's cheeks glow, and her lips looked like sweet rose petals freshly plucked from the wild vines which grew in vast numbers in the forest.

Shaylee gazed past the dancers at Standing Wolf, who did not notice, for he was attentively watching the dancers, among them his friend Good Shield.

Shaylee had recently asked Standing Wolf why Good Shield wasn't married.

Standing Wolf had explained that Good Shield had chosen to live a life of celibacy in order to keep his strength and cunning so that he was able to help the people who had taken him in as a child.

Of Sioux descent, his parents had died in a skirmish with the Chippewa. Standing Wolf's mother had found Good Shield hiding in the brush, emaciated and weak, orphaned at age two.

He had since been raised as Standing Wolf's brother.

Standing Wolf had told Shaylee that no man could ever have been as devoted to a people as Good Shield had been to the Blue Clan of Cherokee. He never seemed to feel that he had done enough to repay their kindness.

Standing Wolf had also told Shaylee that he had encouraged his friend to take a wife. A man of Good Shield's goodness should bear many sons in his likeness.

Thus far Good Shield had not found the woman of his desire.

Shaylee was so glad that Standing Wolf had found his!

She looked over at him and smiled. He was dressed, oh, so handsomely today for their wedding. His wedding attire was doeskin and heavily fringed and beaded. He wore a colorful woven belt with tasseled yarn ties. He also wore arm and wristbands made from a mountain lion skin, to which shells were attached.

His moccasins were adorned with quills, cloth, and beads, and since he was a man of status, a chief, the moccasins had been died a vivid red.

Also because he was a chief, a renowned, revered man, he wore a necklace of mountain-lion skin with the hair left on and with small horn bells attached.

A headband made of otter skin held his long, thick black hair back from his face.

She gazed at him, wanting to be with him so much; Shaylee's patience was beginning to run thin. But she made herself look attentive as she again watched the dancers.

Shaylee knew she should be studying the dance steps, for now that she was one of the Cherokee, soon to be their chief's wife, the Blue Clan of Cherokee's Beloved Woman, she would be expected to dance along with them during upcoming ceremonies.

She had been told that only the most special dance was performed on a chief's wedding day — the "eagle dance," named for the golden eagle, which was prized by the Cherokee. It was the great, sacred bird called "the pretty-feathered eagle." The eagle feathers used for the dance had been preserved from years long past.

Shaylee had been told that the performers of the eagle dance had been chosen from among the most athletic young men. Their bodies were painted and their heads decorated with feathers.

They had arranged themselves in lines of four to six warriors so that they looked like a platoon of soldiers. A long, shrill war whoop was sounded by the dancers, immediately after which they moved forward in quick time. As they danced, they answered in a short chorus to the singing of a person appointed for that purpose, who today was Good Shield.

Shaylee noticed that although the motions of

the dancers' feet were quick, they proceeded at a slow rate by mincing their steps.

They halted frequently, and before setting off again issued a war whoop that was so shrill it stunned Shaylee's ears.

She looked around her and saw that no one else seemed as affected by the loud whooping. Unlike herself, they were all accustomed to it.

Surprising to Shaylee — she had not been told about this part of the dance — the dancers proceeded with their routine as they entered the village council house, where the ceremony would be performed. Once inside, they joined together in a song that was part of the dance as everyone else began filing into the large house.

Standing Wolf came to Shaylee and took her hand. He smiled down at her. "Soon you will be my *a-qua-da-di-i*, my wife," he said, his voice filled with emotion. "I will be your *ei-ye-hi*, husband."

Tears of happiness came to Shaylee's eyes as she gazed up at Standing Wolf. She tried to block out the sadness in her heart at the loss of her son.

Today she would think only of the blessings of having found such a man as Standing Wolf.

She only briefly thought of her parents, with whom she would have liked to share this day, but who were so far away. She wondered if she would ever get to see them again.

They were too poor to travel this far.

And she doubted that she would ever have

the means, herself, to travel to Boston to see them.

But she would wire them as soon as she could to tell them the good news.

She did wonder, though, how they would react when she told them she was married to a Cherokee chief.

They were not prejudiced people, but they might be concerned about how she would live, since they believed that Indians lived in grass huts or tepees, and in poverty.

She would explain that none of this fit the way these people lived.

She hoped that by the time she wired her parents, she could tell them that Moses was with her, and well!

Another cause of sadness was that Standing Wolf's aunt had grown too ill to attend the wedding. When Standing Wolf had said that he would carry her there and place her on a soft pallet of furs, his aunt had persuaded him to go on without her.

When Standing Wolf had mentioned postponing the wedding until she was well, his aunt had scolded him and forbidden him to do it.

Everyone now felt that her days on this earth were numbered. . . .

"Come," Standing Wolf said, squeezing Shaylee's hand reassuringly. "Everyone awaits our arrival in the council house. I have told you what is to be done."

"Yes, I only wish my knees would stop trembling," Shaylee said, laughing nervously.

"Just see my eyes on you and know that I love you forever and ever," he said, framing her face between his hands. "Then you should have no cause to be afraid."

"I'm just so nervous," Shaylee said softly. "I so badly want everyone's approval."

"And you have it," Standing Wolf said, brushing a soft kiss across her lips. He slid an arm around her waist. He slowly walked her toward the open door of the council house, where everyone was quietly awaiting their arrival.

When they reached the door, Shaylee stood alone as Wind Spirit came and escorted Standing Wolf to one end of the open space in the center of the council house. He turned and smiled at Shaylee as another priest came and stood with her at the opposite end.

Standing Wolf, the groom, was supposed to receive from his mother a leg of venison and a blanket, but since his mother was dead, and his aunt was too ill to be there for him, an elderly female cousin did this.

Since Shaylee's mother couldn't be present, Dancing Star came and gave Shaylee an ear of corn and a blanket.

Then Shaylee and Standing Wolf met near the fire in the center of the council house, exchanged the venison and corn, and joined together their blankets to symbolize the mutually supportive functions of the man and the woman in the Cherokee household.

After this was done, and without having said one word between them, they walked together from the council house as everyone silently watched. Alone they went to their cabin and closed the door and the world behind them.

Standing Wolf and Shaylee laid their blankets together on the floor in front of their fireplace where a fire burned on the grate and fish soup simmered over the flames. Close by, Winged Foot lay dozing on a pallet of furs.

"My *u-ne-ga*," Standing Wolf said, drawing Shaylee into his arms. "My *a-ge-ye*."

Then he stepped away from her and bent to a knee, motioning toward two cups that sat on the floor beside the blankets. "Come and drink a special drink with me before we go to our bed," he said, reaching for a deerskin bottle.

"What sort of special drink?" Shaylee asked, trying not to reveal her eagerness to go into their bedroom instead of taking time to drink something.

"It is something for my new bride," Standing Wolf said, his eyes twinkling as she sat down beside him on the blanket.

Shaylee watched him pour an orange-colored liquid into the two mugs, then took one of them when Standing Wolf gave it to her.

"This is persimmon beer that I made during the last persimmon season," he said. His eyes twinkled when he saw her give the brew a questioning gaze. "Drink. Then we will make love."

Seeing that he was insistent, and not wanting

to disappoint him, Shaylee sipped the beer, then took deeper gulps, for it was delicious. It tasted just like her mother's persimmon pies!

"Do you like it?" Standing Wolf said, when he saw her eyes light up.

She lowered the mug and wiped her lips with the back of a hand. "I love it," she murmured. "But why do you call it beer? It doesn't resemble beer in either the taste or smell."

"It is Cherokee beer," he said, taking a sip. Then he set his mug aside. "Our people would not put white man's fire in their bellies."

"I'm glad," Shaylee murmured. "It causes those who drink it to do things they would not normally do."

He took her mug and set it aside, then took her hands gently and brought her to her feet before him. He gently touched her breasts through her dress. "Is the soreness gone?" he asked, his eyes searching hers.

"Yes, yes," she murmured, closing her eyes in ecstasy, her heart pounding as he slowly caressed her breasts.

He slid his hands away, reached down, and gathered the hem of her dress into his hands. Slowly he drew it upward, and then over her head.

He tossed the dress aside, then moved his hands over her breasts, softly kneading them, his thumbs gently tweaking the nipples.

And then, as Shaylee stood breathlessly still, her insides melting, Standing Wolf moved his hands down over her ribs, across the flatness of her belly, and swept a hand between her legs to that moist channel where it seemed her heart-beat was centered. He began a slow caress with his fingers.

While he massaged her, readying her for the passionate moments ahead, he kissed her. As he slid his tongue between her lips, her mouth opened to receive him, and she gave herself over to wild ecstasy and sensual abandonment.

Her body was fluid with fire, her shoulders swaying in her passion. Realizing that his fingers would soon lift her higher than Heaven it-self, and wanting more than that with her husband today, Shaylee managed to find the will to slip away from him.

"Let me undress you," she said. Her voice had a huskiness she had never heard before. But she could hardly control this passion! This joy! The very bliss of being Standing Wolf's wife!

And this was forever! She would have this man as her own until she took her last breath on earth!

His heart pounding hard, his desire of her so keen it was hard to wait, Standing Wolf spread his legs enough for her to bend down and re-move his moccasins, and then his breeches.

He closed his eyes in a wild burst of pleasure when Shaylee enclosed his heat within her fin-gers and slowly moved them over him. She was always thrilled at the way this part of a man could actually grow, as though it had life in itself.

She watched his manhood grow until it was tight, thick and long.

She bent low and flicked her tongue over its tip, then slid her mouth over him and for a moment pleasured him in that way.

But when Standing Wolf found himself nearing that point of no return when he would explode with pure ecstasy, he placed his hands gently on Shaylee's shoulders and eased her away from him.

He yanked off his shirt and tossed it aside, then swept Shaylee up into his arms and carried her to his bed, which he had prepared with thick piles of pelts.

As he spread her beneath him, blanketing her with his body until the naked flesh of her thighs fused with his, his mouth went to hers in a quivering, deep kiss.

Ever so gently he entered her. He moaned with a building pleasure as he pressed endlessly deeper inside her and then began his rhythmic strokes.

Aware of Shaylee's gasps becoming long, soft whimpers, Standing Wolf thrust his tongue into her mouth and flicked it in and out, as her body strained into his, meeting his every thrust with abandon.

Shaylee was almost delirious with sensation. Breathless, she twined her arms around his neck and clung to him, and then could not hold back any longer. She cried out against his mouth as she felt the explosion of rapture claiming her just as he also came to the bursting point. He slid his mouth to the slender column of her neck and groaned his own pleasure as the great shuddering in his loins sent his seed deep into Shaylee's womb.

Afterwards, their bodies subsided in exhaustion together. Then Standing Wolf flipped over and stretched out on his back.

Shaylee turned on her side and lay at peace against him. Neither of them said anything for a moment, and then Standing Wolf turned to her and gently touched her cheek. "Are you hungry?" he asked, his eyes searching hers.

"Not truly," she murmured. She gave him a wicked smile. "But I would like to . . ."

"Make love again?" Standing Wolf said, already feeling the heat rising in his loins at the mere thought of finding ecstasy in her arms again so soon.

"This is our night, isn't it?" she said, smiling softly.

"Yes, White Swan, only ours," Standing Wolf said.

He bent over her and pressed soft kisses across her tummy.

He then moved lower.

As he spread the slight wisps of hair at the juncture of her thighs, he reached for a wet cloth in a wooden basin and washed her clean of their lovemaking.

After dropping the cloth back in the water, he bent down between her legs and his tongue found her throbbing and ready.

The pleasure was so intense, Shaylee bit her lower lip and slowly tossed her head back and forth as he swept his tongue over her in slow caresses.

And just before she found that same ultimate release as before, he rose above her and shoved himself into her.

In two thrusts they again found heaven in one another's arms.

Then Shaylee was the one to roll aside. She closed her eyes and sighed. "I never knew it could be so perfect," she said, her whole body shuddering with ecstasy when once again he caressed her woman's center.

She sucked in wild breaths of bliss, and once again went over the edge into total ecstasy.

She lay there for a moment, her eyes closed, then turned and smiled at him. "I don't know about you, but I don't believe I can eat a thing now," she murmured. She leaned on an elbow and gazed into Standing Wolf's dark, passion-hazed eyes.

"I believe you've worn me out, beautiful, handsome chieftain husband," she said softly. "Would you be offended if I rest awhile, and then perhaps . . ."

"Start all over again?" Standing Wolf said, chuckling. He kissed her, then snuggled her close. "We will sleep together."

"Yes, together," Shaylee whispered, his nearness making her feel so wonderful and complete.

But she could not be as happy as she wanted to be. Deep inside, where the love for her son would always be, she felt sad that he was not with her to complete this perfect evening.

Her life would never feel complete until she had her Moses with her.

As she drifted off to sleep, a tear slid from the corner of her eye.

In her sleep she found herself in the heavens again.

A voice came to her out of the quiet sky. It told her that she had not been told exactly *when* her child would be reunited with her, but to *believe* that Moses was alive and well.

The same wondrous voice, so filled with peace and love, also told Shaylee that her son had his own life to live, his own courage to prove.

"But I feel as though I won't ever see Moses again," Shaylee cried in her dream.

"If you believe, wholly believe, *yes*, you will be with your son again," the voice of God reassured her. "But now I must tell you . . . you will not be with your son any time soon. Again I tell you to have faith and remember that everything does not always happen when you want it to happen. Live your life. Be happy! Take from life what you have been given! Go now, Shaylee. You have a husband. For now *he* is the center of your universe. You are his."

"Shaylee . . . ?"

Standing Wolf's voice, and his hands on her shoulders gently shaking her, awakened Shaylee.

"You were talking in your sleep," Standing Wolf said, drawing Shaylee's eyes quickly to him. "And it seemed as though I might have even heard another voice, but whose?"

Shaylee's eyes widened. "You heard someone besides me?" she asked softly. "Truly? You heard . . . someone . . . else?"

"It was a man's voice," Standing Wolf said. "How can that be?"

Shaylee flung herself into Standing Wolf's arms. "I wasn't dreaming," she cried. "It truly happened! God came to me in my sleep! He comforted me. He also meant for you to hear Him!"

"That was your God?" Standing Wolf asked in awe.

He held her away from him and gazed into her eyes. "My woman, I see such peace in your eyes," he said thickly.

"There is such peace in my heart," Shaylee said. "I now know for certain that I *will* be reunited with Moses. And it doesn't even matter that it might not be any time soon. It is enough to know that he is well and that he will be with me again. For now, my husband, I will concentrate on *you*. You are a gift to me straight from the guiding hands of God."

Standing Wolf drew her into his arms and held her tightly, so glad that she was at peace with herself.

He said his own quiet thank you to the One above.

But the one thing that troubled him was that Short Arrow was still out there, a threat to everyone's happiness. Standing Wolf's warriors had looked far and wide for him, and still the evil, crazed man eluded everyone.

In time, though, he would be found, and he would pay for all the wrongs he had done.

Chapter Thirty-one

My love is majestic,
Sleek and agile,
Proud and tempting,
Wrapped in a fiery
Spirit, bold courage,
Purpose . . . unrelenting.

Shaylee's first day as Standing Wolf's wife had not begun as she'd imagined. She had expected to do her chores in their lodge, perhaps even add some feminine touches to it.

Instead, Standing Wolf had asked her to join him on a shelling expedition. The mussel shells found in the White River were always in demand as raw material for buttons. After learning this, Shaylee was anxious to find many and to be shown how to make buttons herself.

Far downriver from the village, Shaylee was sitting behind Standing Wolf in a small boat called a "sheller." She clung to the sides of the canoe as Standing Wolf rowed them into the center of the river, and then stopped.

The sun was high in the sky and shone its beams into the crystal clear depths of the river, where Shaylee not only saw fat trout resting lazily, but also many shells of all sizes lying on the rocky bottom.

Shaylee looked over at Standing Wolf as he picked up his long-handled net and sank it to the bottom.

After bringing up many mussel shells, he poured them out into the bottom of the canoe.

Shaylee moved to her knees in the canoe. Her eyes bright and wide, she watched Standing Wolf kneel across from her and begin sifting his fingers through the shells, his eyes intense as he studied them. "I would like to take a special shell to my aunt to put shine in her eyes again," he said, his voice breaking. "She seems too ready to die."

"She *does*," Shaylee murmured. "She told me this morning that she has lived this long only because you needed her. She says she is ready to die now in peace and be free of pain because she knows I will be there for you in her place."

She swallowed hard. "I asked Blue Bonnet if she was giving up because in truth, she, might be feeling left out of your life."

"And what did she say?" Standing Wolf asked.

"She said she welcomes the peace that comes with death and she is eager to join her loved ones in the sky . . . that she is so happy that I came along to give her that chance," Shaylee said, her voice breaking.

"The White River holds many mysteries in its depths," Standing Wolf said, quickly changing the subject, which was obviously painful to him. "The river has always been good to us Cherokee. When food is needed and animals are elusive, there are plenty of fish awaiting us here. We give many prayers to this river as a thank you."

He gathered large handfuls of shells and tossed them back into the river. "As for shells, I see none here that pleases me," he said. "We will search further downriver."

He sat down in front of Shaylee and drew his paddle through the water.

Shaylee relaxed her shoulders and enjoyed this special moment alone with her new husband and the wonders of nature all around her. Somewhere overhead in the trees, where the limbs hung down over the water like umbrellas, a woodpecker made its tattoo sounds.

Then elsewhere she heard a mockingbird burst into song, mocking various birds so eloquently.

Somewhere in the denser places of the forest she could hear the yapping of a coyote. A blue-jay's loud squawking soon drowned out every other sound, echoing across the river as though there were two.

Shaylee saw throngs of black-tail deer along the bluff, then looked close to the riverbank where numerous beavers were sliding through the water.

"This is a good place for shells," Standing Wolf said. He stopped and grabbed up his long-handled net.

Shaylee moved to her knees at the side of the canoe and anxiously watched him drag the bottom again. This time he brought up many more shells and dumped them onto the floor of the sheller.

Her eyes were wide and wondering as Standing Wolf moved his fingers through the shells, and then held what Shaylee thought was a perfectly shaped mussel. Even so, he was again disappointed.

He threw all the shells back into the river again and rowed on to another location and sank his net. As he brought up a netful, Shaylee saw that these were larger and finer.

"Search through them for the ones you want for yourself," he said, wanting her to learn how to choose the perfect ones for the buttons she would make for her dresses.

"These shells are more beautiful than those others you found," Shaylee said, running her fingers over the pink smoothness of one which lay in the palm of her hand. She looked at Standing Wolf. "This one will make the most beautiful buttons for my dresses."

He smiled at her ability to accept things as they were and not wish for the impossible. To live the life of a Cherokee, one had to accept less than what whites grew used to.

"*Ho,* the one you hold is especially beautiful, but only because it reflects your face," he said, laughing softly when what he said brought a slight blush to his wife's cheeks. This shyness about her was, ah, so very precious.

Standing Wolf bent over and sorted through the shells.

Shaylee leaned forward and watched as he pried first one and then another open.

Then he stopped.

He brushed everything but one shell from his lap.

He smiled down at what he had discovered, and then smiled at Shaylee.

She gasped when she saw what he had been after. He had found a perfectly rounded cream-colored pearl!

"This is a White River pearl, rare and beautiful," he said, plucking the pearl from its bed of flesh. "It is just one more mystery of our river, and it is the perfect gift for my ailing aunt."

Shaylee opened a palm and sucked in a breath of wonder when Standing Wolf laid the pearl in her hand. "It is so beautiful," she said, studying it. She had never seen anything as lovely.

She smiled at Standing Wolf. "Aunt Blue Bonnet will love it," she said. "I'm so glad you don't want to take it to the trading post and sell it."

"I trade very little at the trading post, and I most certainly would not give them anything as precious as this pearl," Standing Wolf said, his jaw tight. "That would only bring many whites to where I found the pearl. They would ruin the bed of mussels. Then our people would no longer have a means to make their buttons."

"You could even sell your buttons and make a good profit," Shaylee dared to say, although she knew his mistrust of the white traders.

"My people do not need such, as you say, 'profit' from whites," Standing Wolf said, lowering his net into the water and bringing out another large haul of mussel shells. "We are content doing for ourselves."

He turned to her and his eyes were doubtful as he gazed at her. "Will you feel the need to make contact with whites now and then?" he asked, his voice drawn. "Is that why you mention the white man's trading post?"

Shaylee felt the color drain from her face, for she was afraid that she had disappointed Standing Wolf by mentioning the trading post.

"Except for wiring my parents, no," she replied. "I will be more than content to stay among your people. I will learn everything required to make you happy. I already know many ways to make our meals."

She crawled over and placed a gentle hand on his arm. "My wonderful chieftain husband, never doubt how content I am while I am with you and your people," she murmured. "I never want you to regret having chosen me for your wife."

He laid the net aside and drew Shaylee into his arms. "Never would I regret anything about you," he said, brushing soft kisses across her brow.

She clung to the pearl with one hand and twined her other arm around his neck as he brought his lips to hers and gave her a passionate kiss.

Their lips parted quickly when a familiar voice called to them from the riverbank.

Standing Wolf looked and found Good Shield on his horse, waving at him.

Standing Wolf returned the wave, then frowned when Good Shield motioned for him to come nearer. He knew that something had to have happened at the village, for otherwise Good Shield would not have interrupted his private time with his wife.

His heart skipped a beat. His aunt! Had she worsened?

Then something else came to him. Was Good Shield there because he and his warriors had found Short Arrow?

Standing Wolf had sent them out today for one last search. If Short Arrow wasn't found, they were to resume their normal daily activities, but not without sentries posted in various high places to keep watch on his village.

It seemed as though Short Arrow would not rest until he had taken his revenge against Standing Wolf.

"Do you think Short Arrow has been found?" Shaylee asked as she gazed at Good Shield, who seemed intent on telling Standing Wolf something of importance.

She was afraid to think it might be something else that brought Good Shield searching for his chieftain friend. She opened her fingers and gazed at the pearl. It was meant for Blue Bonnet. Would Blue Bonnet never get to see it and hold it?

"*Ho*, the search for Short Arrow may be finally over," Standing Wolf said, taking long, deep strokes with his paddle as he steered his sheller toward shore.

"Is there any way to make Short Arrow tell us where he has taken my son?" Shaylee asked, her voice breaking.

"*Ho*, there are many ways, and when he has been captured and stands before my people, I shall make sure that he pays in the worst way for all of the evil deeds of his life," Standing Wolf said, his eyes narrowing angrily as he gazed over his shoulder at Shaylee.

"I can't imagine you doing anything drastic," she murmured.

"Not drastic," Standing Wolf said. "Just necessary."

He jumped from the canoe and dragged it onto the shore.

He then lifted Shaylee from the sheller and carried her to higher ground, where he stood her amid thick, tall grass.

"Why have you come?" Standing Wolf asked, going to Good Shield and placing a hand on his bare shoulder. "Have you found Short Arrow? Does he wait even now for my return so that I can hand out punishment to him?"

"We again returned from our search empty-handed," Good Shield said, keen disappointment in his voice. "We searched since before dawn, again all places not searched before were searched today. He has totally eluded us, Standing Wolf. I say we wait awhile before searching again. He will make a wrong move. We will then find him."

Good Shield placed both of his hands on Standing Wolf's shoulders. "My friend, Short Arrow is not the reason I am here," he said thickly. "Standing Wolf, it is your aunt. She has taken her last breath of life."

Shaylee saw Standing Wolf flinch as though he had been shot. She reached over and took his hand when she saw the despair in his eyes. She glanced down at the pearl in her other hand and tears flooded her eyes. Blue Bonnet would still have her pearl. Shaylee would put it in a medicine bag and place it with Blue Bonnet in her grave. She would have it with her forever and ever.

"Let us go home now," Standing Wolf said, sliding an arm around Shaylee's waist. He nodded at Good Shield. "We will meet you there. Come to my lodge, my friend. I need your comforting presence."

Good Shield nodded, then swung himself into his saddle and rode away.

Shaylee walked with Standing Wolf to the canoe. Before they boarded it, he drew her into his arms and held her. "I have lost so many loved ones in my lifetime," he said, his voice breaking. "Wife, I cannot let anything happen to you. If I were to lose you, I would suffocate in my grieving."

She held him tightly to her. It was good to be there for him, to comfort him, after all that he had done for her. It was good to have one another.

But still, there was always that emptiness deep inside Shaylee's heart, left there by the absence of her beloved Moses.

Chapter Thirty-two

A summer day's tide,
Our space in time.
Gone for now,
Where all good memories hide.

The sun was warm and high in the heavens. Only a few puffy clouds flitting across the sky disturbed the beautiful, serene blueness of it. Shaylee was picking corn in the garden behind her house, lost in thoughts of where life had taken her. The years had passed quickly since her marriage to Standing Wolf, but they had been good years. Were it not for the fact that Moses had never been found, she could say these had been the very best years of her life.

She paused after laying another ear of corn in the wicker basket at her side and wiped a bead of sweat from her brow. She smiled at the thought of the two children she and Standing Wolf had been blessed with, a daughter and a son. Their three-year-old daughter, who was more white in her appearance than Cherokee, had been named Lucretia Ann, after Shaylee's mother, whom she missed with every beat of her heart.

Her two-year-old son, who was the exact image of his Cherokee father, had been given the Indian name *Wa-ya*, Wolf.

Yes, she had been three times blessed with children but only two of them were hers to hold and to love. Whenever her thoughts strayed to Moses, she made herself remember God's words . . . that Moses *would* be reunited with her one day. She had learned the true meaning of patience *and* faith.

She turned and gazed past her cabin, to a spot where several small children were playing together in the shade of a locust tree, safely in the center of the village. And they weren't without adult supervision. White Wing sat in the midst of them, her old eyes watching, her wrinkled, thin hands patting one and then another.

Surprisingly, White Wing had changed. She no longer practiced sorcery. Old and stiff with a muscular disease, she spent what time she had left on this earth in the service of others, especially the children.

Trusted now by everyone, she was allowed to sit with the children and talk of Cherokee myths to them.

In fact, she was loved by even those who at one time had loathed the very sight of her.

The children called her "Grandmother."

"Moses, oh, Moses, I wish you were there among the children," Shaylee whispered. "I think you would enjoy sitting with your brother and sister listening to White Wing teaching Cherokee myths."

She wiped a tear from her eye and resumed picking corn. "Sweet son of mine, you would now be six. I wonder if you are happy. I wonder . . ."

Knowing that she was only causing herself more pain by thinking about her son, Shaylee forced herself to concentrate on other things.

She shuddered when she saw worms crawling along the corn stalks.

She slapped at gnats as they teased her by landing on her arms, and sometimes her face.

"You tiny varmints, scat!" she said, her eyes narrowing angrily.

She felt lucky that although there were pests of all kinds eating up the garden products, her green beans had been spared. She had already picked and preserved a good amount of "leather britches."

She smiled as she recalled the first time someone had called green beans by that name. The Cherokee had given them that name because of the way they were preserved and stored. The beans were strung on a string in their hulls and dried that way to preserve them for later use. The string ran through the middle of each bean sideways, giving the beans, when dried, the look of a man's leather breeches.

She was proud of everything in her garden. It reminded her of David's garden on a much smaller scale. Every Cherokee house had its own private garden. Corn was planted in the flattest areas behind the homes, but potatoes were planted on the hillside slopes a short distance from the village.

There were also cabbage plants, melons, and squash in her garden. She smiled when she thought of what she had been taught about the melons and squash . . . that they must not be counted or examined too closely while still growing or they would cease to grow.

Also, she had been warned that no one should step over a melon vine or it would wither before the fruit ripened.

And what brought even a broader smile to Shaylee's face was the myth that "a person who had eaten a mayapple was never to go near the melon vines, for the mayapple plant withered and dried up very quickly, and its proximity to the melons would cause them to do the same thing."

Yes, she loved the innocence of these myths, and everything about the Cherokee people themselves. Hers was a life of contentment and learning, for every day she seemed to learn something new about these people who were so precious to her.

She only wished that all whites could experience what she had been given the opportunity to experience.

If so, the Cherokee would be looked on as equal to whites.

She sighed deeply, for she doubted that would happen in her lifetime, if ever. She only hoped that when her children grew up in this world of prejudice and name-calling, they would not suffer . . . because she knew that without a doubt they would be considered "breeds" by whites.

Lost in thought, Shaylee had not noticed how the cornstalks only a few feet away were trembling and shaking. She stopped, then took a slow step backwards when suddenly a wild boar, with its long, sharp tusks, walked into view between two rows of corn.

Shaylee's heart pounded as she stood there awaiting the boar's next move. For weeks now they had been bothered by boars. The animals came and went, but she had thought that the last time they had been run off they had decided to stay away.

Now she knew how wrong she had been. It was apparent that something kept attracting the wild boars to their village.

She should have brought the small pearl-handled firearm that Standing Wolf had given her.

Afraid that her trembling knees would not support her, Shaylee found it impossible to turn and run. Even if she did, the boar would outrun her. Although it was small and fat, it could move very quickly.

And then suddenly its attention was drawn elsewhere. It turned abruptly and strutted away from her.

What Shaylee saw next made her gasp with disbelief. One of the village pigs had gotten loose. It came up to the boar and sniffed, then turned and allowed it to mount it and mate with it.

Now Shaylee understood.

Pigs had only recently been brought into the village to provide food when winters were too severe for hunting.

Split rail fences had been built to keep the pigs in, but they managed to dig their way out, and now Shaylee understood why they had done that. They apparently enjoyed the company of wild boars!

Now that the boar's attention was no longer on Shaylee, she took the opportunity to flee to safety. She almost fell over the basket of corn as she turned to run, then regained her balance and hurried from the garden. She nearly collided with Standing Wolf as she ran around to the side of the cabin.

Shaken, Shaylee stopped and fought to get her breath. Standing Wolf must have seen what was happening in his garden, for he had his rifle and his eyes were lit with angry fire.

"It's so horrid," Shaylee said, placing a hand to her throat. "We . . . we . . . can't allow the children to see such goings on. Please, Standing Wolf, do something. Please do something before the boar gets a chance to run away."

Seeing how distraught Shaylee was, Standing Wolf leaned his rifle against his leg and took the time to hold her, to calm her.

"I thought it was going to attack me," Shaylee sobbed out, clinging to him. "I'm ashamed to let you know how afraid I was."

"It is not shameful to be afraid," Standing Wolf said, leaning away from her and gently touching her face. "The boar's tusks are sharp. They could —"

"Don't say it," Shaylee said, covering her mouth with a hand to hold back a gasp of horror. "Please just go on and do something about it."

He brushed a kiss across her lips, grabbed his rifle, and ran into the garden, but stopped when he discovered that both the pig and the boar were gone.

Shaylee also saw that they were gone. She went to Standing Wolf. "Since the pig went with the boar, do you think that will keep the boar from coming back?"

"There are many pigs and many boars. No, wife, I do not think that our troubles are over just yet," he said. "I will hunt the boar again. Also I can set traps."

Shaylee paled. "But you abhor traps," she said, her voice drawn. "You don't even own any."

"I have traps," Standing Wolf said, sighing

heavily. "I have those I confiscated from Short Arrow. They are the sort also used by white trappers. Until now I saw them only as a reminder of what greedy men were capable of. Now I can use them myself, but for a much different purpose. I will kill what is a threat to our people, not to take pelts."

"The children," Shaylee gasped out. "Until the boars are stopped, our children are not safe."

"As long as they are watched carefully, they will be safe," Standing Wolf said. "But we must make sure that our young braves who are anxious to learn the art of hunting are warned not to wander into the forest alone."

"Although you have made Wolf a small bow, and have given him blunt arrows, he will not be going into the forest alone for many years to come," Shaylee said, turning to look at the children, who were even closer to White Wing, listening, their eyes wide with curiosity. "And our daughter is such a petite, tiny thing, I doubt she will ever even want to learn to ride a horse, much less be taught to use weapons."

"For her protection she must learn both, but much later," Standing Wolf said, walking with Shaylee toward their front door. He stopped and handed her the rifle. "Take this inside and bring my bow and quiver of arrows. I shall be in the council house where the traps are hidden beneath the floor boards."

"Are you certain you want to do that?"

Shaylee asked, again recalling how he had talked against traps time and again.

"It is the only way," Standing Wolf said, turning to gaze into the forest.

"But what if some other animal should — ?"

He slid a gentle hand over her mouth. "Sometimes loss comes with gain," he said softly. "Should some forest animal stray into the trap before the boar, I shall make certain it does not suffer a slow, painful death, as often happens when whites leave traps for animals. They are known to leave the animals in the traps for weeks at a time, suffering hunger and pain."

"That's so horrible to think about," Shaylee said, shuddering.

"That is why I confiscated as many traps as I could," Standing Wolf said. He nodded toward the council house. "I will be at the council house, but I will stop first at Good Shield's lodge and ask him to join me."

"I'm glad you won't be going out there alone," Shaylee said. "As long as the boars are running wild so close to our homes, no one is safe."

"Their end will come soon," Standing Wolf said. "I will use bait they will not be able to resist."

"What bait?"

"Muskrat."

"Good," Shaylee said, laughing. "They are also a pest I detest."

Laughing good-naturedly, Standing Wolf walked away from Shaylee. She watched him, his long, thick hair bouncing down his muscled bare back. He wore only a breechclout and its flaps were lifted from his legs by the gentle breeze, revealing the muscles of his legs flexing with each step.

She was concerned about his going into the forest, where surely many boars lurked, but she knew that this was the only way. Their children were not the only ones who must be protected. There were many villages, scattered here and there along the White River. In those villages were many innocent children who might be at the mercy of the long, sharp-tusked wild beasts.

She shuddered at the thought that her own son Moses might be out there, perhaps not far away from her village, vulnerable to many different kinds of danger.

At the age of six, wouldn't he be riding horses, learning how to shoot, and wandering where the grasses were green and tall, and where creeks tempted a child to play in them?

She thought of the tadpoles that she had seen more than once in the creeks. She smiled as she recalled the time when Standing Wolf had explained that the children kept tadpoles as pets. She had even gotten some for her children. They were still alive in their jars at their bedsides.

"I wonder if Moses knows about those tadpoles," she whispered, stopping to turn and stare at the river. "I wonder who is teaching him things. Is he being raised as an Indian? Or did the renegade give my child up to a white family?"

She sighed and went inside the cabin. She was becoming restless again about her son, wondering just how much longer she was going to have to wait before they would finally be reunited.

"If ever . . ." she found herself whispering. Doubts were edging in more and more each day around her heart. With doubts came the lack of faith, and if she lost faith, she would lose all hope.

She flicked tears from her eyes and placed Standing Wolf's rifle among his cache of weapons. She started to get his bow and quiver of arrows, then stopped when Winged Foot came to her, his tail wagging.

She bent to a knee before him. "You'd best stay put in the cabin," she said, petting him. "You wouldn't want to be caught in a steel-jawed trap."

She stood up again and gazed at her husband's beautifully carved bow.

"Has someone made a tiny bow for Moses as Standing Wolf made for Wolf?" she whispered, again angry at herself for not being able to control her thoughts. Of late they had come like bursts of gunfire in her brain . . . always about Moses!

"Is that an omen?" she wondered as she took the bow and arrows from the cabin. Could being reminded again and again be an omen of things to come?

Was she about to come face to face with her son again?

She sighed. "Why am I doing this to myself?" she whispered, her voice loud enough to carry to tiny Wolf as he came and grabbed her free hand.

"Who are you talking to, Mommie?" Wolf asked, his eyes shining with intelligence beyond that of an ordinary two-year-old. Everything had come quickly and early for him. He would one day succeed his father in chieftainship and be a powerful, intelligent Cherokee leader.

"Who am I talking to?" Shaylee said, smiling down at Wolf as he walked beside her toward the council house. "Angels, sweetie. Angels."

"I like your stories of angels," Wolf said, giving her a wide grin.

"Me too," Shaylee said, knowing that one day she would share the best of all stories of angels with her children . . . *her* story!

Chapter Thirty-three

Oh, child of mine, where are the years?
Only yesterday we conquered your fears.
One by one I recorded them all,
Into these fond memories, I now recall.

His skin tanned a soft bronze color, his red hair worn long and loose to his waist, and wearing only a breechclout, Moses, who was now called Soaring Eagle, moved swiftly yet stealthily through the tall grass, his hand gripping his tiny new bow, a quiver of tiny arrows strapped to his back.

"Yellow Wing?" Soaring Eagle said as he gazed over at his best friend, Yellow Wing, whose mother Gentle Heart had given him permission to go hunting today with Soaring Eagle. "Everything around us is too quiet. I hear no crickets. I see no grasshoppers. Do you?"

"Our footsteps are not stealthy enough," Yellow Wing said, gazing at his white friend who was now more Indian than white.

He looked at his hair, the color of the setting

sun. He envied his friend such hair, for Yellow Wing's was black, like everyone else's in the Chippewa village.

He knew that Soaring Eagle enjoyed the notice he received by being different until someone called him a "breed," and then, even at age six, he was ready to go to war.

To Soaring Eagle, he was Indian through and through, even the color of his hair. He had told Yellow Wing often how when he looked into the mirror of the river he saw black hair not red.

That always made Yellow Wing smile, for it proved Soaring Eagle's pride in being raised among Yellow Wings's Chippewa brethren.

"My moccasins are as quiet as I can make them," Soaring Eagle said.

The sun felt warm and good on his bare chest.

He proudly wore a beaded headband fashioned of otter that his mother Moon Beam had made for him.

"I wonder where our fathers are," Yellow Wing said. "Why should *we* be fatherless, while all of our friends have fathers to mold themselves after?"

"Fate, my friend, made us fatherless," Soaring Eagle said, sighing. "It is not *our* fault that both died in battle and left our mothers widowed and us fatherless."

"But, Soaring Eagle, that hardly makes sense," Yellow Wing said. "There are no more wars, and I do not believe there were even when we were in our mothers' wombs. There are no scars of warring in our village . . . no scalp poles displaying scalps."

"It is best not to question why or how," Soaring Eagle said. "It always brings up the fact that I am white, which means my *father* was white, and whites are despised by our band of Chippewa."

Caught up in their conversation, the young braves were not aware of something moving through the brush only a few feet away.

Nor did they hear the low grunting sounds as the boar pushed its snout into some leaves and overturned them as it sought food.

"*Ay-uh,* yes, it is best not to talk about it," Yellow Wing said, shrugging. "We are happy as we are, even without fathers, are we not?"

Soaring Eagle nodded; then his eyes widened in fear as a boar with long, sharp tusks ran from behind the brush, its gray eyes looking crazed and bloodshot.

When it saw the children it stopped.

Snorting, it looked from child to child.

"Run, Soaring Eagle!" Yellow Wing cried, yet he was too afraid to move.

"It is best to stand still," Soaring Eagle whispered to his friend, his hand tightly gripping his bow. "If we move, it will attack. If we stand still, it won't see us as a threat and perhaps will go on its way." He swallowed hard. "Yellow Wing, do you see those sharp tusks? Surely they can rip a leg in two."

"See its large teeth?" Yellow Wing whispered back. "Oh, Soaring Eagle, I am so afraid."

"Never admit to being afraid," Soaring Eagle scolded. "Do you want to be laughed at?"

"No one is here but you, and you would never laugh at me, would you?" Yellow Wing said, tears flooding his eyes. "I *am* so afraid. It's going to kill us, Soaring Eagle. Or . . . bite . . . off our heads!"

"I do not think it is going to leave," Soaring Eagle said. "Yellow Wing, start backing up as I back up. If we make enough space between us and the wild pig, perhaps we can turn and make a run for it and get home before the boar catches up with us."

"I wish now for the father who has been denied me," Yellow Wing sobbed.

"So . . . do . . . I," Soaring Eagle said, a sob catching in his throat. "But it is only us, Yellow Wing, and I truly believe that we must start backing away now or soon be attacked, perhaps even killed by this ugly thing with wild eyes and wet snout."

"Now?" Yellow Wing said, trembling with fear. "Do we do it now?"

"*Ay-uh, yes, now,*" Soaring Eagle said, taking a step away from the boar.

His heart pounded as he watched to see what the boar was going to do.

He was relieved that at least for now it stood still.

But the way it kept watching him and Yellow Wing made dread creep up Soaring Eagle's spine. Would the beast attack them?

Just as he feared, the boar lunged forward, and before Soaring Eagle could turn and run, the boar was there, its tusks tearing into his right leg.

Soaring Eagle's screams joined Yellow Wing's frantic cries as they watched the blood oozing from the wound.

Suddenly an arrow flew past Yellow Wing and sank into the side of the boar. Its body lurched to one side, another arrow pierced its head, and it was dead.

Yellow Wing fell to his knees beside Soaring Eagle. He lifted his friend's head onto his lap and held him, tears falling onto Soaring Eagle's pale face.

Yellow Wing looked quickly up as Hanging Dog, a warrior from his village, ran out of the tall brush. His bow was slung across his shoulder as he knelt down and gathered Soaring Eagle into his arms.

"Come!" he cried. "Yellow Wing, come quickly with me. We must get Soaring Eagle to the village!"

Blinded by tears, Yellow Wing followed the warrior, but he was unable to keep up with him.

He kept looking over his shoulder, afraid that at any moment another boar might appear and attack *him*. Boars had been seen frequently near their village.

The parents had warned their children not to stray into the forest. Today Soaring Eagle and Yellow Wing had paid no heed to those warnings.

And surely one of their mothers had noticed and had sent the warrior to look for them.

Yellow Wing felt ashamed at having disobeyed his mother. He knew that he was, in part, responsible for his best friend's injury.

Finally at the village, Hanging Dog carried Soaring Eagle into his mother's wigwam.

Moon Beam's back was to the entranceway as she sat beside her firepit, cutting wild carrots into the stew pot that hung over the fire.

"Moon Beam," Hanging Dog said, drawing her eyes quickly around.

She dropped her knife and carrots on the bulrush mats on the floor and grew faint when she saw Soaring Eagle's leg, where blood still oozed from the wound.

"A boar did this," Yellow Wing said, rushing into the wigwam, panting from his hard run. "We . . . we . . . took our new arrows into the forest to practice."

Moon Beam only half heard what Yellow Wing was saying. All she could hear was her son's harsh breathing. And she could even smell the scent of the boar on her son's body. "Soaring Eagle," she cried, taking him from Hanging Dog's arms. "My son, oh, my son, the wound is so bad! The bleeding is so profuse!"

335

She looked in a panic at Hanging Dog. "What am I to do?" she cried. "Our healer recently died. We have no other!"

She looked past him at the entranceway, wishing her friend Gentle Heart were there to advise her. But Gentle Heart had left earlier to go digging for roots and no one would know where to find her. Years ago the hills were full of herbs. Now they were hard to find. If a woman found a place where there were some, she didn't dare tell anyone else. If she did, there wouldn't be any left when she went back.

Even Moon Beam didn't know where her best friend collected her herbs. All she knew was that Gentle Heart had left the village before dawn, when no one could see or follow her.

"Bird Flying, the Cherokee healer at the village where Standing Wolf is chief, is the one who should see to your son's wound," Hanging Dog said, realizing, though, that Moon Beam would not want to go there. That was her clan's village, where she had resided before her brother Short Arrow had been banished from it. When he had left, so had she, and she had never returned there.

And no one knew she was at the Chippewa village. The Chippewa protected her from her own people, for if her people knew that she resided there, they would come and demand she tell where her brother could be found.

"I cannot go there," Moon Beam cried.

"They would not help me."

"I do not like to think of bringing their people and ours together, either, for any purpose, but for your son's sake, I believe you must," Hanging Dog said. "And remember, pretty one. It was your brother who was banished, not you. This is not the time to think of yourself and how you might be received by your people. It is not even the time to worry about being questioned about Short Arrow. Your son should be your first concern. If going to the Cherokee village of the Blue Clan is what is required to make your son well again, that is all you should consider."

Still clinging to her son, hearing his soft sobs as his head lay limply against her breast, Moon Beam was torn.

Then she stiffened with fear when Soaring Eagle's whole body went limp and he lost consciousness.

She looked anxiously up at Hanging Dog again. "Do you not know of another Chippewa village, or even Cherokee, where I can take my son?" she asked, desperate to take him anywhere but her original home.

"*Ay-uh,* as you yourself know, there are more than one village of our people, *and* yours, in this vicinity, but you also know that they are much farther away than the village of the Blue Clan," Hanging Dog said, his eyes worried as he gazed at the wound. "Time is of the essence here, Moon Beam. Let me take you and your son in my canoe to Standing Wolf's village."

A soft voice spoke up, one filled with desperate fear. "Please go there," Yellow Wing pleaded. "If that is where my friend can be treated so that he will be well again, please take him. If not, he may have had his last hunt with Yellow Wing."

Moon Beam gazed through tears at this small child who spoke with such intelligence, then looked anxiously at Hanging Dog. "*Ay-uh,* I will go with you there," she said. She nodded toward a blanket. "Yellow Wing, get the blanket."

Yellow Wing did as he was told and watched as Moon Beam wrapped Soaring Eagle gently within it.

"I am ready," Moon Beam said, following Hanging Dog from the wigwam.

As she walked away with him toward the river, she looked at Yellow Wing across her shoulder. "Tell your mother what happened and where I have taken Soaring Eagle," she said. "Tell her to pray for my son!"

"I will do that for you," Yellow Wing said, wiping tears from his eyes. "He has to get well! He has to!"

After getting in the canoe and arranging Soaring Eagle on her lap, his eyes closed, his breathing shallow, Moon Beam watched Hanging Dog paddle the canoe out to the middle of the river, then head toward the Cherokee village.

She swallowed hard. She could not help being afraid of her reception at Standing Wolf's village. What if Standing Wolf did try to force her to tell where her brother was? Although she now loathed her brother's evil, twisted ways, she couldn't turn him in to those who would surely kill him for his wickedness.

But, she argued to herself, as Hanging Dog had said, that should be the last thing on her mind. She had to think first and foremost of her son. She had to get him the help he needed or he would die.

And surely no one would hold her accountable for her brother's evil ways.

Then there was the color of her son's skin. She knew that many would want to know all about how she came to have Soaring Eagle.

She saw no other way than to lie as she always had, for she wanted no one to discover the truth about how she had gotten her son. Although Short Arrow had said that the child's true mother was dead, there could be some relative who would take her child from her should they know who his true birth parent was.

Again she would tell anyone who asked about her son that she had been married to a white man and that he was now dead.

She hoped that Standing Wolf had forgotten his animosity toward Short Arrow. She hoped he would not question her about his whereabouts, for she *did* know where his hideout was. They still kept in touch.

But not often. She still loathed her brother's way of life. She had pleaded with him to change. Thus far, he had ignored her.

"*Gee-mah-mah*, mother," Soaring Eagle whispered as he stirred in her arms. "I hurt so, *gee-mah-mah*."

"I know," Moon Beam said, a sob lodging in her throat. "But soon it will all be better. I am taking you to a very wise man who has healed many people."

She felt him go limp again and knew that he had lost consciousness.

She sobbed and rocked him in her arms as she anxiously watched for the first signs of the Cherokee village on the riverbank . . . a village where she had played as a child.

She had not realized until now just how much she had missed her true people!

Chapter Thirty-four

A labor of love, an intense quest,
A desire to instill only the best.
A legacy of immortality I impart to you,
May all your aspirations come true.

Her basket filled to the brim with an assortment of roots, herbs, and delicious berries — blackberries, wild dewberries, and wild strawberries — Gentle Heart walked along the riverbank on her way home to the Chippewa village. Her footsteps weren't hurried, for she had nothing exciting planned for the rest of the day. Her life was filled with nothing but work now.

When she had returned to her true people, with child, and without a husband, she had been shunned. Even her chieftain father had treated her coldly. But it had been a place to live . . . a place to raise her son.

But she could not help resenting this son who was, in part, Short Arrow's. If not for him, she would have been received among her people as a woman of distinction.

Even great warriors would have pursued her!

But as it was, the warriors looked past her as though her beauty was no more than an ant's!

Ay-uh, she *must* find a way to escape this life of boredom and chastisement, especially now, since her father's death. Since his burial she had been shunned as though she were not there, while her son, Yellow Wing, had gained the respect given to the grandson of a revered chief.

Even her father had loved Yellow Wing and doted over him and taught him everything a father should have taught him.

Gentle Heart could not help being jealous of her son: Her father had adored him, yet had shown such disdain toward her, even up to his last breaths of life.

There was one person, though, who treated her kindly. Moon Beam. They were the best of friends, and she was the only reason Gentle Heart had not gone mad from loneliness. If Moon Beam ever abandoned Gentle Heart, she would find a way to escape this life she despised.

And she would leave her son behind, for he would forever be nothing but a thorn in her side!

"Gee-mah-mah!"

Gentle Heart's thoughts were jarred as she heard her son's voice crying her name.

She had not realized that she had gotten so close to the village.

She stopped as Yellow Wing came running down the slope toward the river, his long, jet-black hair flying in the wind behind him, his breechclout flopping on his thighs.

A warning shot through Gentle Heart, for her son was obviously distraught about something. His eyes were wide and she could see that they were blood-shot from crying.

She set her basket down, then fell to her knees just as Yellow Wing came breathlessly and stood before her. She gently gripped his shoulders.

"What is wrong, my son?" she asked, searching his eyes. "What has happened?"

"It is Soaring Eagle!" Yellow Wing said breathlessly. "He . . . he . . . was gored by a boar!"

Gentle Heart felt the color drain from her face. She gripped his shoulders more tightly. "He was what?" she asked anxiously. She knew how Moon Beam adored her adopted white son. If not for him, Moon Beam would be an empty shell of a woman. She had not even sought a new husband. The child, alone, was the center of Moon Beam's universe.

"Gored!" Yellow Wing cried. "We . . . we . . ."

He ducked his head in shame, for he knew that he must tell his mother that he had misbehaved by going into the forest without any adult.

"You what?" Gentle Heart prodded.

Yellow Wing raised his chin and gazed uncertainly at his mother. "We went into the forest with our new bows," he blurted out, wincing when he saw the dismay that came into his mother's eyes.

Normally, he was not the sort of son who disobeyed his mother's instructions. Little did he know that his mother was always watching her son to see if he was growing into the kind of person his father had been. She truly doubted, though, that he would be like Short Arrow, for her chieftain father had taught him that a man's destiny was ruled by his personality and how he chose to use his gifts. Her father had taught the child decency, trust, nobility. . . .

"And because you disobeyed, your friend is now suffering?" Gentle Heart said, her voice accusing.

She looked past him at the village, then again looked into his eyes. "Where is Soaring Eagle?" she asked. "We have no healer at our village. Who is caring for his wound?"

"Hanging Dog is taking Soaring Eagle and Moon Beam in a canoe to the Blue Clan of Cherokee village, where they have a healer who can heal Soaring Eagle's wound," Yellow Wing said. He jumped in alarm when his mother's hands dropped suddenly from his shoulders and she gasped aloud and looked as though she might faint.

"What is wrong, *gee-mah-mah?*" he asked quietly, watching how she trembled as she pushed herself up to stand over him.

He raised his eyebrows as he watched her look suddenly at the river.

Gentle Heart went back and picked up her basket. She reached a hand out for her son. "Come," she said, her voice quivering. "We must go home. I have these roots and herbs to see to."

She felt her son's eyes on her as she walked onward. Of course he had no idea why she was behaving in such a strange way.

Only *she* knew that her best friend, Moon Beam, would be stepping into a lion's den when she arrived at the Cherokee village, for Moon Beam had no idea that her son's true mother resided there, and was the wife of Chief Standing Wolf.

Yes, through the years Gentle Heart had kept this to herself. When Moon Beam began talking about wanting to go and visit her true people, Gentle Heart had been the one to discourage it. As devoted as anyone could be to a best friend, Gentle Heart watched out for Moon Beam's best interests.

She had even discouraged Moon Beam from sending word to her people that she was alive and well. She had made sure that Moon Beam had no contact with any Cherokee, for word could spread to the Blue Clan that Moon Beam had a child . . . and that the child was white.

Wanting to go after Moon Beam, to warn her anyway, Gentle Heart knew that it was too late, for by now Moon Beam had surely arrived at the Cherokee village.

Gentle Heart was not one who prayed to her *A-da-ni-do,* Great Spirit, very often, but today she whispered a prayer that Moon Beam would be spared having to give up the son she loved with all her heart. Gentle Heart did not think that her friend could live with the loss, whereas Gentle Heart found herself dreaming more and more of finding a way to be freed of her duties as a mother. She wanted so much more out of life than . . . a . . . mere child, a child she had never planned to have.

She was most definitely not the mothering type.

Ay-uh, she would soon find a way to relieve herself of such duties!

Chapter Thirty-five

You are an endless source of pride
As you take each new challenge in stride.
You embody an invested part of me,
Reflections of time well spent, I see.

Hanging Dog stayed with the canoe on the beach when they landed at the Cherokee village. Moon Beam's heart raced as she carried her son up a slope of land and then entered the village, where everyone stopped and stared disbelievingly at her.

It had been many moons since they had seen her, but she realized that it was not her they were staring at.

They were gazing in wonder at the blanket-wrapped child that she carried in her arms.

"I need help!" she cried, her eyes searching through the throng of Cherokee. "My *a-tsu-tsu*. My son was attacked by a boar! I have come to seek Bird Flying's help!"

Moon Beam's cries for help brought Standing Wolf quickly from his cabin, as well as

Shaylee, who stayed behind as her husband took the injured child from the woman's arms.

Shaylee studied the woman and knew they had never met.

Shaylee wasn't sure what she should do. Go and offer help? Or wait until Standing Wolf asked for her assistance?

As he disappeared inside the large council house, she decided that he did not need her there. Moments later Bird Flying rushed into the council house along with Wind Spirit.

She knew that the injured child was in good hands. She could resume her task of sewing beautiful shells on a new buckskin dress for her daughter, Lucretia Ann.

As she sat down in her rocking chair beside the fire, she glanced occasionally toward the door. She desperately wanted to go and see how badly wounded the child was. But she didn't want to be in the way. The healer should have as few interruptions as possible.

If it were *her* child, she would want no one getting in the way of the village healer's magic!

She continued with her beadwork, then stopped again when Winged Foot came and sat at her feet. He was gazing up at her strangely, as though he might be trying to communicate something with her.

But when he began wagging his tail and then turned and went to his bed at the far end of the fireplace, Shaylee laughed softly and resumed her beading.

She was so content, she often marveled over it. Her life was sweet and beautiful. Her husband doted on her, sometimes so much she wanted to tell him she didn't need pampering to make her happy. He and her children were her happiness.

When she heard a squeal of laughter, she looked toward the window and smiled. White Wing had gathered the children of the village around her only moments ago. As she grew older, her imagination had become more vivid; even Shaylee loved to sit and hear the old sorceress tell her colorful stories.

Her smile waned, for she could not help wondering who was telling Moses stories. Who was teaching him the values of life? Where was he at this very moment . . . ?

Chapter Thirty-six

Time's face,
Obscure clues,
White velvet,
Shaded hues.

As the child lay on a pallet of furs beside the large lodge fire in the council house, Standing Wolf stared down at the color of his skin, then slid his gaze to his red hair again.

The flame color of the child's hair matched exactly the color of his wife's.

His gaze moved back to the child's skin color, which also matched his wife's.

He then turned questioning eyes to Moon Beam. She had lived apart from his people for so long, no one knew anything about her, especially whether she had married a white man. No one had even known that she made her residence in the Chippewa village.

But one thing that Standing Wolf did know was that she had gone to live with Short Arrow after he had been banished from the tribe.

Probably she had grown tired of being up-rooted along with her brother, so she had chosen to live a more serene life with the Chippewa.

It was hard to understand why she had not chosen to live among her own people. Perhaps she felt too much shame for having allied herself with her brother and his criminal ways.

But Standing Wolf did not know when she had gone to live with the Chippewa. Surely the man who'd fathered this white child had sent her away, or died, or perhaps had allied himself with the Chippewa and lived with them even now.

If so, though, why had he not come today with Moon Beam and the child?

Perhaps one of those surly men who rode with Short Arrow had fathered this child. Was the boy's father an outlaw?

A man of compassion, Standing Wolf looked past all of these questions. He forced himself to look beyond his past ill feelings for her. All that was important now was her child. She had chosen to return to her true people's healer. He would not be denied her.

Standing Wolf quietly watched Bird Flying minister to the boy's leg wound by using a liquid made from the boiled roots of a *sakoni* plant, the plant he had told Shaylee about which was used to protect children from disease.

Seeing that the child, Soaring Eagle, was in

good hands, Standing Wolf turned quietly and left the lodge.

Troubled by his lingering questions, and the fact that the child had so many of his wife's traits, Standing Wolf hurried to his home and knelt beside Shaylee's chair.

"The injured young brave has white skin," he said. "His mother is the sister of Short Arrow."

Shaylee pricked her finger with the needle at the mention of Short Arrow. She could not help it when she was propelled back in time to the day her infant son was whisked from his cradle by Short Arrow. She would never forget watching her son being taken away on Short Arrow's horse. . . .

"How old is the child?" she found herself asking, her fingers trembling as she laid her sewing aside.

She scarcely breathed as she gazed into her husband's jet-black eyes.

Her heart pounded.

The child.

Short Arrow.

Short Arrow's sister.

Could . . . it . . . be?

"I did not ask, but he looks as though he might be a child of six or seven winters," Standing Wolf said.

He gazed down and saw how her fingers were trembling.

He then gazed into her eyes again and saw the shine of tears.

"Standing Wolf, what is the color of this child's hair?" Shaylee asked, her voice breaking, knowing that it *was* possible that Short Arrow had stolen her child to give to his sister!

But why? she despaired.

Why would he give a white child to his Indian sister?

Oh, but surely she was wrong, she argued to herself.

Yet if she wasn't, was her firstborn, her precious son, so near that she could go even now and hold him in her arms?

Was it her son who lay there injured by a boar?

She could hardly wait to hear her husband's response, for if he said that the boy's hair was the same color as hers, she would know the good Lord had finally brought her son back into her life.

Standing Wolf's eyes went to her brilliant red hair, which was being held back from her face by a headband that she herself had beaded.

"His hair is the color of yours," Standing Wolf said softly, moving back as she stumbled to her feet and ran past him.

He waited, then went after her, but not quickly enough, for she was already at the council house.

Chapter Thirty-seven

Spinning life cycles,
Circles and rings,
Omens and dreams;
Uncanny things.

Just before going into the council house, Shaylee stopped and sucked in a wild breath, then clasped her hands together to stop them from trembling. She gazed heavenward. "Is it now?" she whispered. "Will I finally see my son?"

The voice of a child wafting through the open door came to Shaylee like a sweet song, as though it were the voice of God beckoning her inside.

Again she took a deep breath, but this time mainly for courage, for if she was wrong, she would never hope again.

She looked quickly to her left side when a gentle hand slid into hers. She smiled weakly up at Standing Wolf, and could not control the tears that came to her eyes, flooding them.

"Dare I truly believe that this child is Moses?" she asked, flicking the tears from her eyes with her free hand.

"Your answer lies inside," Standing Wolf said, his voice gentle and soothing. "You will not know until you look upon the face of the child."

Shaylee anxiously nodded, then took an unsteady step forward, but again stopped. She gazed up at Standing Wolf. "But, Standing Wolf, he is older," she said, her voice breaking. "He was a baby when I last saw him. Faces change . . ."

"Go. See. A mother would know her son," Standing Wolf encouraged. "You will know yours."

She swallowed hard and nodded anxiously, then turned and listened as the child spoke again, using a language she was not familiar with.

She looked quickly up at Standing Wolf, questioning him again with her eyes.

"The child is speaking in Chippewa," he said, understanding her silent question. "Although white, he has been raised by a Cherokee mother. Yet he learned the Chippewa language because he lived among them."

He paused, then said, "Like Moon Beam, the woman who raised him, he also speaks the white man's language and Cherokee."

Sighing, Shaylee nodded again and took another step further into the large lodge.

She stopped when the child's voice came to her again, saying something that tore at her heart. He had called Moon Beam "mother" in the English language. If he truly was Shaylee's son, oh, how wrong is was that anyone but she should be addressed in such a way.

Standing Wolf squeezed her hand reassuringly. "Go and see," he said, nodding toward the child, who was hidden from Shaylee's sight by Moon Beam kneeling on one side of his pallet of furs, and Bird Flying kneeling on the other side, chanting and performing the magic that would hasten the healing of the child's wound.

Standing Wolf slid an arm around Shaylee's waist and led her onward until Shaylee stood next to Moon Beam. As she gazed down at the child, she gasped. His long flowing hair was the exact same color as hers.

Moon Beam rose slowly to her feet and gazed with concern at Shaylee, and then Standing Wolf. "Why is she here?" she asked in a whisper. "Why is she looking at Soaring Eagle in such a way?"

Shaylee only half heard what Moon Beam said. Her heart was pounding as the child stared up at her, studying her with eyes the same color as hers.

And when he smiled, everything within Shaylee melted, for it was a smile so familiar to her — crooked, just like David had always smiled!

And then she saw something else that made her shoulders sway as lightheadedness swept over her.

The birthmark!

The birthmark in the shape of a butterfly beneath his left ear!

How could any two children have the identical birthmark in the same place?

Oh, Lord, miracle of miracles, this *was* her Moses! There was no question about it.

"Moses?" she said, her voice shaky as she sank to her knees at the side of the pallet. She reached a trembling hand to the child's tanned face. "Son, God has brought you home to your mother."

She so badly wanted to whisk him up into her arms, but too many things stopped her. There was the alarmed look in his eyes and the way he scooted away from her, wincing at the pain in his leg.

And there was the way he reached his arms out for another woman, speaking something to her in Chippewa.

Her heart stung by this rejection, Shaylee fought back tears that scorched her eyes.

"Wife?" Standing Wolf said as he moved next to her on his knees. "It is your son? It is Moses?"

"There is not one ounce of doubt. He is Moses," Shaylee said, her voice breaking. She gave Standing Wolf a pleading look. She was almost frantic from not knowing what to do next.

She should have known that the child would react in such a way. He had been only a baby when he had been whisked away from his cradle and taken on horseback away from her. He had known only this woman's arms who held him even now. He knew only her love. Her voice! Her face!

And his father? Who had been standing in as her son's father? Why wasn't he there even now?

"Moon Beam, you heard my wife," Standing Wolf said, gently touching her shoulder. "You know what she says is true. You must tell her how you got the child. You must then give the child up to her, for she is the true mother. She has loved the child since it sucked the first breath of life into its lungs. She has pined for the child since he was taken from her."

"No!" Moon Beam cried, clinging to Moses. The child's eyes were wild as he gazed across her shoulder at Shaylee. "You are wrong! Short Arrow told me that his mother was dead! I never would have taken a child from a mother! Although I am my brother's sister, I am not like him. I am decent! I care for people! Never would I steal another woman's child!"

Hearing Short Arrow's name brought a quick, seething anger to Shaylee's heart.

She saw him even now leering down at her as he grabbed her baby from his cradle.

She could hear the evil man's laughter as he rode away with the child.

She could even see and smell him as he had bent before her in that cabin at his hideout before going outside and setting fire to it.

But she could also hear his cowardly cries when the lightning bolts had crashed around him before he fled that day, leaving her alone to die an unmerciful death in flames.

"Your brother thought I was dead," Shaylee said, glaring at Moon Beam. "He tried to kill me twice. He failed the first time, so then he tried again. Even now I imagine he believes that my remains lie in ashes."

"No!" Moon Beam sobbed out. "Please tell me that is not so! Please tell me my brother is not *that* cruel!" But now, as Moon Beam recalled the confrontation between herself and her brother that day when he had brought the child to her, she *had* thought that he might have murdered the child's mother.

He had practically confessed to having done it by what he had not said to her when she questioned him about it.

She had taken the child not only because she wanted a child of her own, but also because she knew she was the only one who could take him and raise him, since his true mother had more than likely been murdered.

"Your brother is capable of doing the worst deeds on this earth, the worst of them all . . . stealing my child and giving him to you," Shaylee said, gazing at Moses as he listened intently to every word she said.

She could see his eyes questioning her as he studied her face.

He no longer looked afraid, but stunned.

He now knew that the wrong woman held him in his arms.

He now knew that he had called the wrong woman the most precious of names to all children — "Mother."

Standing Wolf's fingers tightened on Moon Beam's shoulder. "It is best that we talk outside," he said, seeing the confusion in the child's eyes.

"Please do not make me give him up," Moon Beam begged between deep, racking sobs.

"This is not good for the child," Standing Wolf said more tightly. "Come outside, Moon Beam. Let us discuss this as Moses is given time now to understand what he has already heard."

"His . . . name . . . is Soaring Eagle," Moon Beam said, looking slowly from Shaylee to Standing Wolf, then back again at Shaylee. "I gave him a beautiful name. He knows no other."

"His *true* name is *Moses*," Shaylee said, her voice breaking. "I . . . named . . . him *Moses*."

Standing Wolf knelt down beside Shaylee. He held her hand as he gazed into her eyes. "Let us go outside and talk with Moon Beam, and then you can come again and sit beside Moses," he said thickly. "Together we will talk to him. We will see that he understands."

Shaylee nodded, then looked quickly at Bird Flying, whose chants had been silenced by what had been disclosed.

"Bird Flying," she murmured. "Will he be alright? Will the wound heal?"

"It will take time, for the wound is deep, but, *ho*, he will be well, and he will be able to use the leg as well as he did before the attack," he said, watching as Moon Beam gently released her hold on the child and slowly stood up, sobbing.

Bird Flying gazed first at Shaylee and then at Standing Wolf. "What he has to accept about who is his true mother might take longer than the wound's healing," he said. "The heart sometimes takes much time to heal."

He again looked at Moon Beam, then slid slow eyes to Shaylee again. "He has known no other mother than Moon Beam," he said. He reached over and placed a gentle hand on Shaylee's shoulder. "Might he have two mothers now to look after him? Could you share the child? If so, he would be luckier than most children. He would be twice loved."

In her heart, Shaylee instantly rejected Bird Flying's idea. She had been denied her son for far too long! Why should she have to share him now, especially with the woman whose very own brother had caused such havoc in Shaylee's and Moses's lives?

Yet she was so joyful, so thankful that Moses had been led to her, and so grateful that Moon

Beam had given him love and care, she could not find it in herself to out and out deny this woman the child she obviously loved with all her being.

And Shaylee knew that it would be unforgivable to yank the child out of this woman's life. She was all that he had known since he was old enough to know the meaning of the word *mother.*

She would do what seemed best for her son. Yet she still couldn't say the words! She hated even the thought of sharing Moses with anyone except Standing Wolf!

It was eating away at Shaylee that she had not yet been able to wrap her arms around her son and hold him and show him her love, yet she knew, even though it made her heart ache, that she must wait until he was ready to accept who she was. It was enough to have him in her life again. In time, he would learn to love her as a son loves a mother.

Shaylee gazed down at Moses, whose eyes had never left her since he had discovered who she was. She could see much going on behind those eyes and knew that he was trying to sort everything out.

She started to reach for his hand, but had second thoughts. In time, she argued with herself. In time it would all come together and she would never again be denied her child's arms, her child's love, her child's respect!

"Come, wife," Standing Wolf said, reaching

down to take her hand. "Let us go and talk with Moon Beam and then I will come with you and sit beside your son as you tell him about his true family . . . and how much he has been loved even when he was denied to you."

"Yes, I have so much to say to him," Shaylee said, smiling down at Moses. She finally found the courage to reach out and touch his arm. "My dear, dear child, how I have missed you."

She was so glad when he didn't shove her hand away, but instead gave her one of his crooked smiles, which began the healing between them.

She lifted her hand and gently placed it on his birthmark. "A butterfly's kiss," she said, her voice breaking. "The moment I saw the birthmark on the day you were born, I thought of it as a butterfly's kiss."

Afraid that she was going to burst into tears because her joy at being reunited with her son was so overwhelming, and not wanting him to see her crying again, Shaylee rushed to her feet and went outside with Standing Wolf and Moon Beam.

"Come away from the door so the child cannot hear us," Standing Wolf said, walking around to the back of the council house.

Then, frowning, he turned to Moon Beam. "It is time now for you to give me and my wife many answers," he said, his voice tight, his eyes narrowed. "Tell us why Short Arrow brought you the child and why you did not question him further about where he got the baby."

"I . . . I . . . was pregnant with my husband's child when he died. The shock of his death caused me to lose my child," Moon Beam blurted out. "My husband, who was one of the men who rode with Short Arrow, was white." She looked at Shaylee. "I *was* told that you were dead, or I never would have taken the child to raise as mine. And I . . . I . . . have raised him alone. I have not taken a husband. The child was all that I needed in my life. He *is* my life."

Standing Wolf started to tell her that Short Arrow had killed Shaylee, yet stopped just short of saying something that he knew should not be revealed to anyone — that Shaylee had died and then had been given a second chance at life.

Shaylee too, found herself close to revealing a truth that she knew should not be said.

Instead she reached deep inside herself for the compassion that had been tested before, to find the courage to look past how this had all happened, and start anew.

"I believe you," Shaylee murmured. "And it means everything to me that you love him so much. I know that you do, or you would not be so distraught over losing him."

"I feel as though a part of my heart is being ripped out," Moon Beam said, shaking her head slowly back and forth as she lowered her eyes.

She raised her eyes slowly to Standing Wolf. "There is something I must tell you. "I . . . I . . . know where my brother is," she blurted out, now almost hating Short Arrow for having brought her the child and lying to her about the child's mother being dead.

To lose the child now was worse than never having a child at all!

And she knew that Short Arrow was more ruthless now than ever before. To keep himself alive, he was spilling blood all across the countryside as he raided not only white people, but also those of his own skin color.

He had succeeded at eluding not only the Indian warriors who were out for his blood, but also the white sheriffs and the cavalry.

She knew that as long as she kept her brother's whereabouts a secret, allowing him to continue killing and maiming people across the land, she was as guilty as he.

She *must* tell where he was.

If Standing Wolf had known where she was, he would have been at the Chippewa village long ago demanding answers from her.

She sank to her knees, took a stick and drew a map in the dirt, pointing out exactly where her brother's hideout was. She even told Standing Wolf that it was Short Arrow who had tried to frame him by killing Chief Bear Sitting Down.

But she left out one important piece of information — that she also knew Gentle Heart's role in the murder. Gentle Heart was Moon Beam's best friend. She could not tell a truth that would cause the Cherokee people to go for her and condemn her to death for her past sins!

Shaylee was surprised and delighted that Moon Beam was disclosing so much to Standing Wolf. Finally Short Arrow was going to pay for all of his terrible deeds.

"You should have no trouble finding him," Moon Beam said, her voice sounding drained as she stood up and started walking toward the river where the warrior awaited her with the canoe that would return her home.

"Where is she going?" Shaylee asked, turning to look disbelievingly at Moon Beam.

"She has lost much today," Standing Wolf said, glancing at Moon Beam, then at the drawing in the dirt, and then at Moon Beam again. "She has lost a son, a brother, and perhaps her will to live."

Something grabbed at Shaylee's heart. It was a feeling of panic that made her know she couldn't let anything happen to Moon Beam. And not only because Moon Beam had taken such wonderful care of Moses, but because the woman had already suffered too much injustice in her life due to her brother's depravity. She had not asked Short Arrow to steal another woman's child! And once he did, she didn't have to care so tenderly for that child, but she had. She deserved no less than to continue being a part of the child's life.

Even if that meant Shaylee had to share her son.

"Please, Standing Wolf, let's stop her," Shaylee said.

Standing Wolf gave Shaylee a look of wonder, then grabbed her into his arms and gave her a long hug. He ran with her to Moon Beam.

Standing Wolf grabbed Moon Beam by the hand and stopped her.

She turned and looked through misty eyes at him, and then at Shaylee.

"Do not go," Standing Wolf said thickly. "Stay. Be a part of the child's life. Be a part of your people's. You have been gone for too long. You should have never felt as though you could not return."

"I am out of place here," she said, her voice breaking. "I cannot stay."

"You were never sent away," Standing Wolf said, gently framing her face between his hands. "Only your brother was. This has always been your true home. Stay."

"Yes, Moon Beam, please stay," Shaylee said, feeling a peaceful warmth suddenly flooding her senses, and knowing why. God was smiling down at her, blessing her for the compassion she was showing this woman.

"Moon Beam," Shaylee said. "We will share Moses. Can't you see? The child is twice blessed because he has two mothers."

In a state of wonder, Moon Beam gazed at Shaylee, and then looked at Standing Wolf.

"You can truly accept me in our people's lives again, after . . ."

Her voice broke. She was filled with too much emotion to say much else. She was touched deeply by Shaylee's offer, so much so that she wanted to hug her, but she held herself back. Surely the white woman only spoke out of a sense of duty toward her son . . . a child who would be terribly upset if he was suddenly denied the only mother he ever knew.

"You will be accepted by all of our people," Standing Wolf said softly. "You can share the child. It is obvious how well you have cared for him. This is because of a mother's love. Would you deny him this love so suddenly? Do you not know how this would hurt him?"

Moon Beam gazed at Shaylee. "How can *you* be so kind after I have caused you so much grief through the years?" she asked.

"It wasn't you who caused the grief," Shaylee said softly. "It was your brother. It was all Short Arrow's doing."

"Then you do truly want me to stay?" Moon Beam asked anxiously. "You do not resent me?"

"I resent being denied my son these past years," Shaylee said, swallowing hard. "But I cannot resent the woman who cared so deeply for him, especially a woman who never knew the truth of how she came to have him."

"I want nothing more than to stay and be a part of my son's . . . I mean . . . your son's life," Moon Beam said softly. "I thank you with all my heart for that chance. You could have sent me away and asked never to see my face again."

"It is a child's welfare that is at stake here," Shaylee said. "It is because of him that I can so easily ask you to stay and be a part of his life."

"You . . . will . . . share him forever, not only now when he needs me the most?" Moon Beam asked warily. "You will not suddenly order me away after you see that his love for you is secure?"

"My wife is a compassionate, gentle woman," Standing Wolf said. "She is a woman of truth. If she says she will share, that means *i-go-hi-di*, forever."

Moon Beam could not hold herself back any longer. She flung herself into Shaylee's arms. "*A-a-do*, thank you," she sobbed out. "Thank you for not taking Soaring Eagle from me. My heart would never be able to stand his absence. I do love him so. I love him with every beat of my heart."

Knowing that this woman loved Moses so much did worry Shaylee, for she was afraid that perhaps Moses loved this woman as much. And how was Shaylee to know if this woman could be trusted not to try to sway Moses's affections so that he would never love Shaylee as his mother?

Shaylee was, oh, so torn, yet she knew what was expected of her. She must pass another test of compassion . . . this time one that was much harder than the last.

But she knew that she could. It could be no other way.

"Let's go now and sit beside Soaring Eagle," Shaylee murmured, stroking Moon Beam's back lovingly.

She found it so hard not to call her son Moses! But he had not known that name since the day he had been swept from one life into another.

In time, he would understand that name, and so much more.

He would know all that there was to know about his true father.

But he would be raised by a different father . . . Standing Wolf!

"*Ho,* let us go together and I will sit quietly by as you tell Soaring Eagle everything he should know about his true family," Moon Beam said, easing from Shaylee's arms.

"He will never forget you as a mother," Shaylee said, not noticing that her husband was beaming again at this sweet, compassionate side of his wife.

Ho, Standing Wolf knew without a doubt that all was going to be right in the child's life, for Shaylee would do everything to make it so!

Chapter Thirty-eight

Do you know how
To laugh or cry?
To communicate with
Compassionate eyes?
Do you know how
To share with others,
Happiness or sadness,
With gentle gestures?
Caring has dividends
That lie concealed,
For truly I believe,
In giving, we receive.

Shaylee had not left her son's bedside all night and yet she still did not feel exhausted.

Being with him again was so wonderful, she had not even thought to close her eyes and sleep.

After they had talked at length, and she saw that he readily accepted the truth about his parentage, it had been as though someone had lifted a heavy burden from Shaylee's heart.

And she felt so grateful to Moon Beam, for she had raised Soaring Eagle to be a boy of compassion and courage.

Yet she could not help believing that these traits had also been inherited from his true parents, for she had proved both compassionate and courageous in the trials that God and life had put her through.

And her David had been a soft-spoken man of compassion and courage, also.

"Gee-mah-mah?"

Shaylee realized that she had just dozed off as her thoughts drifted. Her son's voice awakened her when she heard the Chippewa word for "mother."

But she was not sure which mother he was addressing. She looked beside her where Moon Beam had sat for a good part of the night, but found her gone.

"Mother, I speak to *you,* the one who brought me into the world, not the one who raised me," Soaring Eagle said, reaching a hand over and taking one of hers. "I have listened to all that you have told me. I am sad that I never knew you through the years."

"But you are with me now," Shaylee said, smiling down at him. "We will make up for lost time."

"It is good that my mother is allowed to stay in this village," Soaring Eagle said. "I have heard her speaking often to Gentle Heart about how she longed to live among her people again.

But because of her brother, she thought she would be shunned forever by the Blue Clan of Cherokee."

"Gentle Heart?" Shaylee gasped out. "She lives in the same Chippewa village as Moon Beam?"

"*Ay-uh,* and also Gentle Heart's son, Yellow Wing, who is my dearest friend," Soaring Eagle said. He tried to rest on his elbow, but the pain in his leg at even a slight movement made him fall back to the bed. "Yellow Wing must be told that I am alright. He . . . he . . . was with me when the boar attacked me."

"I know about Yellow Wing being your best friend, but I did not know that he was Gentle Heart's son," Shaylee said, knowing that even now Yellow Wing should be on his way there to visit with Soaring Eagle, for Good Shield had gone to get him.

But no one had mentioned who his mother was, not even Moon Beam.

"I wish Yellow Wing were here with me," Soaring Eagle said. "He will be so worried about me."

"Your friend will be here soon," Shaylee said, leaning over to brush a kiss across his brow. "Good Shield has gone for him."

"My friend is coming here?" Soaring Eagle said, suddenly beaming. Then his smile faded. "But then he will leave again, will he not?"

"His home is the Chippewa village, not the Cherokee," Shaylee said, her voice drawn.

"I know about his mother's banishment from this village," Soaring Eagle said solemnly.

Then his eyes brightened. In them was a soft, sweet innocence. "Could she be forgiven so that she could return and live here, where Yellow Wing and I could see one another every day, as we have since we were old enough to walk and play?" he asked in a rush of words.

Shaylee did not know how to answer him, for she now realized that her son didn't know the true extent of Yellow Wing's mother's role in Chief Bear Sitting Down's death. Although it had never been proven, everyone knew that she had the same as thrust the knife into his heart herself.

"Wife, Yellow Wing has arrived by canoe," Standing Wolf said as he entered the lodge, saving Shaylee from having to give her son answers he might not want to hear. Sometimes people were forgiven of their crimes, but when one's crime was as hideous as Gentle Heart's, it could never be so.

Standing Wolf knelt down beside Soaring Eagle's pallet of furs. "And how do you feel today, *a-tsu-tsu*, my son?" he asked. He reached a hand to Soaring Eagle's brow. "No fever. That is good. But how is the pain?"

"It is still there, but not as much," Soaring Eagle said, slightly moving his leg, testing to see just how much it would hurt if he moved it. He winced. "I would not dare stand on it."

"You have plenty of time for that," Standing

Wolf said, looking over his shoulder quickly when he heard footsteps behind him.

He stood up and turned. He felt the color drain from his face when he saw Gentle Heart standing with the child, her hand tightly holding his.

Standing Wolf's eyes locked in a silent battle with Gentle Heart's. "You are not welcome here," he growled.

Shaylee stood slowly and stared disbelievingly at Gentle Heart. Her gaze shifted to the young brave at her right side, his eyes anxious as he looked up and silently begged his mother to release his hand so that he could go to his friend.

But she still clutched him tightly, her eyes never leaving Standing Wolf's.

"My son could never come into an enemy's village without his mother," she said venomously. "Although hesitant, I came."

"You knew about the child Short Arrow stole from my wife," Standing Wolf said, his voice tight. "When you walked from this village shamed with banishment, you knew that Shaylee's son had been stolen from her. Being Moon Beam's friend, you must have realized that she had the white child who was Shaylee's son. You are cruel never to have told Moon Beam where the child's mother was. Denying a mother her child is worse even than plotting to murder a chief."

"Moon Beam is my friend," Gentle Heart

said, her eyes filled with spiteful anger. "I would do nothing to take away her happiness, especially after she had accepted the child as her own."

As Gentle Heart stood beneath Standing Wolf's angry, cold stare, she knew that she could not live without achieving the vengeance she had sought earlier.

Yes, she must still find a way to see Standing Wolf suffer as she had suffered over his rejecting her and later banishing her.

Her gaze shifted slowly to Shaylee. Her heart skipped a beat. Yes! That was how it would be done. She would kill Shaylee! Ah, what heartache Standing Wolf would feel! It would be a heartache worse than dying himself!

She again looked into Standing Wolf's eyes, defying him, "Why do you think I would do anything to hurt my friend when the one who would have benefited in the end was already my enemy?

"No," Gentle Heart continued. "I would not have ever told Moon Beam where the child's true mother was."

"Yet you allowed her to bring the child to our village so Bird Flying could care for the child's wound," Standing Wolf said, curling his fingers into tight fists at his sides.

"Had I been at the village, I would have stopped her," Gentle Heart said, her eyes taking on a strange gleam as her plot to kill Shaylee grew in her mind. "But I was away digging roots and gathering herbs. When I heard where she had brought her son, my heart sank. I knew that the child would not be hers for long and that her life would be torn asunder."

"As usual, you are wrong," Standing Wolf said, his lips curling into a mocking smile. "She has come, she knows everything, and she is staying among her true people, as is the child."

"Although everyone now knows that the child belongs to your white wife, you will not force Moon Beam to give the child back to her?" Gentle Heart said, her voice cold as she again gazed at Shaylee, and then at Soaring Eagle, who lay quietly listening to everything that was being said.

"The child now has two mothers to love him," Shaylee said, taking a step closer to Standing Wolf. She slid her hand into his.

Gentle Heart's free hand tightened into a fist at her side as she watched the affection between the man who scorned her and his white wife. Her lips quivered into an evil smile, for only she knew that soon this man would be widowed!

Moon Beam came into the lodge just then and knelt beside Soaring Eagle's bed. "Your friend has come to you," she murmured. She turned and reached a hand out for Yellow Wing. He questioned his mother with silent eyes. She nodded and released his hand.

Yellow Wing ran over and fell to his knees on the pallet opposite where Moon Beam knelt.

"My friend, I did not sleep all night from worrying about you," he said, giving Soaring Eagle a fast hug.

Then he sat down, his eyes wide, as Moon Beam slowly lifted the blanket away from Soaring Eagle's wounded leg.

Shaylee watched Yellow Wing wince as he saw some spots of blood that had soaked through the bandage.

Shaylee saw the child's concern. She went and sat beside him. "He will be alright," she said, taking Yellow Wing's hand and squeezing it reassuringly. "But he will not be hunting with you any time soon, will you, Soaring Eagle?"

"At least not until I know all of those boars are gone from the forest," Soaring Eagle said, laughing softly.

"Tell me everything that has happened since you were brought here," Yellow Wing said, glancing from Shaylee to Moon Beam, catching them smiling at one another.

"It is all good," Soaring Eagle said, reaching his other hand out for Shaylee.

Her heart soared as he twined his fingers through hers. It still seemed so unreal that she had her son with her again. Suddenly those years they were apart were erased from her heart.

And she could hardly wait for him to meet his brother and sister. She had wanted him to get used to her and Standing Wolf first, but soon she would introduce the rest of his family.

A new voice exclaimed Gentle Heart's name.

Shaylee looked quickly at the entranceway and saw White Wing inching her way into the lodge, her old legs just barely carrying her.

When White Wing and Gentle Heart broke into tears as they embraced, everyone in the lodge became quiet.

Then White Wing eased out of Gentle Heart's arms and gazed at Yellow Wing. A sudden proud smile quivered across her thin, old lips. "He is such a handsome young brave," she said, then looked at Gentle Heart again, her eyes anxious. "Are you here with the child to stay?"

Gentle Heart's jaw stiffened. She glanced at Standing Wolf, then Shaylee, then hugged her aunt again. "No, I have only come today to bring my son to be with his friend for a while," she murmured. "Yellow Wing and Soaring Eagle are best friends."

White Wing looked quickly at Standing Wolf. "Does banishment for my niece have to last forever?" she dared to ask. "Do you not see how the two boys love one another? If you deny Gentle Heart, you also deny both children."

"Yellow Wing is welcome here any time he wishes to visit Soaring Eagle," Standing Wolf was quick to say. "He can even stay, if he wishes to. But Gentle Heart? No. She chose her own life road long ago. It no longer leads here. That she was allowed to come today was only because the children needed to be together.

But it can never happen again."

"But you are such a compassionate man," White Wing said, her voice breaking.

"Compassion goes only so far and then it must stop," Standing Wolf said. He went to stand before Gentle Heart. "You know that what you did was unforgivable. Now either decide to allow your son to come and go as he pleases to my village, or take him now and live with your regrets as you have been living since you chose to plot against your chieftain husband."

Gentle Heart held her chin high. "I have only one regret," she hissed. "Knowing you!" She turned and rushed from the lodge.

Standing Wolf turned to White Wing. "White Wing, I have spoken and I will not change my mind," he said tightly. "Now I give you a choice. You may stay with our people, but if you do, never again speak in behalf of your niece. Do you understand?"

White Wing nodded, then embraced Standing Wolf. "And I do understand," she murmured. "I will stay. I am needed here."

"It is good that you will stay, and yes, you are needed," Standing Wolf said, hugging her. "The children of my village have grown to love you and would miss you. As would I."

She hugged him again then turned and left the lodge to talk to Gentle Heart and explain how things must be.

Shaylee put her arms around Standing Wolf.

"I can tell that you did not enjoy sending Gentle Heart away, or denying the old woman a relationship with her," she said, only loud enough for him to hear. "But you were right, Standing Wolf. That woman wronged so many people. I even feel that she is dangerous."

Then she eased herself from Standing Wolf's arms and turned and gazed down at Yellow Wing. "One thing that she has done right is to raise a child who shows deep caring for others," she said softly. "It is clear that Yellow Wing is a wonderful young man."

"I will see to it that when Soaring Eagle is well enough to hunt and ride, he will be with his friend as often as he likes," Standing Wolf said. "Yellow Wing can stay weeks at a time with Soaring Eagle. They will remain as close as blood brothers. The river provides swift travel for those who are anxious to be with one another."

"I am so happy that Moses is with me again," Shaylee sighed, a wonderful contentment spreading through her. She smiled up at her husband. "With *us*."

"White Swan, you must remember that he only knows himself as Soaring Eagle," Standing Wolf softly reminded.

"Yes, I know," Shaylee said, turning to gaze at her Moses, who would be Soaring Eagle to her as soon as she could put the name Moses into the storage place of her heart where other wonderful memories were kept.

"I go tomorrow with many warriors and will not stop until Short Arrow is found and destroyed," Standing Wolf said somberly.

Knowing that her husband would be placing himself in danger dimmed Shaylee's happiness, yet she knew that what he must do would be not only for himself, but for everyone who ever came face to face with that evil man, for no life he touched was ever the same again. There was always sorrow and pain left behind wherever Short Arrow traveled!

Perhaps it would be over soon. Because of Moon Beam, Short Arrow's hideout had been disclosed!

Chapter Thirty-nine

Simple times I love,
Easy moments, known.
Honest feelings felt.
Humble caring, shown.

Knowing that Soaring Eagle had improved greatly, and that Moon Beam was there to care for him, and having left her two smaller children in good hands, Shaylee felt that it was alright to leave the village to follow Standing Wolf and his warriors to Short Arrow's hideout.

Dressed in her loosest buckskin dress, which gave her more freedom while riding a horse, Shaylee rode far enough back from Standing Wolf and his warriors so that her husband would not realize that she was there. Shaylee had been unwilling to wait at the village and have no role in Short Arrow's capture.

She had waited too long already to see him get his comeuppance!

She would never truly be able to accept that she was safe unless she actually saw him taken, for through the years he had managed to elude capture. How could it be any different now?

She had not been with Standing Wolf now for a full day and night. Before war, or possible confrontation with an enemy, the Cherokee warriors had to celebrate a fast day. This consisted of a day and a night that were given over to prayer and fasting. During that time, no warrior would eat or sleep, or be with his woman in any respect.

It had been hard to sleep without Standing Wolf beside her in their bed, especially knowing that he was going to be placing himself in danger.

Shaylee jumped and brought her horse to a quick halt when she heard gunfire up ahead.

She was relieved when she saw that it had nothing to do with Standing Wolf. The gunfire was some distance away from him, but Standing Wolf and his warriors stopped for a moment, then rode onward again.

She followed, but was more cautious this time to watch her surroundings. She now realized just how dangerous it was for her to be out there alone and at the mercy of the madmen who roamed the area, killing and maiming.

She slid a hand to the pistol that lay in her right pocket. Although she was not practiced at shooting firearms, surely she could use one to defend herself. She shuddered at the thought.

Chapter Forty

While silence cries out
Her voices we do not hear.
Instead by choice of soul
Ignore its taunting fear.

Standing Wolf sank his heels harder into his steed's flanks, then wheeled his horse to a stop when he was finally able to see where the gunfire was coming from. A short distance away, to his right, where the trees thinned out, he saw a gun battle in progress between a sheriff's posse and Short Arrow and his companions.

Standing Wolf narrowed his eyes as he tried to keep track of Short Arrow, but the horses were creating dust, sending it flying like brown clouds into the air, blocking his view.

Suddenly the fight stopped and the dust cleared, revealing to Standing Wolf the sheriff, who was dismounting to check on his fallen men.

Standing Wolf smiled when he saw that Short Arrow's men had suffered a much greater loss.

But his smile waned when he discovered that not all of Short Arrow's men were dead.

A slight cloud of dust off to his left told him that at least one of the renegades had escaped. Could it be Short Arrow?

He wheeled his horse to his left and rode off, his men following.

Chapter Forty-one

Last resort's desperate fall,
Destruction's rot,
Dismal recall.

Shaylee had just started to follow Standing Wolf again when he and his men had stopped a second time. The gun battle was still going on, the burst of gunfire making her wince as it wafted through the forest.

Shaylee had just drawn a tight rein and stopped again, but this time she felt as though she should go into hiding since she wasn't sure what to expect of Standing Wolf next. She edged her horse into the denser forest and waited in the shadows.

She tensed and tried to see through the break in the trees when the gunfire suddenly stopped. She wanted to go out into the open to see if Standing Wolf was alright. But she felt too vulnerable now with so much gunplay going on. Her heart pounding, she decided to stay hidden in the trees for a few more moments.

It was now that she saw the foolishness of her having come today. Here she was, a mother of three children, putting herself in danger.

She wondered who had won the gun battle up ahead and if Standing Wolf was still only watching, or joining in the fight?

Should she make herself known to Standing Wolf?

Or would she be distracting him at a critical moment when he might be in danger?

Suddenly Shaylee was aware of horses approaching. The sound of hooves pounding the earth came to her from the depths of the forest.

She became disoriented as the sound echoed around her.

First it seemed to be coming from directly behind her.

Then it seemed to be coming from her left side, then her right.

Panic seized her.

She knew she couldn't just stay there and wait to see if it was her husband approaching her, or those he had been hunting. For the sake of her children she must hurry back home.

Just as she lifted her reins, she knew she was too late. The sounds of horses were upon her like large claps of thunder. She could only hope that it was Standing Wolf, or else she might not live to see another tomorrow.

Her hand trembling, Shaylee yanked out the small pistol that she had taken from Standing Wolf's weapons.

Breathing hard, dizzy with fear, she spun her horse around just as Short Arrow's horse came to a shuddering halt face to face with her. Yet still she heard the pounding of more horses' hooves. She died a slow death inside as she thought of who she would surely see in a matter of moments. Short Arrow's outlaw friends!

Did this mean that Short Arrow had killed Standing Wolf?

Were her husband and his warriors dead at the hand of this vicious, heartless man?

But for the moment, it was only herself and Short Arrow.

As they sat on their steeds glaring at one another, Shaylee held her pistol steady on Short Arrow.

And when he smiled smugly at her, as though he knew she couldn't pull the trigger, she suddenly realized that he was right. Although she had waited for the day to see this man pay for what he had done to her, her son, and the Cherokee people, her finger felt frozen to the trigger. Now she knew she couldn't take this man's life, even though he had torn her life asunder six years ago.

"I hate you so much," she hissed out. "I have wanted you dead for so long!"

"Yet your courage fails you?" Short Arrow taunted, grabbing his pistol from his holster and aiming it at her.

Shaylee screamed and lurched when a

sudden gun blast filled the air.

She thought he had pulled the trigger and that she should be feeling the bullet's fire in her heart.

But instead he cried out with pain as he dropped his pistol, blood oozing from a wound where a bullet had grazed his flesh.

Shaylee looked quickly over her shoulder as Standing Wolf and his men rode up behind her.

She smiled with relief and lowered her pistol as Standing Wolf drew a tight rein beside her.

"Shaylee?" Standing Wolf said, in his eyes a keen puzzlement when he saw the pistol in her hand. "Why . . ."

That was all he got out before someone shouted his name.

He looked quickly around and saw almost in slow motion that Short Arrow was sliding his rifle from his gunboot.

Standing Wolf had foolishly thought that Short Arrow was surrounded by enough warriors not to try anything.

But as though he welcomed death, beckoning it to him as honey lures bees to their sweetness, Short Arrow raised his rifle, then dropped it as his body jerked with two gunshots. He followed the path of the rifle to the ground, where he finally lay with his eyes open in a death trance.

Quick with his firearm, Standing Wolf had sent one of his bullets into Short Arrow's chest. Good Shield rode out into the open with his rifle smoking, proving that he had joined his friend in downing their enemy.

Shaylee was stunned speechless as she looked from Standing Wolf to Good Shield, then stared down at Short Arrow, hoping that he was truly dead and not pretending.

But by the way the blood was seeping from the wounds, and by the way his eyes were locked and still, she knew that he was dead, and felt relief surge through her.

Standing Wolf edged his horse closer to Shaylee's. As their eyes met and held, he took the pistol from her. "Angels do not carry firearms, now do they?" he asked, his lips tugging into a soft smile.

"No, I don't believe so," she said, gladly relinquishing the deadly thing to her husband.

"I need not ask why you are here," Standing Wolf said, sliding his pistol into his saddlebag. "You wanted to share in his comeuppance."

"Yes, but now I know I shouldn't have," Shaylee said, sighing heavily. "I wasn't thinking of our children when I put myself in such danger."

"You were never in any true danger," Standing Wolf said, smiling over at Good Shield as he stopped beside him.

"What do you mean?" Shaylee asked, seeing how Standing Wolf and Good Shield exchanged knowing smiles.

"I knew all along that you were trailing me," Standing Wolf said. "I only allowed it because Good Shield was assigned to ride behind you and keep you safe."

"Truly?" Shaylee said, looking from one to the other, then laughing softly. "I should've known. Sometimes I believe you two have eyes in the back of your heads."

As one of the warriors bent down and hauled Short Arrow's body up from the ground, then placed him across the renegade's horse's back and tied him there, Shaylee went quiet. Her thoughts drifted back to that day when she had briefly looked upon Short Arrow's face. There had been such evil lurking there, especially in his eyes. Now it was finally over. She would never have to think about him again. She was totally free now to enjoy her family and know everyone was safe from Short Arrow.

Shaylee's breath caught in her throat when Standing Wolf wrapped his arm around her waist and swept her onto his lap. "Wife, let us go home," he said, brushing a kiss across her brow. "Our children await us."

"Yes, our children," Shaylee said, snuggling against his chest. "Doesn't that sound wonderful, Standing Wolf? Our . . . children . . . ? And to know that Moses is there, one of them, is so wonderful, I feel as though I might burst from the joy of it."

"Wife, you must remember to call him Soaring Eagle," Standing Wolf reminded softly.

"Yes, I know," Shaylee said. "But to me, inside my heart, he will always be my Moses."

"I understand," he said.

"After we sit awhile with our children at Soaring Eagle's bedside, I want to show you just how much I love you, husband," Shaylee said, her eyes twinkling as she gazed up at him.

"You are speaking of making love?" he said, smiling at her.

"Is there any better way?" she asked, giggling.

His smile waned. He frowned down at her. "But not tonight," he said, his voice drawn.

Shaylee leaned forward. Her eyes wavered. "Why not?" she asked. "Don't you want to make love with me?"

"More than anything," Standing Wolf said, guiding his horse, down a path that led to the river, where he would then follow it to return to his village.

All of his warriors except Good Shield were behind him, following his lead. Good Shield rode at his right side, a noble man of distinction in his own right, a man who understood everything about his best friend, especially why Standing Wolf must leave his wife alone in their bed tonight.

"Wife, when a Cherokee warrior kills a person, touches a dead body, a human bone, or a grave, he is considered unclean for four days," Standing Wolf explained. "The warriors are even required to take an emetic that makes them throw up. Then they bathe and put on clean clothes. They are not permitted to sleep with their wife for three more nights."

"I . . . must . . . sleep alone . . . for four nights?" Shaylee gasped out. She looked into her husband's gorgeous dark eyes. "I'm not sure I can. I have already been kept from you for a full day and night."

"You don't have to sleep alone," Standing Wolf said, smiling. "White Swan, bring our children to our bed. They will keep you company."

"I adore them so much, but I will hunger so much for our nearness," Shaylee murmured.

"It will be a good opportunity for you to bring the three children together in a loving way," Standing Wolf said. "I am speaking, of course, of including Soaring Eagle. He is well enough to be moved from the council house to our bed. He will feel the love of not only you, but also his brothers and sisters. And then when I am able to join you, we will take one more night, together, with the children. After that, the bed will become ours again, alone."

"Do you know just how special you are?" Shaylee said, tears of joy spilling from her eyes. "You are so warm-hearted, compassionate, loving —"

He laughed softly as he placed a gentle hand over her mouth. "Enough, my wife," he said, his eyes gleaming. "You will make this Cherokee chief blush."

Shaylee laughed, then snuggled against him and felt more at peace with herself than ever before in her entire life. But she knew that she still had a major hurdle to overcome — to give Soaring Eagle every reason in the world to be happy about the changes that had occurred in his life.

Thus far he seemed content enough, but there were those moments when she had seen a faraway look in his eyes.

She wondered what he was thinking about.

She was glad that he had been too small, that day when Short Arrow shot her, to have understood it.

At least he was spared such nightmarish memories as that!

"While I am away from you, I will go out and collect the traps that I placed to catch the boars," Standing Wolf said dryly. "After seeing how young ones stray from villages when they are not supposed to, I must make sure none stray from ours to be caught in a steel-jawed trap."

"I'm so glad you are going to do that," Shaylee said, shuddering. "It's a horrible thought to imagine someone getting into one of those things."

She went quiet then as they rode onward toward their village, her mind filled with so many things that made her joyous.

After they reached the village and the Head Priest had blown his shell trumpet to call together their people, Shaylee soon forgot everything except the celebration of Standing Wolf's success.

She watched Standing Wolf and his warriors go off, alone. The dancing had already begun in the center of the village.

Shaylee's two children came and sat with her.

Her heart soared when Soaring Eagle was carried to her and he sat snuggled in a blanket beside her as Yellow Wing sat on his other side, enjoying the celebration.

Before he had left to spend the necessary time away from his family, Standing Wolf had told Moon Beam about her brother's death and where his body had been taken. She was with Short Arrow now, far from the village, where he would be buried alone, and without honors.

Chapter Forty-two

I am truly happy
With my now, this minute.
Its truth, its beauty,
Its many joys.
Its loneliness and sadness
All led me to this,
Its contentment, its peace,
Its lasting happiness.

The days had passed quickly. At peace with herself and her world, her patience and faith having brought answers to her prayers, Shaylee stood with Standing Wolf beside Soaring Eagle's bed.

The moon rippled like spun silk through the window at Soaring Eagle's left side, leaving a soft glow on his face. With him asleep, and curled slightly on his left side, it was easy for Shaylee to see him as that small baby lying in his crib when he slept the same way, so soundly and peacefully . . . so trustingly.

Once his trust had been shattered.

Now?

She would do everything in her power to keep it intact. It had been many weeks now since the boar attack . . . and since Short Arrow's death.

As though God had reached down from the heavens and touched her son's heart, he had welcomed Shaylee into his life as though she had never been gone from him.

She choked down a sob of joy and twined her fingers through Standing Wolf's. She could feel his eyes on her, watching her.

She turned and smiled up at him, then melted inside when he slid an arm around her waist and drew her close to him.

"I'm so happy," she whispered so only he could hear. "Thank you, my love, for making it possible."

He brushed a soft kiss across her brow, and then their eyes were brought back to the bed, where on one side, to Soaring Eagle's left, lay another young brave who did not sleep as soundly. Yellow Wing. As he tossed in his sleep, he seemed to be saying something.

It tore at Shaylee's heart to watch Yellow Wing, for only a few days ago his mother had been buried. Yellow Wing had asked to come and live with the Cherokee so that he could be near Soaring Eagle. Moon Beam had quickly offered him her home.

Now Yellow Wing had a true chance at life, where he was loved. And he would one day be able to get over the loss of his mother.

Some nights he slept in Shaylee's and Standing Wolf's lodge, for he was as close to Soaring Eagle as any brother could be.

But other nights the boys slept in Moon Beam's cabin so she would not feel left out of Soaring Eagle's life.

"*Gee-mah-mah* . . ." Yellow Wing sobbed.

Her heart almost breaking, Shaylee gave Standing Wolf a sorrowful look.

He nodded to her.

She went over to the side of the bed where she could reach Yellow Wing.

Her heart aching for him, she sat down and drew him into her arms.

As he opened his eyes and gazed up at her through tear-streaked eyes, she smiled reassuringly at him.

"You are loved," she murmured. "Oh, so loved. You have Moon Beam. You have us. And you have all of our people who are now yours."

Soaring Eagle stirred awake. Rubbing his eyes with his fists, he sat up, then saw Shaylee with Yellow Wing. Standing Wolf sat beside Soaring Eagle and lifted him onto his lap.

"Soaring Eagle, Yellow Wing had a bad dream," Standing Wolf said, drawing his fingers through Soaring Eagle's long red hair. "Your mother is making him feel better."

The child's grief was easy to understand. Only a few nights after Gentle Heart had left Yellow Wing in the Cherokee village so that her son could be with Soaring Eagle during his recovery, Gentle Heart's body had been found in the forest near Standing Wolf's village.

When Standing Wolf had gathered up all of the traps that had been set to catch boars, he had overlooked one.

Gentle Heart had gotten a foot caught in the trap, at her ankle, and had bled to death.

No one knew why she was there alone, but it had not taken Standing Wolf long to figure it out. She wore a sheathed knife and was on her way to a village where there were two people she hated. He believed she had planned to kill either Standing Wolf or Shaylee, for it had been obvious of their last encounter that she still held much hate in her heart for Standing Wolf. She was surely blinded with jealousy for Shaylee.

One thing was for certain, she had been driven by madness into finally attempting vengeance against the only man she had ever truly wanted.

"*Gee-mah-mah,* I did not tell you a dream that *I* had while I was recovering from my wound," Soaring Eagle said, easing from Standing Wolf's lap. He crawled over and rested on his knees close to Shaylee, facing her.

"Tell me your dream, son," Shaylee murmured. Always when Soaring Eagle called her "mother," her heart sang. She was so thrilled to be with him again.

She had to actually force herself not to touch

and hug him all the time, for she knew he was a proud young brave who did not want to look like a baby who needed mothering.

It was truly enough for her that he was there any time she wanted to look at him, to savor every nuance of his nearness.

Yes, she guarded her emotions well so that she would never embarrass this son who was with her again, and was everything to her.

Something else she had to guard — the feelings of her two other children. She didn't want them to have any reason to be jealous of, or resent, their older brother.

Even tonight, before she had come to Soaring Eagle's room, she had first gone to Lucretia Ann and Wolf and told them each a story before saying her good nights.

Older brother, she thought to herself. She loved the way that sounded whenever her young daughter and son spoke adoringly of Soaring Eagle.

And they did adore him.

They argued over who would sit next to him when they ate.

They watched him as if he were some kind of god as he walked among the new friends he had made at the Cherokee village.

Often she found them actually walking behind him in his shadow, as though they wished to be that much a part of his existence!

Now she focused on what her oldest son was saying. She only wished that his true father could see what a fine boy he had grown up to be. But surely David was looking down from the heavens, proud of his son.

She could not help smiling at times when she thought of her David wondering over this son of his who was now more Indian in his manner than white.

"In my dream I was soaring like an eagle amid beautiful white clouds," Soaring Eagle said, as though seeing it all again in his mind's eye. "I was so at peace with everything. I no longer felt pain. It was as though I had left my pain behind in my bed."

Shaylee's pulse began to race as she recalled her first time in the clouds.

But she had been *dead!*

Oh, Lord, did that mean that her son had . . . died . . . for a moment while lying there in the council house, when everyone had thought he was asleep?

His voice pulled her back to the present and she listened more carefully, believing he had been summoned into the heavens, but surely for only a moment or two, or someone in the council house would have noticed that he had stopped breathing!

"While I was soaring in the clouds, a voice spoke to me," Soaring Eagle said softly. "It was the voice of a man, a voice of gentleness, of kindness. He said that he had beckoned me there for a purpose."

He paused and reached a hand out to

Shaylee, who took it.

She twined her fingers through his and felt the same sort of grace that she had felt while in the presence of God, as though she were there now with Him, being comforted by Him.

"This voice told me that I was my mother's gift from God," Soaring Eagle said, smiling at Shaylee. "*Gee-mah-mah*, He said that you had waited a long time to be reunited with me after I was so wrongly taken from my cradle that day. He said that first you had been tested, and then I, your son, had to have my own test. You passed your test of compassion. I passed my test, that of courage, the day the boar came to me out of the forest. He said that now I could be with you, my true mother, forever. He told me to cherish you, for you had suffered my absence long enough."

Shaylee put her free hand to her mouth and stifled a sob behind it.

She now recalled how God had told her that her son had his own test before him, a test of courage!

After so many years, it had come to pass!

And being the brave young man that her Soaring Eagle was, he had proved that he was worthy of being as blessed as Shaylee!

She felt her husband's arm slide around her waist.

She felt her son's hand in hers.

She knew that this moment was true rapture.

"Mother, I love you so," Soaring Eagle said,

sobbing as he removed his hand from hers and flung himself into her arms.

The room was quiet and serene as Shaylee and Soaring Eagle clung to one another. When he eased from her arms and wiped his eyes, he gazed over at Standing Wolf. "And it is good to have a father," he said, then suddenly flung himself into Standing Wolf's arms.

Shaylee wiped joyous tears from her eyes. Standing Wolf's gaze met hers as he looked over Soaring Eagle's shoulder at her. Never did this man allow anyone to see him cry, for he was a chief.

But tonight?

He let them flow freely down his cheeks, his pride in this moment causing him to beam.

She was so proud for her husband she felt that she might burst.

But she knew that one person might be feeling left out. She put her own feelings aside and turned to Yellow Wing and held her arms out for him.

Yellow Wing came to her so quickly and hugged her so eagerly, he almost caused Shaylee to topple over backward.

She laughed softly and wrapped her arms around the child, but her heart ached for him and the suffering he was going through over the loss of his mother. But she knew from experience that this, too, would pass. She only hoped that he would never realize the sort of woman his mother had been. That would begin a new kind of sorrow in his heart!

She would guard against his ever discovering the truth about his parents, who were the worst sort of human beings who ever walked the earth.

In the end, both had died the death they deserved. Short Arrow had been downed by bullets. And Gentle Heart had died alone, her spirit surely even now moving restlessly from place to place.

Soaring Eagle eased from Standing Wolf's arms. He rested on his knees as he gazed up at him. "*Gee-bah-bah,* both I and Yellow Wing have been thinking about our future," he said, drawing Yellow Wing from Shaylee's arms.

Yellow Wing scooted over and rested on his knees beside Soaring Eagle, his eyes also on Standing Wolf, anxious, for he knew what his friend, his *brother,* was about to say. He clung to every word spoken by his friend, anxious to hear Standing Wolf's reply.

Proud, Shaylee too listened to her son. She was so proud, she had to fight back joyous tears that again burned her eyes. This moment was, oh, so very, very special!

In the other bedroom, where her other two children lay, her daughter was cuddled close to the doll her father had made out of White River red clay that had been hardened in the sun. Shaylee had made clothes for the doll out of quilt scraps.

Her tiny son had gone to sleep looking at a

jar on his bedside table, watching his pet tadpoles darting around in the water, chasing moonbeams reflected in it. Shaylee would never forget that day when she had heard what she had thought were turkeys gobbling, when in truth it was turkey frogs making the racket!

"*Gee-bah-bah,* Yellow Wing and I wish to dedicate ourselves to a life of hunting," Soaring Eagle said, drawing Shaylee's thoughts back to him and just how grown up he now seemed, especially since he was talking about things that would change him forever. He would no longer be a young brave. He would be a warrior!

Chapter Forty-three

Double star,
Blend our dreams,
Souls, spirits . . .
Eternal things.
Make us one,
Laughing, crying,
Joined together
Until all is one.
Let us drift through time
As a single star.
Double star,
Blend our dreams,
Souls, spirits . . .
Eternal things.

Winged Foot came into the room, leapt on the bed, and crept into Soaring Eagle's arms.

"To dedicate one's life to hunting is quite an undertaking," Standing Wolf said, smiling at how his bear dog had taken so quickly to Soaring Eagle. It was as though they had been friends forever. "It takes many years to achieve that goal, and there are many things that a young man must sacrifice during his time of training."

"We understand that," Soaring Eagle said, glancing at Yellow Wing. "Do we not, Yellow Wing?"

"*Ay-uh,* but we do not know everything that is required," Yellow Wing said. "We have not sat down and talked at length with anyone about our decision. We still have some years ahead of us before we can begin our training."

Soaring Eagle turned quick eyes to Standing Wolf and let go of Winged Foot as the dog crawled down and lay at the foot of the bed and soon was fast asleep. "We have wished for this since we knew it was something great that a young brave could achieve," he said. "What held us back from talking about it was . . . was . . . that neither of us had a father to train us."

"Soaring Eagle, it is good that you have accepted me as your father with such trust and enthusiasm," Standing Wolf said, placing a gentle hand on Soaring Eagle's bare shoulder. He looked over at Yellow Wing. "Yellow Wing, I believe you, too, will soon have a father. I have seen Good Shield watching your mother only as a man who is interested in a woman watches her."

He chuckled as he saw excitement enter the child's eyes. "My friend Good Shield has waited a long time for the woman he would want for a wife," he said. "I think in Moon

Beam he sees this woman."

"Oh, Standing Wolf, I am so glad to know this," Shaylee said, her eyes dancing. "Moon Beam talks endlessly of Good Shield. She is in love with him."

"Then I see a wedding in their future," Standing Wolf said, approving of his friend's choice in women, because Moon Beam had proved herself worthy of such a fine man as Good Shield.

He smiled at Yellow Wing. "And know this, Yellow Wing, both Good Shield and I will always be there for you," he said. "Together we will teach you everything that is taught Soaring Eagle. As young braves who love one another as brothers love, you will be nothing less than brothers."

Tears came to Yellow Wing's eyes. Deeply touched by Standing Wolf's kindness, he dared not try to speak. He knew that he would then truly burst out in tears. He eagerly shook his head, then scooted closer to Soaring Eagle.

"Now tell us everything we should know about what is required of us to become great hunters," Soaring Eagle said, his eyes anxiously peering into Standing Wolf's.

Standing Wolf dropped his hands away from the young braves and rested them on his lap. He laughed softly. "There is too much to tell in one night, but I shall tell you partly what you will need to know," he said, glad when Shaylee scooted closer so that he could slide an arm around her waist. He could feel her eyes on him. He could feel their warmth and he could see her soft smile without looking at her.

"Although I am the first person you chose to share this endeavor with, there is someone who should have been approached first," Standing Wolf said, looking from child to child, seeing their intent stares. "A priest whose business it is to train young braves for this task is the one you should seek out when it is time for you young men to begin your training. Then on the appearance of the first new moon in March, the priest will give you, his pupils, a certain purifying drink. He will then ask you to flush your bodies with the drink. This is an enema, and after you are purged, you will be sent to the river where you will immerse yourselves seven times, then put on clean clothing. You will then be ordered to hunt, and when you have killed your first buck, you will take the tip of the tongue to the priest to offer as a sacrifice."

He paused, then continued as everyone still intently listened, "The same ritual will be repeated at the appearance of the first new moon in September. For four years thereafter you will be consigned to the care of the hunting priest, and during this extended period, you will not be allowed to have sexual relations with women."

He smiled softly when he heard them both gasp, for sex was never mentioned openly. It was a taboo subject for children their age!

"There is more I will tell you and then you young braves must return to your beds and sleep," Standing Wolf said softly. "This same priest will teach you the sacred prayer formulas for hunting and about bird and animal natures and habits. He also teaches you how to make the special calls to lure the birds and animals closer. He will help you make the power-infused luring masks for hunting that never fail to bewitch the game, which allows the hunters to get within killing distance."

Knowing that Shaylee must be recalling the turkey mask she had found that day beside the cavern, bloodied by the head wound inflicted by Short Arrow's war club, he turned slow eyes to her and smiled.

Then he turned to the young braves again. "And then there is the tent for sweating," he said, but sighed. "But that is something the priest must tell you."

He reached over and drew Soaring Eagle into his arms and hugged him, then hugged Yellow Wing, then took Shaylee's hand and asked her to stand with him. "Your mother and I will now go to our own room," he said thickly. He chuckled. "I doubt you will get much sleep, for I know the excitement of planning for one's future."

"You will be proud of us both," Soaring Eagle said, stretching out beside Yellow Wing.

Shaylee bent over them and pulled a blanket across them, leaving it to rest beneath their arm pits. She bent lower and brushed a soft kiss across each of their brows.

"Sleep tight," she murmured, then turned and left the room with Standing Wolf.

As they walked down the steps to go to their bedroom on the first floor, Standing Wolf turned and placed his hands on Shaylee's waist. "Let us go outside and talk beneath the stars," he whispered, his voice carrying no farther than Shaylee.

"Yes. It is such a beautiful night," Shaylee whispered back. "A night just made for lovers."

When she saw the seductively wicked glint in her husband's eyes, she knew that was exactly why he had suggested they go outside. They had a special knoll upon which they sat when the moon was full. It was private. It brought out the passion in one's very soul.

Giggling, she clung around his neck as he swept her into his arms and carried her down the staircase.

After they were settled comfortably on the knoll on a blanket she had grabbed just before leaving the cabin, they looked far down below where they could see the White River glistening in the moonlight. They could hear all of the night sounds, the turkey frogs the most distinct. Then Standing Wolf gently removed Shaylee's clothes and laid them aside.

She, in turn, removed his.

As he kissed her, his hands on her breasts, he blanketed her with his body and pressed her down on the blanket on her back. "Although your body has carried three children in its womb, you are still small, delicately boned, and slender," he said huskily.

"I always want to stay that way for you," Shaylee murmured.

"And your hair smells sweet," he said, his fingers lifting strands of her red hair and bringing them to his nose.

"I slit a grapevine today and caught the juice of it in a bottle to put on my hair after washing it," she whispered, his tongue now lapping one of her stiffened nipples. "It . . . makes . . . my hair soft."

"Not only is your hair soft, but also your body," he said huskily, his hands moving seductively over her silken flesh. He flicked his tongue over one nipple.

Then he sank his lips over it and sucked it, making Shaylee almost mindless with pleasure.

She ran her hands over his back, and then lower and around to where she felt his thick, long shaft resting against her leg. She twined her fingers around his manhood and slowly moved them on him.

His mouth came to her lips in a quivering kiss, his moans of passion coming from the depths of his throat as she continued to pleasure him with her hand.

When he pleasured her in kind with his fingers, caressing the core of her womanhood, she opened her legs wider. She led him inside her, then sucked in a wild gasp of rapture when he began his rhythmic thrusts.

She twined her arms around his neck and rode with him, her body lifting and moving with each of his thrusts. She was soaring with joy as their urgent mouths and hands fueled their desire even more.

Fiercely, he gathered her in his arms and held her as he moved inside her more deeply and more rapidly, lifting her up on waves of desire.

With a moan of ecstasy she pressed herself up against him, her skin quivering with the warmth of rapture that overwhelmed her.

His mouth seemed more sensuous than ever tonight, hotter, more demanding. It was as though it was their first time together and they could not get enough!

He had her crushed so tightly against him now that she gasped, but she did not pull back. Her body was yearning for release.

"White Swan, I love you so much," he whispered into her ear as he drew his mouth from her lips. His hands cupped her breasts. He kissed the soft curve of her neck. "Come with me. Fly with me!"

"Yes, yes . . ." she managed to whisper, so huskily she scarcely recognized her own voice.

She reached between them, and as he withdrew his manhood slightly from inside her, she ran her fingers over his pulsing satin hardness, then shoved him back inside her and drew in a ragged breath as the pleasure exploded.

Their lips met in a frenzy of kisses as their bodies jolted and quivered together, and then they lay on their backs, their hands intertwined, their eyes watching the stars.

"Do you know what is so wonderful?" Shaylee said, sighing contentedly.

"Tell me," Standing Wolf said, gently stroking the satiny flesh just beneath her breasts.

She turned misty eyes to him. "It is so wonderful to hear all three of our children breathing beneath the same roof, and to know they are safe, because for so long I was denied my Moses," she said, her voice breaking. "Standing Wolf, I feel so wonderfully blessed."

"White Swan, I am the one who is blessed," Standing Wolf said, sliding an arm beneath her, drawing her closer. "That you came to me that day in the cavern is still magical to me."

"Yes, magical," Shaylee said, sighing as she gazed up into the heavens.

She started to reminisce aloud about how they had come to be together that day, but stopped and gasped when she saw something in the sky that she had never seen before. She had heard of them, but had never seen a double star . . . two separate stars in the sky coming toward each other, suddenly blending into one larger star as it fell toward the earth.

"Did you see that?" she cried, sitting quickly up. "Did you, Standing Wolf?"

His eyes still on the sky, he sat up beside her. "Yes. I saw it."

Then he turned to her and held her face between his hands. "White Swan, tonight we experienced something spiritual," he said, gazing deeply into her eyes.

"Yes, and surely it was a sight sent to us from the good Lord above," Shaylee murmured. "You see, my love, how we both are blessed?"

He drew her into his arms and held her.

She looked over his shoulder at the stars above. She knew that her husband David was there among the stars, serenely happy, as were Standing Wolf's wife, his unborn child, his aunt and parents.

Her children and husband on this earth were happy!

She and Standing Wolf were happy!

And her parents had saved money and were coming to live in the area to be close to Shaylee and her family.

And the special star sent to her and Standing Wolf tonight was proof enough to her that God was pleased with the outcome of her and Standing Wolf's lives!

She melted into Standing Wolf's arms as he drew her down again onto the blanket.

She closed her eyes as he gave her a slow, sweet kiss, the sort that came with total contentment.

8 H

CP
2/04

MG
7/03

1/03
NF

ML   11/02